The Halftone Man

More Literary Works by the Author

Novels

Spine
The Buckseller
P O D

Collections

Unvisited Spaces
& Twelve Other Stories

THE HALFT NE MAN

F. E. MAZUR

Royalty Ridge
Springfield, KY
2016

This is a work of fiction. All of the characters, events, websites and their messages in this novel are either the products of the author's imagination or are used fictitiously.

Royalty Ridge Books
1610 Royalty Ridge
40078

ISBN-13: 978-0-9979101-0-0
ISBN-10: 0-9979101-0-0

Cover Photo/Design by the Author

First Print Edition: August 2016

halftone: a photoengraving made from an image photographed through a screen having a lattice of horizontal and vertical lines and then etched so that the details of the image are reproduced in dots

ONE

It was an incredibly remarkable phenomenon and he was uncertain what to expect if the impairments worsened. The fact was, with his vision and hearing at their present stage of decline, Eugene Banish was able to ascertain the truth of matters more clearly than ever before. Of course, these were not those truths assigned to animal and insect, or innocent children. They were not the beautiful unadorned truths that were illuminated in the Apollo 8 photograph of his planet and that should have embarrassed any leader contemplating war or terror. And they did not include the humbling truth of exploded tissue of which he possessed an unforgettable, singular awareness. Neither were they the body of truths inherent to music, geometric lines and forms with their arithmetical x and y, nor the glorious spectrum with its rainbow of colors and countless hues, all at which he quietly marveled. These truths that he discovered uncoiled unwillingly out of the minds of deceitful men and women. And he had been standing first in line at a neighborhood market while on a visit to his daughter's home when he recorded this unique transformation inside himself.

"Sir, you did not give me a twenty. You gave me a ten."

Oh, he had heard all the words the young woman in the thick, ugly mascara and blue smock had uttered, and he supposed he could have described her general tone to anyone showing an interest and he would have received a nod. But the faintest inflections intending to deceive a fellow human being, these were suddenly no longer available. Sharpened subtleties passed down as some kind of legacy from one generation to another over the course of history, they were now silent to an aging man. Auditory distillation was this new process, the purification of the human sound and the unmasking of the conniving heart behind it. Not so different from the computer editing of a black skyline of cacophony, removing a peak here and there and maybe a whole valley that would not meld to the rest.

He glanced at the LED display above the register that showed the change he was to receive. He regretted that he had not given it his attention the moment he had passed the bill to the woman.

"No, Miss. It was a twenty I handed you, I'm quite sure of it. As a checkout clerk, you're supposed to lay the money on the register before making change. Not slip it immediately into the drawer."

"That's what I did!" the woman said accusingly, while rolling her eyes to the others in line. "You were staring at the Wall of Values, not to mention something else."

"Look, I'm not homeless, but I'm not a wealthy man either. I need my money." He moved his head to one side to better see her nameplate partially concealed by a lapel.

"There you go again!" she scolded him while swinging her bosom away from his line of sight.

"Dara," he said pointedly, refusing to be baited, "I want my money."

"You did not give me a twenty!"

"The hell I didn't!"

"Will you take your items and go? There's others behind you waiting to check out and they shouldn't have to wait all day."

There were, indeed. And for a ridiculous moment he considered that he might be part of an unscripted commercial or some kind of Candid Camera thing or even one of those new reality TV shows he'd seen his daughter watching. Because in the express line behind him were a woman older than himself who could have been mistaken for Phyliss Diller, if you were unaware the comedienne was no longer alive; a tall black gentleman purchasing several kinds of citrus fruit and reading the tiny stickers on their rinds while nervously alternating his attention from their content to the register area; a conservative-haired white man withdrawn under a sunken chest who was holding a tabloid and a package of allergy medicine and unaware that a fly sat upon his shoulder; and bringing up the rear, a teenaged, Latino-looking girl with mirrored sunglasses propped on her head in such a manner they resembled tiny solar heating elements intended for pre-ignition of her brain. He stared at these fellow shoppers to learn if they might side with him, but not a one was. Instead, they all were pretending to be on another planet; and it was precisely at that moment that he realized how his vision was presenting to himself the uncluttered basics, displaying a halftone of minimal light and dark spots, a veritable three-dimensional news photo of human beings whom he likely would not recognize if he were to see them outside in the parking lot a few minutes later with every detail saturated and complete. So he looked back at the halftone manning the register, and now he realized neither had this young woman named Dara made a mistake. She had committed this crime on others, and there would be no unaccounted money in the register drawer come the change of shifts. She knew this, and now he knew it too because the intended clutter of her smug deceit was being kept from his eyes, the same as it had been kept from his ears, because of a most unusual change to his chemistry.

"You should be ashamed," he said.

Forgoing the bagging, he snatched up a roll of paper towels that was slipped under an arm, the plastic jug of milk, plus a woman's item his daughter had asked him to pick up and exited the store, but not without another glance at those in line behind him whose faces, while continuing to feign an unawareness to each other of the skulduggery they had just witnessed, were starkly revealing to himself.

Still early in the sixth decade of his life, declining vision and hearing were the only impairments with which Eugene Banish was forced to contend, if you overlooked a crooked index finger damaged more than twenty years earlier while he was wrestling with his dog, the only animal his wife had permitted in the house, a chow so exquisitely feminine that she could not bear to see it sit out in the heavy rains and other inclement weather. But although he was fit and healthy, because of his offhand admission following their mutual bereavement—thank God, he later told himself, he had mentioned nothing about the "truth" revelations—his daughter had worried his increasing loss of hearing and sight would land him in serious trouble. Her husband Riddell could not believe the old man was continuing to drive and so he surrendered, more willingly than either Paulette or her father ever would have predicted, to allotting him a room in their house.

At first, Eugene had contested the offer. Though he told this to no one, and never would, he had enjoyed the time alone after the death of his wife. In their last years together, following his early retirement from the aluminum company, they had expended their waning energies to snipe and argue throughout much of every day, he once telling her that she was the "blight of his life" to which she'd responded, "You mean the height of your life, because you weren't going anywhere and you've certainly proven it." And in that same stretch of misery his distress once had him calling emphatically for the question: *Do you even like this woman any longer?* — a question he deliberately and fearfully forced from his consciousness because although it lacked the silliness of the childish questions from his early years, *Who's buried in Grant's Tomb?* and *What color is the little brown jug?* — still there was the suggestion that it was from that category of inquiries which answer themselves. He had wept at the funeral as he knew he would, but later in the mirror he would say he was relieved, and it was true he was breathing more easily and the chronic headaches had gone away and not returned, just as had the knot at the back of his neck. Yet at the same time, he was not persuaded into thinking the pleasant feeling would endure. He knew what his Ginger and he could not accomplish in life, the mutual dismissal of a hundred and more petty irritations, would be accomplished in death. Only four weeks without her and when he gazed into the bathroom mirror this time, he began to cry, and the tears might not have stopped without the phone call from a telemarketer offering a free trip on a cruise ship and for which he held no interest.

The room assigned him at his daughter's home was modest but comfortable. Besides his bed and compact mahogany desk, transported from the white Cape Cod Ginger and he had occupied for three and a half decades, was a newly acquired cushioned platform rocker and ottoman, and Paulette and Riddell had agreed to his radio and Sony CD player, so long as he used the headphones. Opposite the door was a large walk-in closet and next to it a window. Because the room was in a corner of the house, he had a choice of windows to look out. Neither glass revealed an expanse of sky and the reason was that the house was snugged midway up a long roman-nose slope with tall pines and larch populating three of the four sides. If sky was what he was after, he left the house and hiked to the top; the elevation was grudging but not impossible. Once there, he had his choice to sit on a large rock, or on a bench he had cobbled together out of some thick fallen branches, or he could dare to climb an unknown bowhunter's out-of-use tree-stand. The view here was simple enough, as were the sounds. Immediately below him were the new houses built on old property cut from failing farms, one hundred acre tracts now ashlars of fives, while way to his left he could see and hear evidence of the four-lane Route 56 bypass skirting the Steel City's most outlying communities of Kensington and Arlion.

Last night's rain had relaxed to an atomized drizzle and this autumn morning, as he stood at the top of the slope staring at a small slice of the distant bypass, occasional drops were forming on the limbs of the trees above him, then falling onto his hair, still rich with color despite its age and always displaying the effect of being freshly tedded, like hay that had lain wet in the field. He had already counted seven concrete delivery trucks inside of twenty minutes, their slowly tumbling barrel shape easy to identify in spite of the visual information missing because of the accumulating mist. Some massive pour was underway. Probably more repair to the bridge lanes crossing the Allegheny and the entrance and exit ramps on Tarentum's west end, he thought. On the Lodge Road that intersected with the bypass he noticed a white van as it pulled off onto the shoulder and seconds later a young man got out who awkwardly clutched several large plastic containers that would soon be filled with the most perfect water from an always respondent spring above the road's opposite shoulder. Below on his right construction of a new home was starting, and he could hear the occasional pop of a nail gun and the whine of a circular saw. This scene he watched also with interest because the person acting the part of the general contractor and issuing direction to all the others appeared to be a woman. He could not discern this from the distant person's looks, but rather from certain points of elegant gesture. Moving parallel to the flow of a narrow creek, swollen after the night's downpour, the same creek that crossed a corner of Riddell's and Paulette's property, were two figures on horseback.

Below him the front door to the house closed, the air forcibly whooshed out of the tight aluminum frame, and seconds later sounded the lively bark of Brownie, his daughter's American cocker. The dog had picked up his scent and was pedaling quickly up the slope to join Eugene.

"Oh my, lookatcha! She's not going to let you back inside the house all muddied up like this."

On arrival the small dog jumped up and crashed its front paws on Eugene's pant legs, leaving several muddy marks, but Eugene didn't seem to mind. He ran his hands briskly over the dog's coat, finishing with a noisy flapping of its long ears, which were terribly knotted from running through high weeds.

"I don't know why they named you Brownie. Burdock or Sticktite would have been more on target."

The dog opened its mouth and started to chew on Eugene's hands and fingers, and he allowed it. He had allowed every dog he'd ever known to do the same, often initiating the matter with some by inserting his hand between their jaws. It was their way of checking a person out, researching if the roughhousing was really roughhousing, or were you thinking of breaking their neck perhaps. It was a simple, but pretty good test of one's intentions because soon enough the dog would put additional pressure behind the teeth and one had the option of staying in or pulling out. Unlike people, dogs never judged any human being to be a fool. They never questioned for a second that you possessed the knowledge you could be instantly and seriously bitten. So, if the person's hand was staying put, the activity, they concluded, must be in fun. At least, such was Eugene's take on it.

"Come on," he said to the dog. "Let's get on back to the house. I'm becoming soaked myself."

The cocker ran ahead, but repeatedly sliced off the path like a fine horse into attractive spots on either side. Eugene could smell the must underneath the soil and the bleached earthworms dying on the paved walk and gravel driveway below. When they reached the small landing constructed of aging railroad ties before the door to the house, he took a good look at the dog, which was now sitting anxiously, waiting to follow him inside. Its fur was already thoroughly wet and stringy, and a dark muddy brown, almost the color of dried blood, extended upward from each paw for about four inches. Small clumps of rich earth were wedged throughout its toes like clusters of grapes.

"Now listen, Brownie. Don't make a scene. Once inside, make a dash for my room and stay there. Understand?"

He opened the door and entered onto another landing, this one of black slate that divided the upstairs from the TV room and basement. The dog squirmed ahead of him and scampered up the carpeted steps. Out of nowhere stormed a woman in a dull yellow shift with auburn hair bunched at the back of her head, a woman too big for her frame, Eugene's daughter.

"Oh no you don't, Brownie! You're not coming up here. Dad, you should know better."

"I told him to go to my room and remain there."

"You take him back outside and put him in the garage is what you do. Can't you see? He's already dropping mud on the rug. And look at your pants!" She bent down, instantly annoyed just like her mother had been, and snatched up two brown clumps before there was any chance of them becoming smeared into the nap of the carpet. "Well, Dad, what are you waiting for?"

"It's cold out there, Paulette, and it's damp. He's already starting to shake."

"He's a dog. He'll be all right."

Eugene frowned, but reached up the steps and grabbed the cocker. A flash of child crossed behind his daughter.

"Who's that?" he asked.

"If it was wearing purple," Paulette answered while reaching down to pluck a wad of mud from the top of his trousers, "that's Marshall. Have you met Pippa Goodwin since you've been here...? Well, she's a friend from our time at church, and she's taken a part-time job where Riddell works. I've volunteered to watch Marshall for one day each week to help her out. No telling how long that will last, but I'm sure it'll be a while."

The purple flash appeared again, heading back whence it had come, this time making sputtering sounds like an airplane in distress.

Eugene addressed the dog. "Why, he's no bigger than you, Brownie."

"Now you heard me, Dad! He's not coming up here!"

TWO

Four silver maple trees, each with an annually whitewashed trunk as thick as a whiskey barrel, separated the house from the garage, which offered three bays. Riddell's motorized aluminum fishing boat this day was in the farthest, Paulette's blue minivan in the second, and the first was empty because her husband was at the Hollowell trucking terminal where he was employed as the chief dispatcher who made arrangements for the pickup and delivery of various steel products manufactured throughout the Alle-Kiski Valley. Eugene stepped through a windowless door on the side and Brownie padded after. He could hear the dog's long, untrimmed nails clicking on the concrete floor.

"This is where you got to stay till you dry off some," he said to the dog.

He searched along the walls of the garage and located an old rusty milk canister converted to rag bin, which stored numerous pieces of discarded towel his son-in-law used to wash the cars on Saturday. He extracted these and gave the dog a swift, massaging rubdown. Then, using his fingers, he began pulling away the balls of moist dirt from inside the paws.

"They ought to clip you. Except this time of year I guess you'd freeze your little rump off. So we'll scratch that idea."

The dog listened to his every word and Eugene believed if it could speak, it would indeed respond sensibly. He gave it a final tousle on its head and went back outside, toward the house. He could hear the purple flash suddenly screaming inside.

"I patted him down and removed the mud from his paws," he reported to his daughter in the kitchen. "He'll be fine in just a little while."

"Like Riddell says, you're *always* angling for that dog."

"He's a nice dog. I don't think either one of you appreciate him enough."

"We appreciate him just fine, Dad.... Sit down. And don't go getting any of that mud I see on your pants, on the chairs. Have you eaten anything this morning?"

"Where's Marshall?"

"I asked, have you eaten anything?"

"Yes, I made some toast while you were still asleep."

He stuck his head through the entrance to the other rooms. "There you are, you little dickens."

The child was on all fours, pushing around a shiny toy tractor-trailer. Painted on one side was the name of the transport firm for which Riddell worked. On the other was a religious declaration by the firm's owner: *"Our God Reigns."*

"Are you sure he isn't yours?" he turned back and teased his daughter. "I see a resemblance."

"Riddell wanted me to ask if you're ready to sell your car."

"Why?"

"Here. Sit down. Have a cup of coffee. Leave Marshall be! Don't disturb him like I know you're wanting to."

"Why is your husband eager for me to get rid of the car?"

"Riddell isn't eager," she said. "In fact, he says if you're going to hang onto it, then he might just sell his own and begin using yours."

"He might want to replace parts of his exhaust before putting it on the market," said Eugene who then rose from the kitchen table and disappeared to the back of the house. He returned in about a minute.

"Were you searching for the title?" inquired Paulette. Eugene didn't immediately comprehend his daughter's question as she routinely moved kitchen items off the counter and into the cupboards. "I saw it sitting out one day with some other papers soon after you moved in. I put it with our own important documents so that it wouldn't get thrown away by accident."

"What I did," he informed her boldly, "was remove the gun from your bedroom."

An orange tumbler slipped from her grip. She caught it before it could hit the floor. "You did what?"

"You have this little feller here and I was willing to bet that Riddell's .22 pistol was still inside the stand beside the bed. And I was right."

"It isn't loaded."

"You think that matters?"

"How did you...?"

"I'm a snoop, what else? There's not a whole lot to eat up my day anymore, now that I'm not living at home."

He could see she was angry, but so was he a bit. Taking in a child and not thinking to put the gun out of reach! Riddell was just as irresponsible. His daughter hadn't made this decision to baby-sit without his approval, he was sure of that.

"Dad, you can't go sneaking around this house. You can't just rummage through our closets and drawers anytime you want because you can't come up with something to keep yourself busy. Riddell's likely to hit the ceiling when he hears of this."

"Who said to tell him?"

"You know that I tell him everything."

"Not this time. This time, I'll tell him."

"What did you do with the gun?"

"It's in a safe place. Like I said, I'll tell him. I'll tell him where it is and plenty more. What time does he knock off work?"

"You know full well what time Riddell gets home."

The child came running into the kitchen, stopped, grinned a goofy, then spun around and ran back. Eugene went after him while imitating a mosquito, and caught him at the waist. He lifted the boy up to the ceiling where his screaming mouth bit into a cobweb, then dropped him as quickly.

"How old is he?" he called back to the kitchen as the child was attempting to spit out the dry filament.

"Three, going on four," came the answer.

He had been joking with his daughter when he said the boy resembled her, but the truth was the little feller did. The wide-open eyes like big marbles—boulders, they were called when he was a kid—the hair's daring twist and off color, the high-set dimples, and that forehead like ceramic tile! His wife had owned a similar one, but she'd always arranged a blonde curl or a set of bangs to hang in front like a subtle foliage design in order to obscure its glossy surface. Paulette wouldn't, and Eugene continued to believe, apart from her weight, it was still the single thing preventing his daughter from appearing pretty.

When Riddell arrived home from the terminal, Pippa Goodwin, a delicate creation with a peppering of freckles, was there to pick up her son, and Eugene was talking to her.

"I was telling my daughter that she and Marshall share

similar features."

"Dad! No mother wants to hear that sort of thing."

"Actually, Paulette, it's not strange your father thinks that. I've more than once told Marshall's daddy, Mr. Banish, that he and your daughter could be siblings."

"Are you serious?" cried Paulette.

"Baby, look at those foreheads on my son and you. The two of you could rent out billboard space."

Riddell interrupted her laughter. "Tell me Eugene is selling you his car, Pippa."

"Excuse me?" And by these two words alone and the exceptional tone in which they were uttered it seemed instantly clear to Eugene that Pippa Goodwin not only had landed the job on her own at the trucking firm without his son-in-law's help, but also that she loathed the husband of her friend.

"Eugene, Paulette ask you what I told her to?"

"I've something I want to discuss with you," said Eugene, directing the crooked finger at his son-in-law.

"We have to be going," announced Pippa Goodwin. "Thanks again, Paulette. It was a pleasure to meet you, Mr. Banish. I'm sure we'll be seeing more of each other."

As soon as the woman and her son were outside the house, Eugene whirled about to confront his son-in-law.

"We've got something to talk about! Did you know that little boy was coming here today?"

Riddell grinned lazily, the minor act enduring for at least six miles of the earth's rotation, and what Eugene saw in the drawn and bony face confirmed what he had merely felt at his daughter's wedding decades ago. He wished he could have recognized it back then, but at the time his eyes were seeing everything, understanding little.

"That's what I thought," he said.

"Are you agreeing to sell the car?"

"Very well, we'll do the car first. No, son-in-law, your wife's daddy is not quite ready to surrender up his wheels."

"You're not planning to drive it anymore, I hope." Riddell looked to his wife. "He isn't, is he?"

"Maybe not as much," allowed Eugene.

"You know you're heading for trouble, don't you?" warned Riddell, stepping forward and sticking a finger into Eugene's face. "But whatever. One I thing I do know for certain is this. You're not backing up on the house."

Eugene sucked in his cheeks and looked toward a window.

"What's so goddamn funny?"

"Nothing. Just sell the house. Sell it within the range I set and inside the time we agreed upon and you get the percentage I said. If not, it gets turned over to a realtor."

"You sure that house is worth it?"

"It's worth it. Just sell it. And don't go walking off. Remember, I had something to say."

"So get it out. I'm hungry. I've been working all day."

"I used to work all day too."

"You worked in that goddamn plant along the river. Nobody ever works all day in any goddamn plant."

"I worked all day on a garbage truck, too!"

"Right," Riddell drawled behind a slow roll of his eyes.

But he had. And it was his first job and it was good work, hard work, and it had put him in the best of shape. Three sons, the Shanks, who were friends of his brother, had recognized that Brell Township was growing and every house couldn't bury their garbage in the backyard forever. So they pooled their savings and bought a dump truck, a Mack. It was dark green and they painted the wooden sides of the bed a brilliant red. Never once had Eugene ever seen the vehicle anything but clean. In truth, it could have passed for spiffy, a simple dump truck used to collect and haul the garbage of American families. Whenever it wasn't in use, the Shanks washed and waxed it.

"What was your job?" Riddell asked over a silly grin. Pulling the lever for the compactor?"

"Why not talk in the kitchen," said Paulette. "I'll get something on the table for you."

"There wasn't any compaction in those days," answered Eugene. "The cans were heaved into the air and their contents dumped in the bed."

A Shank drove the truck and the stick on the floor was set in its lowest gear so that the truck crawled up the middle of each street like a caterpillar, the brakes rarely struck. Above, standing atop the ever-mounting heap of garbage in the bed, was sometimes another Shank but more often a shirtless teenager, if the season were summer, of seventeen, eighteen, nineteen years old. Two additional young employees, one on each side, each also in the greatest shape of their young lives, were on the street and Eugene was one of these. All the cans in those early years were formed of metal and he would remove its lid, then lift the open container of twenty, twenty-five, sometimes even thirty pounds above his shoulder and shoot it to the employee on top who caught, upturned, and emptied the contents all in one motion, before dropping it back into Eugene's hands. Then that fellow on top would swing around in a half-circle and repeat the process with the employee on the opposite side. Eugene really never had an appreciation of their efficient collaboration until the day he was ill and the youngest Shank filled his shoes. That day was also the day of collection for the street on which he lived and Eugene watched the smoothest operation he would ever see. He'd never forgotten it.

"You don't really care to hear about it, do you, son?"

"I'm not much into garbage, ol' man. But hey, I'm glad

to see it made you happy."

"You could have benefited from a job like that when you were a kid. Then you wouldn't be the skin and bones you are today."

"I think I can take you without too much trouble."

"Riddell...?"

"Set it on the table! I'm starving."

Eugene trailed his son-in-law into the adjoining room. From the refrigerator the younger man slid out a longneck bottle of Rolling Rock, then changed his mind and put it back.

"So what's on your mind, Eugene? Got a hankering to listen to some of your classical crap without the headphones? Or are you in the mood for some of that early drivel they still call rock 'n' roll? *'One two three o'clock, four o'clock rock!'*"

"I removed the .22 from your bedside stand when that boy was here," said Eugene.

Riddell stood stock-still a moment, then pivoted like a tiny robotic doll, his face a serious question. Paulette silently watched her husband.

"Say again?"

"I removed—"

"—Why the hell are you scratching around in my drawer, old man? Who gave you permission to go picking through my things?"

"You should have stored the gun somewhere else. You knew the child was coming."

"The goddamn gun isn't loaded!"

"Yeah, your wife said the same. But there's shells right beside it."

"And you think a little knob like Marshall Goodwin can figure out how to insert them."

"Kids figure out adults, they sure as hell can figure out

guns."

"Old man, you listen up and you listen up good. You go through my things like some worthless slithering snake ever again, you'll be out of here whether the house is sold or not. And don't think I don't mean it. Where's the gun now?"

"It's in my closet."

"Get it. Bring it here."

"All right. But you make certain you put it in a safe place when that child is around. I'll be checking."

"You remember what I just told you, old man!"

Eugene left to retrieve the gun from his room at the far corner of the house. Riddell seated himself at the table and a plate after changing his mind again about a beer. He and his wife stared at each other.

"Old people," he grumbled. "They're a major pain in the ass. There's one down at the terminal whose oxygen I'd like to shut off."

Paulette smiled at her husband at the same time she shook her head.

"Here," said Eugene, who had quickly returned. He handed over the pistol. "But tell me, son, because I'm genuinely curious. Why do you keep it so close to your bed and yet unloaded?"

Riddell, looking up from his dinner and meeting the eyes of his father-in-law, pretended he didn't understand the question, and maybe he didn't, thought Eugene. At least not consciously. But Eugene did. His son-in-law might not have brains enough to know that a child could figure out how to load the gun and accidentally shoot himself or someone nearby. But he did have sufficient sense cautioning himself against setting up the right circumstances.

"That's nothing you need to concern yourself with," said Riddell. "You think about selling that Plymouth. That's what you need to concern yourself with. I'm sick of seeing the goddamn thing in my driveway every morning when I get my ass ready for work."

THREE

Throughout the rainy fall and into the dreary winter months of January and February of the new year Paulette sat the child for one day of every week, sometimes two days, and prior to the boy's arrival, Eugene performed a safety inspection of the house, although he had long ago ceased sliding out the drawer to his son-in-law's bedside stand. Soon after their exchange of words, Riddell had transferred the gun to the top shelf in his own closet. But there were other things demanding attention. The toilet seat wasn't dropped. A can of Drano stood in plain view on the bathroom sink. Cabinet doors were left invitingly open. Paulette at the end of a day would have left the vacuum cleaner at the top of the steps with its lengthy cord trailing diagonally across the stairway to the floor below. Riddell, in search of a mouse hole, had ripped away the bottom molding in one of the rooms off the hallway and Eugene had discovered a half-dozen finishing nails pointing straight up. Some of the things he corrected, he guessed, might qualify him in the eyes of some people as a fussbudget, but there were others for which there was simply no excuse. Not with a child in the house. And why didn't his daughter know better, she had raised two children! His wife certainly had. Probably some bad influence from Riddell, he concluded, and it wasn't clear if he meant this in any way as a joke.

It was no joke whatsoever that three-year old, going-on-four, Marshall Goodwin required watching-over. Eugene wondered how his mother Pippa maintained her sanity. There had been no letting up on his racing about inside the house. From one end to the other, he menaced the dwelling like an angry miniature razorback. Now, even when he paused to play with a toy car or a plastic truck, it was only to get a good grip on its roof. Once accomplished, he raced the vehicle throughout both the first and the second floor of the house, banging it against sofa and chair, table and hutch, ramming it into the washer and dryer, screaming it at Eugene and at Brownie too, all the while on knees that pounded the floor with the pneumatic sound of a small jackhammer.

Paulette eventually asked her father if he might take the boy outside and permit her a break.

"On the nicer days. Let him run out there and work off his energy. Please, Dad. That would really be a big help."

Usually, Eugene took him to the top of the slope. Once, after a snowfall, he had searched the garage and found the sled previously used by his grandson Junior, who was now married and raising twins on the opposite side of the country. But Marshall was afraid once he sat on the sled and gazed down the slope, and Eugene didn't press him. He imagined the kid slept well at night. Why provide the child the ingredients for a possible nightmare! Instead, the boy started loping down the slope's other side, and Eugene skidded about ten feet behind. There were times he was unable to restrain himself from laughing at the tyke. Like when Marshall would turn around to learn if he was still close behind. The boy would continue to walk, only now he was doing it backwards and like so many kids, forgetting to allot the matter the required extra attention. Soon enough, he went falling on his rear end with his tiny stick arms and legs flailing out to the side, eyes wide open as their young owner experienced primitive flight. Eugene wondered if Pippa Goodwin caught him laughing at her son, would she be upset.

They went all the way to the bottom and the child wanted to keep on going, but Eugene stopped him and circled him back up the snow-covered hill. Every few feet during their climb the child pointed over his shoulder to something in the distance and shouted forth some garble. A couple times he pointed far away, then at Brownie. Eugene more than once scoured the landscape behind them but could find nothing to solve the mystery. All he saw that wasn't natural were the many homes on land that was previously cropland and pasture.

That evening during dinner, Paulette began telling her husband how Marshall was afraid to slide down the slope.

"Maybe he was scared you were setting him up, Eugene," joked Riddell. "Did you make him go in the end? Get him to look some other way, then give the sled a nudge?"

"Daddy didn't force him, Honey, no," said Paulette.

"Why not? It's what I done to Riddell Junior when he was just a little shit. I remember, too, he didn't think I would!"

Riddell laughed at his memory. Eugene was aware his son-in-law, despite the non-existent relationships he had with his own two children, regarded himself as good with kids.

"He wanted to trek down the other side," explained Eugene. "So we did. Is there anything unusual out that direction? I looked but couldn't see anything, yet there was definitely something out there that was of interest to him."

"You looked but couldn't see!" exclaimed Riddell, shaking his head. "You can look all you want and you still ain't gonna see. When d'ya you think that detail might sink in?"

There were times it was best to simply ignore his son-in-law, and Eugene recognized this as one of them. He swung his attention back to his daughter, waiting for her to answer his question.

"Seeing something, I don't know," she said. "Maybe it's what he was hearing, like all those dogs at the new shelter. They relocated a month ago in among those new homes, and the people are complaining because they can hear them bark day and night. There was a story in the paper. It would drive me nuts, I know that."

"Where is it?"

"It's in among that distant stand of pine. You can't see it from the road, so you probably can't see it from up above either. That was the idea of relocating. Get it away from the really big residential areas. But they never thought because it's so normally quiet out here, the sound of all those dogs would carry and soon become a nuisance. On some really quiet nights I've heard them myself."

"Auschwitz," Riddell remarked, stuffing a forkful of mixed vegetables into his mouth, but still managing to pronounce the "w" as a "v". "That's the reason they're all barking. Them unlucky hounds know their big day is already penciled in on the calendar."

On the next few occasions Eugene climbed the slope he listened to see if he could hear any dogs. It was no surprise he couldn't, but he had been hoping.

"What about you, Brownie? Your brothers and sisters down there trying to communicate?"

The bobbed tail on the cocker wagged faster as it always did when Eugene spoke.

If the noise from the animal shelter was what the boy had been hearing, Eugene thought it somewhat odd, but

only because Marshall seemed to show little interest in Brownie. Eugene had tried to generate that interest, too, and Brownie, he could see, was willing—one more human to pay attention to you, nothing wrong with that. He even showed Marshall the trick of letting the cocker take his hand and fingers into its mouth to establish a mutual trust. Yet, nothing came of it. The boy didn't dislike the dog, however. It just seemed to Eugene, and to Paulette too, that Marshall was a small boy much absorbed by himself.

FOUR

Riddell Parker, too, was much taken with himself. At least that was the view in the eyes of the people who associated with him, who were mostly the men and women from the local trucking firm. He held no particular social distinctions except for making sport of others and uttering occasional sayings. These sayings, which seemed to miss the prime ingredient for all three adage, aphorism, and maxim, became annoying to his father-in-law because of their repetition. Perhaps the worst of them was the one Eugene first heard when his daughter had been dating Riddell who, at the time, often cruised up helmetless to the house astride a motorcycle: *If you ain't been down, you ain't been around.*

Even today, so many years later and minus the CH, Riddell managed to resurrect the saying, particularly when the local news stations reported such an accident. In the last year alone, Eugene had heard it and on that occasion he was messing with pencil and paper and in seconds produced a cavalier sketch "just for the hell of it," he explained to his daughter when she asked why, that showed a wrecked Harley-Davidson with an accordioned Riddell Parker almost half the size of the motorcycle standing alongside, a part of his head missing and blood dripping off his stick-like body from a half-dozen places onto pavement. Printed overhead in a balloon were the famous "words of wisdom."

All of the sayings, however, were not of the absurdly macho variety, and some Eugene even fancied and repeated to himself. His favorite was: *Whoever has the money, has the money.* The first time his son-in-law had muttered it he had rolled his eyes.

"Hey, old man, you think about what I said. You hear me? You think about it."

Later, Eugene did, more than what the younger man would have expected. He thought about it specifically in regard to his son-in-law. Riddell was no deadbeat by any definition as the bills were paid and generally on time. Nonetheless, there was the infrequent collector telephoning who was told to get lost. For when Riddell had a question concerning a particular bill, he forbade his wife to write out a check until the creditor provided a satisfactory answer. And he never, ever, would mail it to a collection agency because he said he had initiated no business with them. "Whoever has the money, has the money," he would bark at the caller. "And guess who has this money, bub?"

Since he had confessed to prowling inside the house, Eugene was soon listening to a newer saying and one he supposed Riddell had heard from a fellow worker and then fixed up for himself, a spin-off from the familiar *mi casa, su casa*. Every time his son-in-law poked his chest and said "Riddell's house is Riddell's house," Eugene wanted to remind him that Paulette had a stake in the place as well, but his daughter would wave him off.

"He knows that, Dad," she had told him.

Eugene thought he probably did. His problem with his daughter's husband was a simple one. He liked him and he didn't like him. He imagined an equal ambivalence was harbored in return. But the trouble with their ambivalence, he sensed, was its too close resemblance to a balancing scale and, sooner or later, more weight was certain to get lowered onto one side; and although he couldn't have explained why if questioned, something was telling him that side was bound to be the wrong side.

It was obvious what Riddell meant by his new saying, but all of what was implied was not. Eugene understood it to mean it was Riddell's house and being a guest, he should keep his nose out of things and not ask too many questions. It meant that, certainly, but Riddell was not intending even the smallest reciprocity. He believed he had the right as the homeowner to go into his father-in-law's room and crawl like a cockroach through the old man's things any time he had the itch.

"Hon, what are you staring at?" Paulette inquired from the hallway.

"Have you seen this?"

Riddell held up a large, sorely yellowed piece of paper resembling parchment. He held it between his thumb and forefinger as though it were a soiled handkerchief. Newsprint pictures and stories, similarly yellow from age, were attached to it. An entire book of like pages rested on Eugene's dresser and with his other hand he picked up another sheet. One of its pictures instantly detached and beelined to the floor.

Paulette stepped into the room to join her husband. A conspicuous strand of hair lay curled on his shoulder and she reached to remove it.

"Where is your old man, anyway?" he asked while rejecting her hand with a well-practiced slap and a flash of overworked annoyance.

"I don't know. He said he was going to catch a thief, whatever that means."

Riddell shook his head. "So what about this?"

"It's his scrapbook," said Paulette. She not only

recognized it; she could smell its antique mustiness.

"He ought to donate the goddamn thing to the Smithsonian. Or the garbage crew. Whichever shows an interest. Look at it! The damn thing's a relic. Most of the items were torn out of newspapers and they're at least forty, fifty years old. Take a look at this picture with the young girls in it. Judging by the number of ponytails and the clothes they're wearing, this got to be half a century or better."

"Grandma started it, I remember him telling me that," she said. "But he took it over when he became a teenager. Something of a hobby for him, I guess. Have you looked through all of it?"

"Are you crazy? I'm amazed he hasn't tossed it. The damn thing's falling apart. You know any of these girls with the ponytails? I'm thinking one of them might be your mother. That one second from the left."

Paulette briefly studied the yellow and obviously brittle picture. There were names in the caption, but the paper had once been scored and folded prior to gluing and so had never lain flat and frictionless and most of the letters were no longer readable. Each of the girls was holding a coffee or juice can, the corrugated kind that rarely appeared on today's grocery's shelves. In place of the identifying label was a wrap-around for a polio charity.

"That isn't her," she said.

Growing up, she had opened the pages to her father's scrapbook on occasion, but she had never dwelled on the history contained therein. The book had been a curiosity, nothing more, Eugene sometimes sitting down with her to volunteer an answer to a question she hadn't asked or point out some fact about his mother or father. Back then she had been the typical teen who was more interested in pictures and stories of herself and her friends. Only recently, after setting her father's clean laundry into one of the dresser drawers where he had placed the scrapbook with its broad gray covers and green shoestring binding, was she moved to look at some of its content with scrutiny.

The halftone on the yellowed newsprint that had captured the seven young girls, the one at which Riddell was continuing to stare, she had previously studied at length, then followed with a close inspection of another old photo showing a king and queen of some event. This was the same photo that lay on the floor and she bent to retrieve it.

"Take a look at this one," she said. "A close look."

"Wow! She's a beauty. The picture's faded, but that still comes through loud and clear!"

"Now look at the other one again. The girl on the far left? You think they're one and the same?"

Riddell moved his head from one picture to the other, several times. Paulette caught herself chuckling because he reminded her of the Egyptian dancers she had seen in some terribly old movie who locked their flattened hands beneath their chins and then bobbed their heads from one side to the other as a score of hungry men watched and drooled.

"Could be. In this one she's angled to the side and so it's hard to say for certain."

He picked up the rest of the scrapbook from the dresser and thumbed through its dying pages.

"Careful, Honey. It still means something to him."

Some of the items had strips of scotch tape holding them together and the tape had darkened to obscure the portion of the newsprint behind. Two other pictures slid out and onto the floor and Paulette quickly recovered them. Not all the pictures were cutouts from newspapers. Others were the actual photographs used to create the halftones, yellowing Kodak and Agfa prints with each of their four corners tucked under tiny black stays that resembled the underbelly view of a miniature Stealth fighter.

"You know what these remind me of, some of these pictures?" Riddell said. "They remind me of the kind of thing you see tacked on the wall in some basement dump of a sporting club. Not this one though. Who's this little girl?"

The newspaper picture he held up for her to view was small and, again, the caption underneath was mostly illegible. The image, too, had lost much of its detail.

"Do you know her? She looks like she might have been a sweetie."

"No, I don't know her, and neither did he. It's a child who was sick, I remember." She had forgotten all about this moment with her father, but now it came rushing back like she could never have expected. "He was rearranging items in his wallet, and I saw him pull out pictures of Mom and me. But then he pulled this out and flattened it, and I asked who she was."

"And so who was it? Some young movie prima donna, like a Shirley Temple, that he had a fatherly crush on?"

"No, Hon. It wasn't anybody but a little girl who wasn't even in school yet. She stole his heart because she had a terrible disease and would soon be dead."

"So why did he tear it out of the paper and carry it around in his wallet?"

"As a reminder."

"A reminder of what?"

"That he had nothing to complain about, Hon. That if he ever felt sorry for himself, he should feel ashamed."

Probably he should feel ashamed anyway, thought Riddell, toting against his ass all that time the picture of some little kid who was neither kin nor friend. He soon tired of the scrapbook and its pictures, much as on some days he quickly tired of his father-in-law, and left the room.

Paulette remained behind and continued to look. Another of the photos located a page or two further down, equally yellow and worn around its creases, showed a man with a severe and bloody injury lying stretched out along a dirt path that intersected with a paved road. The man's face was mostly hidden from the camera. When this picture had been ripped from its newspaper, the caption had been left behind. Why was this saved, she wondered. Who was the injured man? It wasn't her father, she was certain, and she didn't think it was Val, his brother, either.

She then went deeper into the book and it became clear it offered a chronology, however unmarked. The cutout pictures showed less yellowing and those that were actual photographs had been properly fixed, which wasn't always typical of early photofinishing. She stopped on a black-and-white photograph she mistakenly believed was her grandmother. In fact, it was Eugene's grandmother, but the mix-up was understandable as the prominent features of either woman were in the other. Toward the end of the book she recognized a picture of herself, a baby picture clipped from a pennysaver that had sponsored a contest. On this and several other neighboring pictures there was writing scrawled in ink, sometimes black or blue, other times red or even green, evidence of her mother's careless hand and now an instant reminder to Paulette of an altercation between her parents. Her father hadn't objected to her mother identifying any of the pictures, only he wanted her to perform the small task neatly. Instead, spiteful Ginger had scratched down names and an occasional date without regard to aesthetics, in some instances even into the soft emulsion of the snapshots themselves.

Very carefully she began to replace the pages, not tapping them on the dresser top or between her palms, but matching them one and two at a time to the others already in order, all the while continuing to look at the halftones and prints. She couldn't help but notice how often her father had made the newspaper, during his teens especially. One showed a typically posed baseball team, the players wearing many different buttoned-down shirts, and she could still immediately identify him in the first row in his 7th Street Sportsmen uniform, a selected all-star at the age of thirteen. Another showed him, Number 8, left-handedly hooking a basketball over the outstretched arms of a T-shirted opponent. The leading words to the caption read, "SHOOTS ... AND MISSES." She remembered Eugene had told her that he had played in a church league, which was the explanation for why the opponent was not wearing a uniform. Yet another showed him with a girl of similar age and they were staring into a paper bag. The caption informed the reader the pair was co-chairing a corn roast.

She collected all the pages and slid them between the gray covers. The braided shoestring binding was now useless because the holes in the pages were no longer complete and had not been reinforced.

"Riddell! You nearby?"

"What is it, Sweetie?" he answered from the kitchen.

"Did you find this on his dresser? Or had you dug it out?"

"It was already out!" he hollered back.

FIVE

On that same wintry night his scrapbook was undergoing examination by his daughter and her husband, Eugene had attempted to catch the grocery clerk Dara in the act of thieving. But while he was waiting fourth in line to the register, the young woman suddenly broke away and informed a fellow worker she couldn't stand it any longer, she was sick to her stomach and was returning home. He waited a week and tried again, only to learn from that same fellow worker, a much older and feisty woman, that Dara was lounging offshore. She and her boyfriend had driven down to Florida to visit "a brother or sister or some such," and then they were intending to fly to a "cozy island." Eugene detected a mistrust of Dara in the worker's voice.

"Must be nice," he said.

"You're telling me. Wish I had the money to get away from the cold and slush. She and her live-in both smoke like a transit bus, too. Go figure that for saving travel bucks."

Eugene nodded his understanding and he thought, *I could tell this woman how Dara does it*; and he might have done exactly that if she had not relented in her suspicion.

"But it could just be him," the woman said. "You've heard why some people go to Florida, no doubt. To carry drugs across state lines for a big payoff? Well, I know her mother, and I can't believe such a wonderful lady would have raised a criminal. But nice girls sometimes become involved with them. All I'm saying there is, that's what happened to me. Except I got rid of my loser the second I learned the truth."

Eugene had never doubted since their first encounter, already several months in the past and while he was still living in his own home, that the young cashier would endeavor to rip him off again, presented the chance. She had considered his earlier questioning an affront to her pilfering abilities, and he was sure she would remember him and make herself feel good again by stealing from him a second time.

On his third attempt, he found her at the express register, back from the tropics and proudly showing off her tan.

There were few customers throughout the store and no customers behind him, and the man in front, with only a bag of apples and a box of pearl tapioca to be checked out, was complimenting her on her fresh and healthy look, which now included a deep run of beckoning, shadowy cleavage. Eugene reminded himself to study the Wall of Values running on the opposite side of the row of registers, to pretend his mind was somewhere else, although he would be sure to peek at the LED display this time.

"D-H-forty, six-twenty, three forty-two American Flyer," he repeated silently to himself.

The man with the tapioca and apples exited the register and the market, and Eugene, fraudulently listless, pushed his items toward the clerk even as she activated the black conveyor belt. He did not regard her but for a second as she scanned each item, and his look was as vapid as could be mustered.

"Eight seventy-three."

With a limp hand he slipped the special twenty from his wallet and passed it to her, Jackson up. He ignored her, continuing to stare at the Wall of Values as though he were puzzled, while at the same time observing that the LED display showed ten dollars as the amount tendered.

"Are you aware your store's display is excluding a family-size can of values?" he said, thinking in this day and age, when the evangelicals were claiming the high ground on everything, the line was worth at least a smile, if not an outright laugh.

"One twenty-seven is your change," said the clerk, furnishing him with neither.

Eugene stared at the money awaiting transfer from her hand to his own. Beneath a furrowed brow, he raised his eyes to meet hers.

"That was a twenty I handed you."

The woman took a step backward. "It is you, isn't it?" she said.

"You've cheated me before. I'm not about to let you do it again."

The woman shook her head once, twice, like she couldn't believe this was happening to her a second time, and attempted some anger.

"Would you like me to show you what you gave me, huh? Would you?" She went into the register's drawer with the ferocity of a claw hammer in a villainous hand and whipped out a worn Hamilton. She held it out in front of his face, so near that the ragged bill's fusty odor was suffusive enough to mask the usual smells of the market. "This. This is what you gave me! You didn't give me a twenty. You gave me this ten-dollar bill. And if you ever looked at your money, you old coot—and I'm not going to apologize for that—you would have noticed that some previous owner of it once wrote out a telephone number in the corner."

"A twenty," Eugene said with unruffled calculation. "I

gave you a twenty, young lady, and you know it."

"Well, then you're just going to have to prove it because I'm tired of messing with you and getting called a thief."

"Where's the manager?"

"You want the manager? All right, we'll summon the manager." She lifted her head and raised her voice. "Jerry? Would you come over here? Jerry?"

Eugene shifted his attention in the direction she was calling and saw a single head pop up from the raised cubicle near the front of the store. He was unable to tell the age and height of the manager until the man stepped down from the cubicle, and then he saw that Jerry was about the same age as his son-in-law and almost identical in his shortness. The manager walked toward the cashier and him, and Eugene could tell by the subtle swagger that this Jerry was of the type who is automatically suspicious of the customer.

"Is there a problem?"

"This is the store manager," Dara said to Eugene. "You can deal with him." Then to Jerry, proceeding on the overworked basis that the best defense is a good offense, she said, "This is Riddell Parker's old man. He's accusing me of stealing money from him. He's done it before. So don't go telling me to be nice to someone who thinks I'm Jimmy Skilling, or whatever the name of that Enron guy was."

Jerry failed to repress a smile. *He obviously likes his employee Dara and her cleavage,* thought Eugene.

"What makes you think she took money from you, Mr. Parker?"

"I passed her a twenty. She attempted to return me change for a ten," Eugene answered, foregoing, for the moment, a correction to his relationship with Riddell.

Jerry cocked his head and rubbed his brow, which was the size of a tablet. "Look, if that's all there is to it, that's easy enough," he said. "When she cashes out at the end of her shift, if she's ten over, we'll send it along. Are you living with your son? Is that where we can find you?"

"Excuse me, but you've already let something slip your mind. I didn't say she made a mistake. Your clerk here, Jerry, is a thief. Have her cash out now."

Even as he said it, Eugene was sure this suggestion would not be abided, and in fact the furrows in Jerry's face reconfigured almost instantly like a computerized line animation to remind Eugene which of them was the store manager with authority. Now Dara was repressing a smile, though barely.

"She's a few more hours before the shift changes, and so we're not going to do that, sir."

"In that case, open the cash drawer and look at the twenty on top. You'll find its serial number to be D-H-forty, six-twenty, three forty-two A-F."

Jerry hardened his gaze at Eugene, held it for a few seconds, then threw it at Dara. When she failed to move to open the cash drawer, he reached past her and did it himself. She peered over his shoulder at the twenty-dollar bill.

"D-H-forty, six-twenty, three forty-two A-F," Eugene repeated, pleased the baseball mnemonic of Designated Hitter and the other of the toy train he played with as a child had worked!

"The drawer was open," Dara said to Jerry, who was now looking at his employee with *What the hell is going on here?* written all over his face. "He read it and memorized it while I was putting his items in a bag."

"You could have, sir," said Jerry, still not wanting to believe an accomplished thief was on his payroll.

"If you'll turn the bill over, you'll find my name, address, and telephone number printed along the bottom margin."

Jerry slipped the bill from its assigned compartment in the register and flipped it. "Eugene Barish?" he said, puzzled.

"Banish," Eugene corrected him. "Eugene Banish. And just for the record, I'm not the father to Riddell Parker."

Jerry looked back to his employee.

"I have it on good authority," she said.

Eugene reached out his hand and gimmeed his fingers. "I'd like the rest of my money. I'd like it now."

SIX

The call came two days later, a chilling middle-of-winter day with the clouds low and synovial and making everyone wonder if the sun would ever shine again in Upper Brell. Paulette answered.

"Hello. May I speak with Gene?"

A woman's voice, it seemed overly familiar even though it was faintly hesitant. She hadn't heard anyone ever refer to her father as Gene. Always, it was Eugene, or sometimes Banish. To the best of her recollection there had never been a diminutive or a nickname.

"Yes, he's around here somewhere. I'll try to find him. May I say who's calling?"

"I'm not sure," said the woman. "We may be old classmates. And then again, maybe not. Probably it's best if you don't say anything."

Paulette caught herself suddenly looking at the phone from inches away.

She found Eugene downstairs in the TV room. He was reading *Martze* to Marshall who was half listening, half giggling, the latter a reaction to Brownie who sat on the carpet to one side of the sofa, licking the dangling right hand of the boy.

"Dad, there's someone on the phone. A woman."

"Her name isn't Dara, is it?"

"Who?"

"Does she sound angry?"

"No, she sounds very nice. Do you not want to talk with her? I can tell her you've disappeared."

"No, I'll take it," he said.

"Ouch!" cried Marshall, whisking his hand up and away from Brownie.

"What's the matter, Marshall?" Paulette asked.

"He tried to bite me," said the boy.

"Oh, he did not," said Eugene. "Brownie's not going to bite you."

"He did to."

The cocker was lifting up its nose toward the boy and Marshall slapped a hand at it. "No, no," he said in a whining tone.

"Now stop that," said Eugene. "I'll be back in a few minutes and we'll finish the story."

"Come on, Brownie," said Paulette. She reached down to pick up the dog. "You get on outside awhile before you get yourself into trouble."

Upstairs, Eugene took hold of the phone.

"Hello. This is Eugene Banish."

"This is Myra Songer. I used to be Myra Fassett?" There was a moment of silence, and then the woman asked, almost sheepishly, "Is my name familiar?"

Eugene realized he was smiling to himself because of a couple things. One, the woman sounded much as she had in high school. Two, if she'd not identified herself, his memory of her most likely would never have emerged.

"It is," he answered. "I graduated from high school with a Myra Fassett. Are you one and the same?"

"I am," said the woman, and he overheard a soft note of relief in her voice.

"How are you?" he then asked. "If my math is correct, the last reunion is already about twenty-five years ago."

"At least," she said. "It was fun."

"It was fun."

He was trying to determine quickly why the woman might be calling, and one reason only was coming to mind. She had been a teenager talked about. Although he had no firsthand knowledge that what had been circulated about her was true... well, if it was then, it might still be true today. And if some people thought that didn't matter at his.... He became aware his head was slowly shaking. More than forty years after the fact—or rumor—and he was still reacting the same. He was an idiot, a shameless idiot!

"How are things with you?" the woman asked.

"Oh, they've been better," he replied. "My wife died a while back, and I'm now living with my daughter and her husband. How about yourself?" Even as he asked it, it occurred to him that she had contacted him at the Parker household.

"My husband and I divorced many years ago and I never remarried."

To that he was uncertain what to say, and so another silence developed, a silence that he did not want to be the one to break.

"The reason I'm calling, Gene? It has to do with my granddaughter, Dara."

"Oh," said Eugene.

"I'm not calling to complain, believe me. Dara got what she deserved. I have friends who shop at Sparkleman's and they've told me stories about receiving the wrong change from her. But in the end they always dismissed it as their own error and that, I think, is what Dara counted on. However, when I heard from my daughter that you were the one responsible for getting her fired—and Linda is not of the same mind as me when it comes to Dara—I thought it was the best comeuppance that could have happened.

You see, when we were in school, the rest of us thought of you as being honest and incapable of lying, and these aren't qualities Dara has ever believed exist. I tried talking to her once over Linda's objections, but Dara, I could tell, thought her grandmother was an old fool. So I suppose I'm calling to kind of thank you, Gene."

"I didn't realize she had been fired," he said.

"Yes, she was let go."

"For some reason she mistook me for my son-in-law's father."

"Did she?"

"Yes, she did.'

"Well, you've probably been together in the store a time or two."

"He grew up on the other side of the river in West Deer," he said, knowing her explanation was false on its face.

"Linda's always lived in the Valley," she replied. After a pause from both of them, she laughed and added, "So it seems you have yourself a mystery to solve."

"If I do, it's not much of one," he allowed. Then unexpectedly he found himself saying, "Why don't we get together this afternoon. For a coffee or something. I'm not doing anything."

"Coffee…? Well, all right," she said, unable to keep an unexpected moment of fluster out of her voice. "A coffee would be wonderful. We'll have our own reunion, so to speak. We never really talked at the last."

He suggested a small eatery not too far from himself, but she recommended a shiny reconstructed diner called Emcee's that had been featured in the local paper. It was situated just off the other side of the bridge, whose repairs were recently completed, which meant he would have to drive the bypass with its faster speeds and he had been avoiding that, but in the end he submitted to her wish.

At mid-afternoon he swung the gray Plymouth into Emcee's front parking lot and saw immediately that she had arrived ahead of him—the years hadn't spoiled his immediate recognition of the woman. She was sitting alone in a booth to the far left of the gleaming metallic entrance and although he felt sure she had observed him turning in and knew that it was him and no one else, she was waiting for him to come inside before she smiled, or waved, or offered a greeting.

Her back was to him as he approached the booth, and he wondered if she had been in any minor turmoil deciding whether to face the entrance or face away.

"Myra?"

She half-turned and raised her eyes. "Hi." It was soft, straightforward, not brimming with enthusiasm, but neither was enthusiasm absent.

There was nothing on the table in front of her and she saw that he noticed.

"I only just got here myself," she said. "It's so good to see you."

He nodded. It was good to see her too. He had felt some reservations forming about this as he was crossing the bridge, although he couldn't answer himself why, but now they all fled. Still, neither made a move to touch the other in any manner.

"Have you never been here since it opened?"

"I read about it," he said, dropping to a seat. "But my daughter's house is a few miles on the opposite side of the bridge. Which reminds me. How did you know to call there? I meant to ask you on the phone."

"Again, one of my friends. She was in the store when you called my granddaughter's bluff. She's seen you in the company of your daughter who doesn't live too far from one of her children. When she mentioned the last name, I just thought it could be you."

"And where do you live? Somewhere nearby?"

"Oh no. I live on the other side of the bridge as well. I own a home on Van Buren. You must be familiar with it."

"It's one of the oldest streets in Lower Brell. One of the steepest, too. Great for sledding when you were a kid if there was a little daredevil in your blood."

"I've been to Emcee's before and liked it very much. It's the only reason I suggested we meet here. What do you think?"

"It's nice," said Eugene, casting a surveying sweep about the interior. "Plus, we get a view of the river and that's always a plus." Outside, between the pale ice that each day was stretching itself further from the banks, a chugging white tug with the name *Dickey Lee* painted in green along its bow was pushing two long barges full of rusted amorphous metal past them down the Allegheny River toward the Acmetonia Lock and Pittsburgh.

The diner was mostly empty at the mid-afternoon hour and a waitress with hair compressed to her skull, who had been in the backroom performing double-duty with the greasy dishes, emerged wiping her hands in a towel and asked what they would like to order. Both ordered coffee, Myra one of the new trendy flavors, as the diner offered a handful; and when Eugene decided he would have a sweet roll, so also did she.

They talked for much of the next hour, commiserating briefly on their current situations, more inclined to speak of their younger days. Although it had been a relatively small school they had attended—one hundred-three graduates in their class—both realized neither knew the other well, even in their memories. The truth was, they had talked more at their last reunion, which still wasn't anything to speak of, than they had in high school. They had shared some classes, Geometry and Latin I, but neither course had served to catalyze anything more than a simple acquaintance between them.

Eugene was suddenly ashamed of himself for having permitted the same thoughts to rush into his head about this woman, the same thoughts that had rushed in when he was young and his hormones had been trying to control him. Very likely those thoughts had been wrong. What had he really known about her? Probably nothing more than most of his classmates. But like them, he had talked about her behind her back as though she were putting out for every guy in the county. Thank god, though, he hadn't talked as much. Hopefully, that would be worth something in the land of redemption.

"You're looking good," she said, her head slightly cocked to one side, as though the statement were the end to some careful analysis.

"You're looking good as well," he said.

"Does that mean Gene Banish is capable of lying after all?"

He couldn't help but release a smidgeon of laugh. "Come now. You look wonderful. You certainly haven't transmogrified into a tons-o-fun like some others I've run into."

"Transmogrified?" She couldn't keep herself from smiling her appreciation of his use of a favorite word. "You must read Calvin and Hobbes!" she said, elated. "That's the only place I've ever seen that word. I do wish Bill Watterson hadn't retired."

In some way he thought he could probably think of her as attractive, which was a quality he was thankful he possessed. As he'd grown older, his interest in women remained with those who were his age or somewhere around it. Sometimes he glanced at younger women, those in their twenties and early thirties, but he felt no real desire as he did when he stared at a female who had retained some of her good figure and had a few dashing lines of gray streaming from her temples.

"Anyway," she said, "if I'm debatable, clearly you are not. If I didn't know you were my age, I'd guess you were at least ten years younger. You look very good, Gene."

"Looking good, maybe," he said. "But all's not well on the inside. The eyes seem to be going. The ears, too."

"Well, I can sympathize with the first," she said. She touched her glasses, ovals in a gold wire frame. "My third prescription in under six years. A friend—you might remember Vera Elspaugh, she was two years behind us—she once told me that failing vision sometimes reverses itself a few degrees. Mine seems determined to plunge in one direction only."

"How did you come to live in Lower Brell?" Eugene inquired.

"My marriage. You'd think we would have crossed paths at one time or another."

"My daughter actually lives in Upper Brell, and my wife and I had a home in Arlion. But it wouldn't have mattered. It's all changed, gotten too big everywhere throughout these parts since we were young. Sprawl and more sprawl. Except for a young paramedic and her abusive spouse who live at the corner of the street, I don't think my daughter and her husband are even remotely aware of the people who make up their neighborhood."

As they ate their sweet rolls, Eugene watched her delicately wipe her fingers with a napkin. She caught the attention of the waitress and signaled for refills of their cups without asking him. Myra Songer was a nice woman with a kind face void of deception and any intention to manipulate. Eugene realized she must have been nice when they were together in school as well. It was easy to miss a lot when you were a stupid kid. Thank God, the adults at the time hadn't told him his generation knew more than theirs, else he'd still be stupid.

She angled her head again. "Can I ask you something? Something many of your female classmates wondered about?"

"Oh-oh."

"It's personal. Maybe I shouldn't be asking."

"I like to think I've grown up by this late date," he said, smiling. "Go ahead. Ask away. I promise, I won't be offended."

Despite his invitation, she remained hesitant. But at last she said, "Why didn't you ever date anyone in high school?"

"I didn't go to the prom either," he replied. "And that's one of my regrets."

He thought she might respond to this because at the time there had been a lot of urging by the principal and various teachers for every student to attend. There had been a great deal of matchmaking underway, mostly to make sure no senior girl was wallflowered.

But when she did not, he explained, "Things were … well, they were just screwy for me back then. I used to think I covered it up, but probably I didn't."

"You often did look sad to me."

"There were things happening in my family at the time, and they weren't good things. I was the youngest, and it just got all screwy for me." He made up a smile. "What can I say?"

It hadn't told her much, very little really, and he could see she was aware of the fact.

When he re-crossed the bridge and swung the

Plymouth into the driveway later that afternoon, he saw Brownie being dragged unwillingly from the front door of the house. Riddell, bent over and obviously angry as great explosions of white cloud were issuing from his mouth in the icy air, had a tight grip on the dog's collar and was dragging the animal relentlessly toward a large pine where a thin chain was attached. Eugene got out of his car and went inside to find his daughter.

"What's happening with Brownie?" he asked.

Paulette was grinning. "Tell me. Is she a widow or divorcee?"

"I asked about Brownie."

"Oh, Riddell's just tying him outside for awhile."

"What did he do?"

"He laps up his water too fast. Two minutes later he's throwing up on the rug. Riddell and I are tired of the mess."

The front door opened and his son-in-law re-entered like a man who had been caught in a deluge. He mounted the steps quickly, skipping every other.

"Goddamn it! If that animal wants to drink and upchuck like some wasted junkie, we might think about putting his water bowl outside!" He went over to the spot on the rug. It looked like an egg had been dropped, except the center was the color of bile. "Look at this shit."

"I was getting it," said Paulette.

"Thing like that's going to happen sometimes," said Eugene. "Why do you two have a dog if you don't expect that?"

"It's a goddamn good question," cursed Riddell, steaming past his wife for the kitchen where he ripped off several paper towels.

"Give them here," said Paulette."

"Out of my way. I'll do it. I would have done it when it happened."

"Now what's that supposed to mean, Hon?"

Eugene started for his room.

"Daaad!"

"What is it?"

"Won't you answer my question?"

He was disgusted with both of them because of their unsympathetic regard for the dog, but he was also disgusted with his own daughter because he believed she was thinking the same thing about Myra Songer that he himself at first had been thinking.

"There's nothing to answer. She and I went to school together, that's all."

"Well, don't go marching off," said Riddell, stooping to sop up the cocker's vomit. "I've got a surprise for you."

"What sort of surprise?" inquired Eugene, suspicious.

"First, you tell me you're not planning on getting married again. What's with this 'She and I went to school together'? You seeing someone all of a sudden?"

"What's the surprise, Riddell? Just answer the question."

"Hey, I don't want you bringing some new bride to live here. You're enough to handle as it is…. I've got a contractor coming by the next day or so. I'm finishing off the top of the garage. Turning it into a rental apartment. I've thought about doing it for some time, and now I've made the decision."

"How's that a surprise for me?"

"Hell, you can move out there! Play your Mozart and Jack Scott. You'll have more room to shuffle around, and so will we."

"What about your idea of renting it?"

"You won't live forever, Eugene."

"Maybe you can ship Brownie off to live with me then."

"Oh sure," said Riddell, his eyebrows arching. "It'll make all the difference in the world when he pukes on a rug of mine in the garage, rather than one in the house. Good thinking, Eugene."

SEVEN

Until the consuming sprawl of steady growth firmly established itself in Lower Brell, once several square miles of farmland mixed with the earliest and most constrained of developments that consisted of hundreds of one-story houses, the town had provided no high school of its own. Eugene and his classmates, who walked the warped wooden floors at the W. Stewart Junior High School (back then, teachers held power, so there wasn't much opportunity for running through the halls), were required during the second half of their ninth-grade year to select either of two neighboring high schools to attend when next September rolled around. Unlike his brother Val and their older sister Aletha who had chosen the much larger and populated, racially mixed Kensington, Eugene opted for Arlion, the pride of a smaller community. Explained, his reasons hadn't amounted to much. He had hoped to play varsity basketball, and at the smaller school he presumed his chances would be improved. Mathematically, they were, but he failed to make even the junior varsity team—because of a lack of outward enthusiasm, according to the coach—and in the end was relegated to playing church ball, a league which offered a bizarre mix of teams so that an eighty-five pound seventh-grader of a Presbyterian in a washed-out T-shirt might find himself defending against a fully uniformed, two hundred-pound Catholic leftover from one of the high school football squads. In fact, Eugene had received outlet passes from a muscular teen with a Polish name who would become a starting offensive lineman for the Detroit Lions.

There were yet other reasons besides basketball behind his selection of the small school, but at the time they were wrapped up to resemble more a feeling that he had, and feelings for most kids are never articulated well, and they certainly hadn't been for Eugene. The first of these feelings arose from the fact that his brother had earned a reputation at Kensington High as a troublemaker, although the younger boy had wondered how Val could be any worse than the boys on the athletic teams and in the after-school clubs whose group pictures in the yearbook showed their members prominently displaying the middle finger on their knees and elbows, inside their crotches, and along the sides of their blemished faces as they posed before the camera. Several of his brother's teachers had made evening telephone calls to Eugene's mother and father, complaining of their older son's aggression toward classmates. Without a full awareness of what he was feeling, Eugene nonetheless had some sense that he would be discriminated against the moment he set foot in a Raider classroom. He was unlike his brother in many ways, too, that's why the feeling bothered him. Val fought; he preferred not. He read; Val said he didn't have time, too busy. But the last reason to attend Arlion over Kensington became for him the most meaningful one and one he sensed as strongly as anything in spite of an inability to express it until he was long on the other side of commencement. The family at that time was already sliding toward disintegration, and it would have been a disaster to enter a new environment where he knew so few and would likely never know everybody. Arlion High, on the other hand, had provided him with the impression it was closely-knit, a whole that would stick together. Even today, although it would require some concentration, he believed he still could list off every person in his graduating class. He doubted Aletha or his brother could do the same with even a quarter of their respective classmates.

In the countless scenarios he had manufactured in his mind beginning in those days so long ago, scenarios in which he hoped someone would take the time and trouble to understand him, there had been many who had asked, but Myra Songer, it turned out, was really the first who was not of his own imagining. Yet how had he responded to this woman, an old classmate, who had seemed genuinely interested? He might as well have told her it was none of her business, the reason he had not dated any of the girls at Arlion. As a teenager, he would have expected his friends to show concern had he confided in them, but today, after years of deliberately keeping his own counsel, he believed they would think him foolish. *All this passage of time and you're still not over her? You're continuing to blame it on your family?* It sounded ridiculous even to himself.

He stopped rocking and removed the scrapbook from the dresser drawer, gingerly opening it to the yellowed picture of the young girls holding their remodeled tin cans for donations to a polio charity. The music, a Chopin opus, was kept low in order not to disturb the slumber of his daughter and her husband in their bedroom across the hall.

On paper the girl's image had faded, details lost to the acid. But in his memory she remained there fresh as ever with her warm, watery, beautiful eyes, the creamy flesh, and her auburn ponytail with its gold pins on either side. One more year would make it fifty, a half-century since he had last seen her. There had been times when he had wondered if she were still alive, and yet he would never dwell in such speculation because something told him with all the certainty of a love, the kind both recondite and transcendent, that she was. But where she was and what she was doing, about these he had no idea. He knew she had married right out of Kensington High—a friend had told him this. But was she still?

Right along Eugene had thought of searching her out, for years he had thought of searching her out, yet he never did, and slowly he began to realize the reason, a much too common one: he did not think he was good enough for the woman. This feeling endured well into his forties, when he was already married, until he felt its shame and discomfiture. It was not a feeling that had generated from her; really, to this day he was unsure of its origin, although like many unpleasant things in his life, he was inclined to connect it to his family and its mess without even a feeble attempt at a reasoned explanation.

"Dad? Is everything okay?"

"I'm sorry, Paulette. I didn't mean to wake you."

She had pushed open the door and her head, poking in, looked to him like some giant balloonish insert.

"Can I come in?"

"I thought the volume was turned low enough."

Despite no answer to her question, Paulette permitted herself to enter the room, glancing around.

"It was the repetition, I think, and the strange combination it makes with Riddell."

She tilted her head toward the partially open door, a suggestion Eugene should do the same. He could hear his son-in-law's awful snoring issuing from the other bedroom.

"What is that anyway?" she asked. "It's not Mozart, is it?"

"It's Fredric Chopin."

"What's the name of it? It's really pretty."

"It doesn't have a name, Paulette. It's a waltz in E-flat Major. Number 17 on the CD, in case you want to play it when I'm not around."

Her eyes drifted to the scrapbook he was holding, and she recognized the prominent picture cut from a newspaper.

"She's the woman you met with today, isn't she?"

"Which?"

"The one on the left."

Eugene smiled.

"You're still a very handsome man, Dad."

"Well, thanks for the compliment, but that isn't who I had coffee with," said Eugene.

"She's very pretty. She probably still is."

He stared up at his daughter. The entire generation seemed to be like that. Always certain they knew, when they didn't. He had told her it was not the woman Myra Fassett and without any evidence she had convinced herself it was.

"How did you get like that?" he asked, not expecting an answer and not receiving one.

She stepped closer and reached over his shoulder to turn a page in the book.

"Is this her, too?" She pointed to the picture of a boy and a girl with paper crowns on their heads.

"Where's Brownie?" Eugene asked.

"Asleep in the laundry room."

"I thought maybe Riddell had left him outside in the cold to teach him a lesson."

"He'd only bark throughout the night. Then we'd all be awake till morning."

Eugene carefully closed the scrapbook and placed it back in the drawer. Paulette did not repeat her question.

"Dad. This woman. I don't know if you care what I

think, but I want to say even though Mom is dead, it's okay with me if you see someone. I meant it when I said you're still a good-looking man, and I don't expect your life to stop because Mom is no longer with us. What I'm trying to say is, you don't have to sit in your room late at night pining over some woman out of your past. You've made a reconnection, and for all I care the next time you can bring her to the house. And don't worry about Riddell. He didn't mean what he said. He just worries we won't have enough money."

"Tell him to sell my house."

"Riddell's a good man, Daddy. I'll admit he has his faults, but he's a good man."

"I'm glad you think so."

"I think you think so too."

"Sorry, the jury's still out."

She stared at her father who got up and switched off the music. She disliked how he always refused to give her husband the benefit of any doubt. She thought it unfair, especially since Riddell had opened up their home to him, which was something she hadn't pressured him to do.

"I'm tired and eager to get to bed," Eugene said.

"Okay, Dad, I'll leave you alone. But can I ask you a question before I go? That girl … "

"Who are you talking about?"

"The woman you met with today. The young girl in your scrapbook. How old was she then?"

Shaking his head hopelessly, Eugene said, "The girl in the picture, that was taken when she was in the eighth grade. I was a year ahead. When I enrolled at Arlion, I never saw her again. Do you want to know why?"

"No," said Paulette. "I'm not trying to pry, honest. Goodnight. I'll see you in the morning."

"Goodnight then."

Even so, at the door she paused and, in a soft voice, said, "It's wonderful, though, Dad. It's wonderful that to this day she remains so important to you. It really is."

It was a strange sentiment coming from his daughter, thought Eugene. Ginger had never demonstrated much romance or sentimentality, and Paulette had always been a lot like her mother.

EIGHT

Retired from his work and the daily interactions with fellow employees, Eugene was not always mindful of his beneficent impairments related to sight and sound. Had his vision and hearing undergone the same transformations much earlier in his life, he might have used them to unmask and call out the fraudulent and most duplicitous of the men at the aluminum plant and, consequently, moved himself up onto the corporate ladder as Ginger too often had urged, even nagged, him to do. As it were, living with his daughter and her husband, he interacted with very few people, no matter the day, and rarely were topics of substance or dispute a subject for conversation. Other parties had no reason to lie to him or even to prevaricate, and he entertained no expectations they would. By the time of the arrival of the contractor who was to build a second floor onto the garage, he had mostly forgotten that what he might sometimes see in the faces of others and hear coming off their tongues differed diametrically from what they proffered. Overlooking this unique feature of his aging eyes and ears might have warped into a debilitating practice in which he might have felt sorry for himself and even feared the worst about losing the two, possibly most important senses, had it not been for the visitations of Pippa Goodwin and Lila Shrum, the latter the contractor his son-in-law had hired to work on the garage and the same woman, he realized after meeting her, he had watched from the top of the slope as she moved around the outside of the houses under construction in the diced-up farmland below.

In her white Ford F-250 pickup that displayed her name and line of business, Lila Shrum came often to the Parker property. Usually, one or two younger male workers accompanied her. Curiously, Eugene observed she would always remain longer than he expected. Contractors with whom he once had an association made the rounds of their numerous jobs that were based on estimates, if only to assure themselves their hourly-paid employees weren't sitting on their backsides drinking coffee from a thermos all day. But seldom did they linger at any particular job, as they were fearful the same lack of activity might be occurring at their other sites. Lila Shrum, on the other hand, sometimes stayed for two and three hours, at times unholstering her framing hammer—a 23-ouncer, Eugene couldn't help but notice and be impressed—and labored right along with her men, but on other occasions talked at length with himself and Pippa Goodwin. She was a strongly attractive woman who, despite the blue jeans, work shirt, high boots, and green sweatband, would have looked stunning and natural in an evening gown. She was confident of her work, mature in her every instruction. The biggest anomaly to the immediate world around her was the refinement of her locomotion. Because of it there could be no presumption she was anything but a woman. Little Eva, he mused, would have hooked her into the locomotive dance line without a moment's hesitation. Pippa Goodwin had guessed Lila Shrum was in her mid-to-late-forties.

"Frankly, I'm amazed my son-in-law hired a woman to do this job," he said to her as they stood outside the garage beneath a brilliant sun. "He's not what I would call 'liberal-minded.'"

"Riddell and I go back a ways."

"And don't forget what Paulette told you, Mr. Banish," offered Pippa Goodwin. "She said although Riddell knows Lila is thorough in her work, she won't be dragging out the job 'til the end of time."

"It's one of my stronger attributes, Eugene. Even though you may enjoy talking with me, you wouldn't want to see me hanging around here throughout the summer and into the fall like some stubborn apple on a tree."

Eugene made a face to say that wouldn't be the case at all, and the two women laughed.

"Well, if that's so," said Lila Shrum, elevating her head, "let me just say if I wasn't happily married, I'd be trying to get you to ask me out for dinner and a movie."

Pippa Goodwin tossed her head back and laughed again. "I think she's serious, Mr. Banish."

She was, thought Eugene. But he was sure it was only himself who understood this. He felt without any reservation that he could have wrapped Lila Shrum in his arms right then and kissed her and while she would have been surprised, she would not have objected. Yes, she was married, but her happiness was not yet something she was certain of, despite her words and gestures to the contrary. They were a mix that both hinted truth and hid it.

He thought his daughter Paulette had sensed Lila Shrum's attraction—there had been previous interchanges of the sort—and it was the reason she no longer came out of the house to join their conversations. Now either embarrassed or uneasy, she remained inside. Occasionally, he caught her observing the three of them from a window.

As for tiny Pippa Goodwin's presence in the group, it was entirely coincidental. She was there either to drop off or pick up Marshall, or to visit his daughter, her friend. But by always dallying so long with Lila and him, Pippa Goodwin, it seemed to Eugene, sensed that something interesting was in the jovial offing and was thinking she could figure out what exactly it was in due time.

Lila Shrum Contracting was indeed a firm that got to the job and kept at it like a colony of beavers. The second floor of the three-bay garage was completed in just eleven weeks from the day work started, and this included all plumbing and electrical hookups according to code, plus a small covered landing at the top of the outside staircase, which had not been approved by Riddell.

"I thought you might want to sit out some days. It's nothing fancy, and it's free."

"Know that I thank you, Lila. I'm sure Riddell will too. By the way, I noticed you had your boys pull up some of the decking they had screwed down only the day before. What was that about?"

"Once in a while they put the crown side down and that can cause the boards to cup. They know better. They just forget."

Just then Riddell's car appeared at the top of the driveway and coasted to a stop.

"It's done, isn't it?" he shouted. He got out, leaving the car door open. A wide grin further stretched the taut flesh of the angular face as he took in the finished work. "Hey, the place no longer resembles 84 lumber, that's how I know. You like it, Eugene? It looks great to me."

"Lila built a small deck up there so I can relax," said Eugene, pointing.

"There were some boards left over. I didn't think you'd mind, Riddell."

"How much?"

"Right up your alley," said Eugene. "No coupon required."

"Good! But no barbecuing up there, and that's an

order."

Lila smiled at Riddell's joke and winked an understanding at Eugene.

"I also installed an overhead fan removed from a previous job," she said. "It'll provide the place and Eugene with a little more ventilation, especially on those super hot days and nights."

"So, do I owe you anything?"

"I think you certainly do, Riddell. I'll let you know the balance in a day or two."

"All right," said Eugene's son-in-law, becoming serious. "Just inform me of the amount and I'll have Paulette drop a check in the mail." He switched his attention to Eugene. "Now as for you, Mr. Tenant, I'm going inside, change out of these clothes, and have me something to eat. Then I think me and you and Paulette should head over to the house in the minivan and bring back a few pieces of furniture. You'll need more than what's in your bedroom, and I don't imagine you want to buy any new stuff."

"Have you had any bites on your house?" asked Lila.

"It's his, not mine. I've told him he's asking too much."

"Were you over there?" Eugene asked.

"A friend from Arlion saw the sign and asked me to go with her. She recently settled with her ex and they awarded him the property."

"You should have called," said Riddell. "I would have let you inside."

"The back door was unlocked," said Lila.

Eugene directed a look of disappointment at his son-in-law. "Let's hope the furniture is still there."

"You think I would steal your things?" teased Lila. She pushed Eugene's shoulder playfully.

Unable to suppress satisfaction at his father-in-law's

moment of embarrassment, Riddell laughed and said, "See? You open your mouth, you make a fool of yourself. So take a lesson."

"Not you," Eugene said to Lila.

"Look, if she's really interested…"

"She likes the house. She thinks it would be perfect."

"It's too large a house for one person!" stressed Eugene.

"Now why are you trying to talk her out of it?" complained Riddell. He shook his head to the sky. "You just don't want to pay me the percentage you agreed to. That's what it's about, isn't it? Admit it."

Eugene glanced at the ground and took a very slow deep breath. He said "Excuse me" to Lila. Then he wheeled about and faced his son-in-law. His voice took on a bottomless patience. "I had figured you to realize this on your own, but apparently that's not happening. So here it is in plain language. You're going to get everything, you and Paulette and the kids. Not right away, but eventually. Right now, you'll get the percentage. But once I'm out of here for good, then you get it all. Nor should you worry I'll squander it all away just to spite you. Once more, Riddell. Paulette, you, and the kids will ultimately get all the money I have."

A few unsteady seconds passed while none of the three spoke. Finally, Riddell guffawed and said, "Listen to this old man, Lila. He'd have me believing that I'm an heir to Bill Gates."

Eugene returned his attention to Lila Shrum.

"She has a pair of teenagers she won custody of," said Lila to further explain her friend's interest in the house.

"In that case the house isn't too big. Does she know the price?"

"It was on the sign."

"I'm going inside," announced Riddell. "Lila, let me know what I owe you and I'll have Paulette send out that check."

"I'll back the minivan out of the garage and get it ready," Eugene shouted as Riddell was strutting toward the house.

"The hell you will, old man! Remove the rear seats where it's parked."

Eugene allowed himself to bob with laughter. "A thing like that always gets a reaction," he said.

Lila Shrum again flashed a smile that told him she knew his son-in-law well, but that she also believed she shared a bond with him.

•••

When they arrived at the white Cape Cod and went inside, Eugene was ready immediately to spin about and leave. Although some of the bigger items had been sold before he joined his daughter at her house, the furnishings that remained told the unmistakable story it was his son-in-law who was now frequenting his old home. Riddell possessed not the slightest knowledge of what a house to be shown to possible buyers should look like. Old newspapers that he must have brought with him to read while waiting on a prospect littered the carpet. He had not thought to clean even the most obvious things and Eugene could see a thick accumulation of fine dust. In the kitchen sink sat dirty mugs, a couple with an inch of coffee at their bottoms and their splash of half-and-half now unsightly scum floating like a hawker at the top. Eugene opened the refrigerator and poked his nose into a milk carton.

"If this friend of Lila is truly interested," he said to Riddell, "do what you can to sell her the house. Even if she offers five-thousand dollars under the asking, forget making a counter. Take it, and let's be done with this place."

"You really do think you're some hoity-toity rich bastard. I thought you wanted to get as much out of it as possible."

"Let's just agree to get it off our hands. It sounded like this woman would appreciate the house."

"Good enough. But I still want the percentage on the original price. Just because you're willing to take less doesn't mean I have to. Especially since I'm the one who's been running his ass off to show this place to every bastard who thinks he can get it for a song."

Eugene couldn't help but goad his son-in-law. "You've told me more than once—you even said the same to Lila!—that my asking price was too high. Now you're complaining?"

"But I went along with it, didn't I? You're goddamn right I went along with it."

Eugene paused a moment, then laughed to himself in relinquishment. "Stay cheerful, Riddell. I'll honor my half of the deal."

The van was a mini and with the three of them inside, there had been very little room remaining for transporting items from the house. Riddell said he would retrieve the rest, the heavier pieces, over the next day or two and immediately after the scheduled carpeting was completed, and that he would enlist someone younger from the trucking firm to help.

Eugene moved himself over top the garage soon after the bed was set up and his television and entertainment system were connected.

"Dad, wasn't this a nice thing Riddell decided to do for you?"

"It's wonderful," replied Eugene, his gaze sweeping

the space. "Not too big and not too small."

"Riddell has another surprise. A mini one. Give it to him, Honey."

Riddell pulled his left hand from behind his back and handed Eugene a newspaper.

"You still see well enough to read, I hope. I got you your own subscription to *The Valley Star-Enterprise*. You're not going to want to come over to the house all the time, and I sure as hell don't want to always traipse up here to retrieve the sports page to learn what the Pirates are doing or to see if Big Ben's got himself in trouble again. What's more, since you're starting to get up in age, you'll probably want to keep a sharp eye on the obituaries, to find out which of your friends are kicking the bucket over from one day to the next."

"Riddell, that isn't funny," Paulette chastised him.

Eugene glanced at the newspaper, its headline and accompanying photo of yet another suicide bombing in the Middle East, then slowly surveyed his new quarters. It was gracious of them, something they didn't have to do, and he was grateful.

"Thank you. Thank you both," he said. "I do appreciate this."

"Then why the hell do you look worried?" asked Riddell.

"Do I look worried?"

"You certainly don't look like someone who just got his own pad and doesn't have to shell out a nickel for it. Does he, Sweetie?"

"Are you worried, Dad, that maybe you shouldn't come next door anymore? If that's what it is, put that out of your mind! You come over any time you want. And you make sure you're around when Marshall's there. I count on you."

Even though his son-in-law's remark about the obituaries had been intended as humor, over the past year Eugene in fact had been checking daily the list of deaths recorded in the bottom left box of the front page, ever since he had noticed the names of two men with whom he once worked closely at the aluminum plant. When he remembered, he checked also the hospital admission and discharge column, a continuing feature of the area paper.

And after his daughter and son-in-law had left and he was able to relax in his new surroundings and work his way through the newspaper, he saw that same evening one name he recognized. His classmate, Myra Songer, formerly Myra Fassett, had been admitted to Salyer General.

NINE

"Dad? Are you up here...?"

"Paulette?"

"Whew! Where's the switch to your overhead fan? Twice in two days. This is more of a climb than I need. I don't think Riddell ever considered this when he planned on moving you up here. Turn the fan on, for godsakes. Get some air going."

He went over to the electrical switch on a wall behind him and flicked it upward. He tugged on the fan's chain to put its blades at their fastest rotation and smelled the instant flow of the cooler air from the garage beneath, along with the faint odors of motor oil and solvents.

"Those steps don't tire you out?" she asked.

"My legs are fine. I also don't lack for breath," he said. "But you, my girl, could stand to lose some weight."

Fatigued, she had been staring at the floor, catching her breath, a collection of mail and newspapers in one hand. When at last she recovered and raised her head, she was inclined to smile. "Why, you're all dressed up. Where are you going?"

"I'm leaving to visit someone in the hospital," he answered matter-of-factly. "Is that today's paper?"

She separated the newspaper and his mail from her own and handed the items over.

"You better look inside and see he hasn't already been

discharged. Is it anyone Riddell and I should know?"

He shook his head. He did not want to start a conversation about the woman he had met at Emcee's. He was dressed to go out but still wasn't convinced he should do what he was about to. He'd mulled it over all last night and this morning and felt guilty when he told himself he wouldn't go, but now felt equally uneasy after deciding he would. He just thought the woman would not expect his appearance and would appreciate it. It might even help her to convalesce, although he had no idea why she had been admitted.

He opened the newspaper and found the hospital page. The name was not among those listed as discharged.

"Are you taking the car? Or would you like me to drive you? Salyer is in the heart of some heavy downtown traffic."

"I'll be careful, not to worry."

He could see how obviously she disapproved of his driving anywhere, but she said nothing. Instead, she unrolled her own copy of the paper and studied the front page.

"Did you want something, Paulette?" he inquired after a while. "I was just about to leave."

Her head drooped to one side and he watched her suddenly frown. "Ahhh. Mr. Enrico died, Daddy. You remember him, don't you? He was my favorite teacher. I think he was everybody's favorite teacher."

Eugene closed his own copy of the *Star-Enterprise*, folded it, and looked at the list of deaths on the front page. Mr. Enrico's name and age were at the top. To his astonishment, printed next to the bottom of the list was the name Myra Songer.

"I remember those occasions when he chaperoned our dances. He would always sing this one love song he was

partial to." Then she pretended to imitate Mr. Enrico, a loose fist her microphone, the ceiling her audience. *"Embrace me, my sweet em-brace-able you."*

"Myra Songer," he said, his voice offering little cooperation. "That's who I was going to visit. I can't believe it. She was admitted only yesterday."

Paulette ceased her performance. She required a few seconds to make the connection and glanced back at the paper in her hands and again searched the list of names in the corner.

"Gee, I'm sorry, Dad. How well did you know her?"

Two beads of moisture formed in his eyes, to his surprise. How well had he known this woman? Hardly at all, if he was to be honest. So why, then, was he tearing up?

"Dad?"

Reluctantly, he answered, "You remember. She was the person I had coffee with during the winter."

"Oh. The girl in your scrapbook."

He shuddered from instant annoyance, and the water left his eyes. "No.... Paulette, did you want something or did you just climb the stairs to drop off my mail?"

"Is there anything I can do, Dad?"

"YOU CAN ANSWER THE DAMN QUESTION!"

Recoiling from the volume, she stared at him. It had been a long time since she had witnessed her father so upset. He hadn't been so upset when her mother had passed away.

"I have to run an errand," she said with patronizing calm. "I was just wondering if you would go over to the house and stay with Marshall till I return. He's napping now."

He yanked the knot from the tie and started to unbutton the blue dress shirt he was wearing.

"Dad?"

"I'll walk over in a little while," he said.

"Thanks." She continued to stare at him, deciding on something. "Dad, if you think you'll be attending this woman's funeral, I can drop your suit off at the cleaners. It's probably in need of pressing."

"Get out," he said and waved her away without meeting her eyes. "Just get out." He could easily picture himself running into the granddaughter Dara who thought Myra was a fool. She wouldn't refrain a second from making a scene. No, he would not be going to the funeral. He wouldn't be attending the viewing either.

He listened to his daughter drive off the property as he continued to change into other clothes. Minutes later he shut off the overhead fan and descended the exterior staircase. It was bright outside from a sun that owned the sky and the spring temperature was unusually warm. Patches of marigolds across from the big, whitewashed maples were popping open. Brownie recognized he was on his way as the dog began barking from inside the utility room where Paulette and Riddell locked the animal whenever they left the house.

"I hear you," he called out. "I'm on my way." The little dog improved his spirits every time he saw it. His high school classmate Myra Fassett was dead, but Brownie was most definitely alive.

He entered the house and after peeking in on the sleeping child, went to release the cocker from the utility room, which was much warmer than the rest of the house because Paulette had clothes in the dryer and they were continuing to spin.

"No wonder you're barking," he muttered under his breath. The animal raced out of the overly heated room and past him. He followed, and when he entered the kitchen, Brownie was standing in the far corner of the linoleum

staring back at him.

"Think they'll ever learn you're too short to reach the sink?" He shook his head to himself.

He went over and, after picking up the dog's bone-dry water bowl and scouring the inside rim with his fingers, filled it from the tap. The dog began furiously lapping up the refreshment even before he could replace the bowl on the floor. When it finished, he cautioned, "Listen. Marshall's sleeping and that's a rare afternoon occurrence. So let's not wake him." Sometimes, when he said other words to this effect, he was sure Brownie was nodding. He beckoned the dog to follow him into the living room.

"I just learned that a friend of mine died," he continued in a soft voice. "Correction, she wasn't really a friend. I didn't know her very well. But she was a very nice person and she apparently cared enough about yours truly to look me up this past winter."

Ordinarily the dog would lie flat with its muzzle buried in the carpet, but its awareness that Eugene's attention was on something other than itself prompted the animal to sit up erect and alert, and this response sponsored an immediate rush of truth inside Eugene that he felt embarrassed to admit. It had nothing to do with Myra Fassett, except what she had confessed to him at the end of their meeting: his high school image would come drifting into her mind once a year, she had told him, so that she realized he had a significance in her life she could not explain, but wanted to accept. And that, not Dara, was the real reason she had telephoned.

This truth rushing at him now had to do with the woman with whom he remained in love, despite the passing of fifty long years. How could it be explained that he cared so much about her and yet had never made the smallest effort to see her again? Who had he really been thinking of?

He knelt on the carpet over the cocker who flattened itself, expecting a rub. The dog stretched itself out and Eugene fell prone, burying his nose in the furry spine of the animal as he massaged each of its thigh muscles. The dog issued small pleasing whines that traveled all along the scale, none of greater duration than another. After a time, Eugene rolled on his back and gazed at the ceiling. The cocker, in an unintentional imitation of a seal, while remaining flattened, clumped straightened legs to move itself closer.

"It's time I take stock and realize those who are significant in my own life," he said. He rolled back on his stomach and looked the cocker straight in the eyes. "You are, Brownie. It's not supposed to be this way, I know, with you being an animal with supposedly no soul and no chance for an afterlife, but you're more significant than Riddell. Maybe even more significant than my own daughter. She changed when she married him and she's never changed back. I liked her better the way she used to be." He scratched the dog's head with a single finger, feeling the hard bone beneath the fur. He allowed himself to think of her.

Of course, it was an old image, but at the same time a young image, a pure and unadulterated picture from his last year at Stewart when he was in the ninth grade and she in the eighth. If you kept it intact, memory became the only instrument capable of cheating time. Over the next several days he would think about her with hardly a respite. He thought about her when he first lay in bed at night and there she was on his mind the instant he awoke, and he was certain that he was now, somehow, going to make contact. Yet on the sixth day he was already having doubts. He realized he had no idea how to find her after five long decades. *She could be anywhere. Where do I begin?* Hiring a private investigator entered his mind, not because it was a serious consideration, but because he had seen so many of them on television and had enjoyed watching them all. Mannix, and Harry O with his great voice-over. The Simon Brothers. Rockford and his nutty buddy Angel, who always called him Jimbo, still in re-runs. Even Beverley Hillbilly Buddy Ebsen had a turn at a gumshoe. There was no alumni association like there was at colleges and universities, which eliminated that phone call. And if her high school class at Kensington had ever hosted a reunion, he hadn't a clue as to who might have been the local classmates responsible for its organization.

"It's not likely they would be living in the same place, anyway," he muttered out loud. "The whole country's endlessly mobile. No one seems to ever stop moving."

He soon grew frustrated because he realized he was unequipped to handle a problem such as this and he had always been the kind of man who thought he could handle most things. A person merely had to think and keep on thinking. That's what the brain was for. That's what you could be absolutely sure God gave to you, if you even believed in God, and because of its very nature, expected you to use it and to use it all the time. And so, when he thought he was without ideas, it occurred to him he had read somewhere or heard from somebody that the address of a person could be located on the worldwide Web, and so he drove out to the local branch of People's Library situated off the Lodge Road where he asked for help. He tried the married name he remembered, but she didn't come up; and he tried her maiden name with identical results.

"Maybe she was an early hyphenator, why not try that?" said the young library aide; and they did, but she would not appear.

"If she hasn't remarried and she uses computers, we would have found her name and address. It's probably one or the other, or both," said the aide. "I'm sorry I couldn't be more helpful."

"Thank you all the same," said Eugene.

"Do you know anything about her family? The one growing up?" the aide asked.

"Not much," answered Eugene. "You know… junior high school. You fall in love and there is nobody else."

The young woman smiled with sweet understanding. "Nothing at all? Brothers, sisters?"

"Three brothers, several sisters. But they're likely married with different names. I remember her father was dead. Her mother was raising the family."

"Do you remember her name?"

"Elizabeth. They lived on Lincoln Drive."

"Have you checked that?"

"She'd be approaching her nineties, I would imagine."

"What you're really saying is, you think she's passed on. That might not be the case. For all you know she could still be living in that very same house. I would think that's worth checking out, wouldn't you?"

The woman left him to retrieve a phonebook beneath the circulation desk.

"Good luck," she said, handing it over.

Eugene could hardly believe his eyes. There continued to be a listing for Elizabeth Hardinge on Lincoln Drive. And if he wasn't mistaken, except for the area code and the absence of a lettered exchange, the number was the same one he had dialed when he had asked his first love, very nervously, to go rollerskating at the Mellowwood Rollerdrome, which today remained a pile of rubble as the grandsons of the owners were continuing to wait for new development, and the money that accompanied it, to expand into their area of the county.

He glanced at his watch—it was around noon—then left the library to find a phone, which was no easy task. He felt both excited and afraid. The voice that answered belonged to a younger woman.

"Hello?"

"I wonder if I might talk with Elizabeth Hardinge. Mrs. Hardinge."

"Let me see if she is feeling up to it."

"Excuse me, are you family?" he asked, in case he was incorrectly judging the age of the voice.

"No, I'm her nurse."

"I'm sorry, I don't mean to be a bother. Perhaps you can help me." He introduced himself and mentioned that he had attended school with Mrs. Hardinge's youngest daughter. "W. Stewart Junior High School. I doubt that's familiar to you since it hasn't been in existence for quite some time."

"Actually, I went to Stewart myself," the nurse responded quietly. "Part of its final class."

"Small world," said Eugene. And after a pause: "I'm trying to find Connie Hardinge and renew a friendship. Unfortunately, I haven't any idea as to where she might be living."

With this there was a longer pause and he presumed the woman was thinking, *Is he legitimate?* or was this some stalker or psychopath on the line? He appreciated her caution. It couldn't be overdone in today's unpredictable world, and he wanted nothing harmful to come to Connie Hardinge.

"Give me a second," the woman finally said.

Connie Hardinge, he presently would learn, was residing inside the state in a small community whose name was not unfamiliar to Eugene, but whose location was. A short while later, he purchased a map at a convenience store and estimated it was a four-hour drive, all on slower, two-lane roads. No phoning, he told himself—he couldn't risk a rebuff. Of course he wanted to hear her voice, but more than anything, he wanted to lay eyes on her.

It was just under eight miles, the distance from the community library to the Parkers', a pleasantly winding drive through some of the last untainted country within Lower and Upper Brell; and returning, he began to make plans, although these resembled mostly an unsettling disarray of thought and conjecture because there were so many factors unknown to him. Was she still married, remarried? Was the husband civil, was he even alive? If so, was he well? How might he react to a man out of nowhere suddenly appearing on his doorstep asking to see his wife? What would he, the visitor, say if the husband were to come to the door? The mental image he was percolating put Connie and himself alone in the living room or the kitchen of her house. First, put her alone at her door, and then an invitation for him to come inside where the reunion would really begin. What about her? Really, what if there was something wrong? What if some terrible event was unfolding in her life at this very moment? He realized this as a possibility, but because of the nurse was quick to discount it. Their telephone exchange had been minimal; still, he had sensed in the younger voice a thoughtfulness. She would not have flung a virtual stranger at the daughter of the woman for whom she was caring if there was trouble. Even so, what if there had been tragedies in the past? What if she had gone through a lot in her life and it now showed on the surface? What, he thought, if she looked nothing like she had, like he remembered her, if she looked old and worn-out? He had taken on age easily and he knew from others that he continued to look considerably younger than he was. Some had placed him in his fifties, a few even in his forties. There was some vanity in his thinking, he realized this as well, but it was a possibility to be aware of because, when the moment arrived, he didn't want to look surprised. In no way did he want to hurt Connie Hardinge.

During the last mile of the drive he grew optimistic about his upcoming visit and stuck to the items he could control. For one, he needed to replace the Plymouth's rear tires, he told himself, as the ones presently on his car Riddell had transferred from his own.

"I'll be putting on plenty more miles than you, Eugene, so that's the reason for the switcheroo."

"Look, if you're short..."

"No way. I just hate to see things go to waste. These tires of yours will dry-rot in no time if they don't get much use."

Naturally, that wasn't true—it would be another ten years till his top-of-the-line radials showed signs of the summer heat—but this occurred soon after moving from his home to his daughter's and he had let it go.

Also, he made up his mind to leave early in the morning whenever he did finally go, and he did not intend to tell Paulette or her husband until the last minute, as they would be sure to try and stop him from driving such a distance. He had some worries regarding this himself, he admitted, but they were the reason he planned to drive only while the sun was up. Consequently, he would be staying over once he got there, probably in a motel, unless the reunion went so well that she invited him to remain at her home overnight.

All this and more was he thinking, and so it would have been the farthest thing from his mind, what was happening at the home of his daughter, when he turned into the driveway. Pippa Goodwin, he observed, was outside the house and hurrying toward her car. She seemed upset and appeared to be crying. Marshall ran in front of her and she kept pushing at his back. Every time he glanced over his shoulder, she forced the boy's head to look the other way. Eugene couldn't make anything of it, and when he got out of his car and stood beside the door, although the woman and her child were already behind him, he raised his voice and inquired if there was anything wrong.

"I asked him not to do it, Mr. Banish!" Pippa Goodwin cried out, choking on the words. "I told him the skin isn't even broken. It's just a little red. But he won't listen."

Again, Marshall, nearly losing his balance, disobeyed the actions of his mother and stretched his head back over his shoulder. Eugene could see the child's eyes were directed at the pines on the far side of the house, and in the next instant he spotted the cocker sitting on the ground, its entire body trembling with fright. In front of the animal stood Riddell, who then took a single step that positioned him behind and slightly to the side of the dog, and Eugene watched as his son-in-law, projecting an image of brilliant clarity as there was not the faintest intention to deceive, raised the revolver and eased it behind the right ear of Brownie. The muffled eruption from the small caliber followed, barely sending a ripple through the late-afternoon air, but the dog rolled over onto the dark earth.

With every stride Eugene took he stumbled.

"He's not sufferin'!" Riddell exclaimed when his father-in-law neared the pines. "One slug was enough."

Eugene approached in his last steps with deliberation and firmer footing. At last he stood over the dead animal he had considered a friend and companion. He knelt to touch its tawny fur. Blood was draining out its mouth.

"What are you looking at me for? You think I should have called out the vet? Get real. I wasn't about to shell out no thirty bucks for someone to stick a needle in his neck when a bullet does just as well."

Eugene moved his gaze from Riddell's sickening face to the gun.

"Hey, old man. Be thankful it was the .22. I could have used the 12-gauge, and then you wouldn't have recognized him from hash. You gonna say something, or just continue to kneel there like some wild-eyed jihadist?"

"Why?" said Eugene, struggling.

"If you have kids around, then you can't put up with a dog that bites. Simple as pie, Eugene."

"Paulette go along with this?"

"She had no say in the matter. I told her after we married if she had any ideas about taking on like her ol' lady took on with you, she had another thing coming. Of course your daughter's a trusting soul. She doesn't believe her friend would ever sue us. But I'm not anywhere near as trusting when it comes down to money. Pippa Goodwin's a single mother and if she had a chance to get a piece of me, you can bet she would. Take a look at that wreck she's driving out of here. Take a good look."

"You could have found a home where there weren't any children, if that was worrying you. You could have given Brownie to me. I asked you to."

"You get your own hound, Eugene. This dog was my responsibility."

His son-in-law was making Eugene sick.

Riddell flashed something resembling a smile. The old man was half nuts, as far as he was concerned.

"Go ahead, make your goodbyes, or say your last words. I'll be right back."

More blood was flowing out of the brain and into the cocker's mouth. Eugene watched it pool on the earth beneath its nose and soil the tip of its left front paw. He began to cry.

Riddell was back too efficiently. From his hand hung a green garbage bag and he began snapping it in the air to open it.

"What are you doing?"

"What do you think I'm doing?"

"Get away from here!"

"Hold on now, old man. Don't go getting threatening."

"Get away, Riddell! Or so help me…."

Riddell hesitated and squinted, more to himself "You old fool, you think you know something about killing, do you?"

Eugene held his reply as he met the gaze of his son-in-law. Then he raised a finger and pushed away the tears from both eyes. Had Riddell possessed Eugene's altered vision, he would have realized the action of his father-in-law carried neither shame nor apology.

"All right, if you're wanting to bury him, if that's what's bothering you, go do it," said Riddell. "What do I care! Only you make sure he's buried deep enough so some other animals don't dig him up overnight. I don't want to discover a chewed-up carcass in my driveway when I leave for the terminal at sun-up."

TEN

The picture in his mind would not fade—the execution of his little companion. The ambivalence he had felt for his son-in-law was gone. Riddell, on feet firm but nimble, had taken a single stride from the front of the terrified dog to its back, then brought the gun up from his side, straightened his arm, and with no sign of doubt about what he was doing, released a bullet into Brownie's brain. A distant photograph from some magazine, or maybe an early newsreel watched inside the Kent theater in Arlion when he was just a child, of the Nazi Joseph Goebbels flashed to Eugene's mind and stuck there, finally warming to a kind of putrid infarction. The ankle-length coat of the skinny Aryan psychopath had been the only thing missing from the tragic scene in the pines.

Riddell and his daughter, he would soon reflect, had never been, would never be, admirers, much less lovers, of things animate. Rather, they were possessors, and this was the reason Brownie was dead, this and the cocker's unfailing loyalty. Earlier dogs without its kind of devotion had left the Parker boundary, never to return. Cats, too. Why, soon after their marriage, Riddell had delivered to the couple's new home an Irish Setter, and Paulette, a Sylvester-resembling feline a friend had wanted rid of. Yet within months both pets were lost, and Eugene remembered, when he had encouraged his daughter and son-in-law to place an ad in the *Star-Enterprise* and visit the area's shelter, Riddell had responded, "Forget that! They don't want to be here, they don't gots to."

"But perhaps they didn't run off," Eugene had tried to reason. "Maybe they took a wrong turn. My heavens, son, don't you remember when you forgot the route to your new home the second time you drove out?"

"They don't want to be here, they don't gots to."

Another dog, a mix of several breeds, which had been initially in the house, was later forced to stay outside in a terribly confining pen because, according to Riddell, it was "stinking up everything." When the opportunity for freedom presented itself, this creature too disappeared.

In the end, Eugene was sure all the animals had run off and their reason wasn't hard to understand. Very likely it was the same reason Junior had departed the region in favor of some obscure town in Northern Oregon, declining a job his father had wrangled for him and accepting the same kind of work for several thousand dollars less. He had no doubt either as to why his granddaughter didn't visit. She, in fact, had used the words, which he, along with Ginger, who at the time did not know she had less than six months to live, had been on hand to hear.

"Neither of you love me. Neither of you want to help me. All you and Daddy really want is to own me."

She would keep the baby, marry the father, and the new family would move from the Valley. Where they lived today wasn't far from St. Andrews, Connie Hardinge's place of residence.

Dogs, cats, and children, all gone. And as for those creatures that were unable to leave, the tropical fish and the budgies, they died and were quick to do it.

Even Almighty God, it seemed, had tipped His hat and said "Farewell" to the Parker household, catching on a few years after their church marriage that the young couple's use of "my" in "my God" revealed a possessive not of their simple acknowledgment of Him, but rather of their intention to control the Prime Mover of the Universe.

In the days and weeks that followed the death of Brownie, Eugene was again on hand to listen to his daughter and Riddell, only this time without their knowing that his presence was nearby. And as they spoke of him, their exchange flashed him the warning: *From here on out, you best be wary!*

"He wasn't just drizzling salt water, Sweetie! What I'm telling you is, the floodgates were open and over a dog that wasn't his! That a child might get bitten and we could have our keesters sued, that didn't faze him in the least. He just stood there shedding tears and threatening your hubby."

Eugene mistakenly had expected his daughter to defend him.

"Remember the young girls in his scrapbook, Hon? It was one of them who died not long after she got in touch with him. I know he cared about her, but he hadn't seen her, I don't think, for a very long time, and yet he started crying, like immediately when he learned the news of her death."

"I know he's your old man, Sweetie, but behavior like that is goddamn weird, you gotta admit. Normally, it takes a little time for a thing like that to sink in."

"You should have been there, too, to see how he got upset with me, his daughter who cares about him, simply for asking a question regarding the poor woman's funeral. He actually ordered me out of the apartment.... Hon, maybe living above the garage all by himself, maybe that isn't a good thing."

ELEVEN

On the morning following the alarming conversation of his daughter and her husband, Eugene departed for the small upstate community of St. Andrews. He had awakened in the dark, showered and dressed, then waited patiently inside the apartment until Riddell drove off to work. He then crossed the driveway and slipped into the house where he positioned a post-it note on the kitchen telephone for Paulette to find after she got up and began her ritual of putting away the dishes she had washed and dried in the rack the night before. As would be all of his future communications to the couple, the note was brief.

"Driving up to see a friend. Back in a few days," it read. *"Eyesight this sunrise the best in years."* He had included this last bit of information after recalling Riddell had an acquaintance who was a state trooper, and his son-in-law had once threatened to inform the lawman of Eugene's questionable vision if the old man ever dared to drive more than a few miles outside of Upper Brell.

To reach St. Andrews he had marked out a northerly two-lane route on his map. It now wound him through the more mountainous regions of the state so that he soon acquired a fundamental composure, one he had not experienced for too long a time. It was strong, unexpectedly enthusiastic, forward-looking, and resulted greatly from the discovery that his only offspring would conspire with her spouse to control and limit him. Disconcerting as this information was upon first overhearing it, he realized he held the upper hand so long as he remained alert.

A second part of this composure flourished from the thrill of leaving sprawl behind. Developments diminished with every mile, as did people, while the car rolled reassuringly under him and the engine performed without a flaw, and shortly he was driving through country rife with tall trees, thick brush, and clean meandering streams. He saw cats languishing on porches and dogs greeting each other. Either would have been an unwelcomed anomaly in the housing plans of the Brells where he rarely saw even the occasional feline cutting across a lawn or the trotting, carefree hound pause to claim an azalea or rhododendron bush. In truth, in the well-groomed front lawns of those houses it was a rarity to see a human form, and yet there were thousands of them.

The third and final part of this new composure sprouted naturally from the anticipation he was experiencing of seeing once again the woman with whom he had been in love for most of his life. In his mind he realized the possibilities that could prevent the reconnection from happening. He warned himself that she could be vacationing, or visiting her children who might live out-of-state. They might even pass each other on the highway if today she was driving down to see her mother, and Eugene occasionally caught himself straining at the occupants of a car on the opposite side of the centerline that rushed by with a woman at the wheel. But in his prolonged buoyancy he discounted all these, as well as other possibilities, and trusted to fate she would be in her home in St. Andrews.

"Excuse me!" he shouted, leaning toward the open window on the opposite side of the car. "I'm searching for

Farrell Lane!"

The portly man, on foot and dotted with perspiration, opened the passenger door on the car and got in.

"A nice day for walking, but I'm already pooped," he said.

Eugene stared with incredulity at his instant passenger.

"Hope you don't mind," said the man, who offered an expression suggesting he would be disappointed if Eugene were to mind.

"Not so long as you don't produce a gun and point it at my head," exclaimed Eugene, and he immediately frowned upon realizing the significance of his words, which, despite the passing of weeks, were still fresh.

The man laughed. "Hey, I never considered Charlton Heston to be much of an actor, although I did like him for the mayor in *Chiefs*." Eugene's puzzled expression caused the man to raise a fist to the roof in order to illustrate a vague NRA allusion.

Eugene decided his passenger was odd, but okay, and directed his eyes to the outside mirror, preparing to pull back onto the road.

"Where to, to get to Farrell?"

"No GPS?"

"No, and it's not on my map."

"Make a right at this next light."

"St. Andrews is bigger than what I expected."

"Yes, we've got ourselves an industrial complex."

"I saw that," said Eugene.

"And a Walmart."

"Saw that, too. A Super."

"You know you've arrived when you get a Walmart," said the man.

Eugene understood his overweight rider was speaking facetiously and grinned at him while making the turn.

"Count three blocks and you can drop me. Then go another block and make a right. You'll be on Farrell. It's a long road. I'm surprised it's not marked on your map. Know where you're going? The number?"

"Twelve thirty-eight," said Eugene.

"That's near the middle, if I'm not mistaken. Who is it? Family?"

"No, it isn't family," he said, but Eugene would not offer the man anything more.

Finally, when he drifted to the curb to release his passenger, the man said, "Sure you don't want to tell me who you're visiting? I could probably direct you right to the house. Tell you exactly what to look for. I've lived in St. Andrews all my life. Not many folks I don't know at least their name."

"Thanks, but I'll find it."

"What's the matter? Afraid I'll go over there and steal her away?"

"What?" said Eugene.

"Just tugging your chain," said the man. "You take it easy, sir, and have yourself a nice day."

Eugene nodded, blinked, then returned the car to traffic. *Another block and turn right.*

Now that he was closer than ever, the earlier anxiety that something would go wrong with the visit resurfaced and he found himself dawdling on Farrell Lane, slowing the car in the one hundred block to under twenty miles per hour. Then, in the six hundred block he decided to check the house number and her last name again, and so he withdrew his wallet and the slip of paper inside; and although he didn't angle to the berm, the car crawled almost to a stop, whereupon others behind him sounded their horns and scooted around, scowling at him as they did.

A civil neighborhood, he mused. *Anger without obscenity.*

But he could delay only so long before the car approached the twelve-hundred block and presently her box number appeared.

Unlike the other homes on the street, the house belonging to Connie Hardinge, a two-story white clapboard structure, sat on a triple lot and rested nearer the back than front among a small stand of mature cherry and poplar trees. The white gravel driveway was wide enough for only a single car and Eugene coasted to its end where there was an apron turnaround. This provided a fresh dilemma. Should he go up to the back entrance, or should he walk around to the front of the house?

The decision was made for him as the rear door to the house opened and a man waited in shadow behind the screen. Eugene tried to read the face on the figure, but he had better luck with his own as he caught sight of it in the rearview mirror.

"Remember when you told Myra Fassett you had grown up?" he said to his image. "Don't make a liar out of yourself."

He sucked in a deep breath to gain control, paused for yet another second, then pulled on the door latch.

"CAN I HELP YOU?"

The voice was strong but absent of suspicion. The man had stepped out of the darkness of the house onto the porch. A sparrow alighted on the lip of the gutter just as he did and while it hopped a few feet to distance itself, it did not fly off. The man shoved his thumbs inside the belt loops around his waist and separated his legs more than was normal for simple standing. He was dressed in blue jeans and a blue T-shirt, which had been ripped in one of the underarms.

Eugene refused to answer the customary question from

his placement beside the car. It would be too easy for whoever this individual was to ruin things. To give himself at least a minor advantage, he strode away from the vehicle and up to the steps that led to the small landing where there were two bright yellow chairs and a table. The man waited on him with an expression that Eugene interpreted as more inquisitive than hard.

"I'm an old friend of Connie Reardon. She was Connie Hardinge when I knew her. Is this where she lives?" he said; then with a sprinkling of humor, added, "Or have I made a mistake and copied down the house number incorrectly?"

The man looked him over from his elevated perch while the sparrow flew off between them. "Are you from the Valley?" he asked.

"Yes. I grew up in Lower Brell, then moved to Arlion after I took a bride. But now I'm passing the days in Upper Brell."

"Step on up," said the man who seemed instantly more friendly. "Allan Hardinge, Connie's brother."

Eugene introduced himself and they shook hands.

"I went to school with a Val Banish who was notorious for getting into fights. He was always accused of starting them, but some of us didn't see it the same way. Your brother by any chance? You sorta look some like I remember him."

Eugene nodded, the kind of nod that was just off the vertical to hint of an apology for his sibling's early behavior, and followed the man inside the house, which placed them in the kitchen.

The brother turned about and faced him. "Did you go to Kensington also? Is that how you know Connie? Or wait! You said you grew up in Lower Brell, so you must have known her at Stewart."

"Yes," Eugene answered. "And that's the last time I saw your sister. After Stewart I went to Arlion High."

"Ah, a racist," said Allan Hardinge.

Eugene was taken aback.

Hardinge laughed. "A number of guys from Stewart—maybe you were one of them—used to select Arlion over Kensington because they figured the chances were better for playing ball. I almost chose it myself, except at the time it was Kensington players who were attracting the college scholarships and so I went there instead. Didn't get a scholarship for my linebacker abilities, though. But I ran into another guy a while back who brought up this racist thing. He said guys who selected Arlion because it had so few blacks were racist."

"I did *attend* Arlion because I thought my athletic chances would improve!" Eugene said emphatically, if not defensively. Arlion had been small. That was the real reason he had gone there instead of Kensington. What was this? This wasn't why he came nearly two hundred miles.

"I'm not explaining this very well. This guy was merely wondering if the fellows who did were stereotyping the blacks as better athletes and that's why they scratched Kensington. So why do I remember this? Only because I found the bottom line to be interesting. Are you acting racist if you take a stereotypical view of a group that isn't negative but complimentary? You see what I was getting at?"

No, in fact, Eugene didn't have the foggiest notion of what the man was getting at.

"Forget it," said Hardinge, who shrugged at his own question, as he must have done on previous occasions. Then, knowing his visitor was becoming anxious, he said, "She's in her room getting ready to leave. She'll be out in a minute."

At this, Eugene felt a burst of misgiving. She was preparing to go somewhere. Would he be an obstacle to her timely departure that she wasn't expecting?

"Will this be awkward?" he asked. "Am I interrupting something, Allan?"

"No, you're not interrupting a thing. Connie will be glad to see you. She'll probably ask you to accompany her to the Leiter Home. It's a nursing home. She visits her former mother-in-law there at the same time, every week. Connie is the old woman's last connection with reality."

"What about her son?" Eugene couldn't help but ask.

"Connie can tell you what she wants about that fellow," said Hardinge, who shook his head, more to himself, and as an afterthought, added, "She doesn't like me saying things."

Then, Eugene heard her voice.

"Allan? Who are you talking to?"

Connie Reardon swept around the corner, faster than anyone would expect of a woman in her sixties, and appeared on the opposite side of the kitchen.

Eugene could not believe how beautiful she was. Nothing had changed in five decades except for the missing ponytail, and although this couldn't possibly be true, it seemed extraordinarily easy for him to believe it was.

She did not recognize him at once, and he realized the nurse had not conveyed his inquiry. To spare her embarrassment, he introduced himself.

"Oh, yes. Eugene," she said, and the honest melody in the voice and the warm smile that accompanied it stirred him deeply. She had not forgotten him.

"I understand you're busy," he said.

"Yes, I'm afraid I can't talk at the moment. Can you come back later in the day? Unless you'd like to tag along."

"I told him," Allan Hardinge said to his little sister.

"If you don't mind," said Eugene. "I'm just so thrilled to see you."

TWELVE

The Leiter Home was located ten miles on the south side of town and they drove there in Connie's car, a recent blue model of a Chevy midsize, conspicuously void of grime on both the exterior and interior, of which Eugene remarked.

She gave no response to the compliment. Instead, she asked, "How did you find me?" while turning the car onto a road that would avoid most of the downtown.

"It wasn't easy," he said. "In the end I searched the phone book. That's when I discovered your mother continues to live at the same address I remember."

"You spoke with my mother?"

"Her nurse," said Eugene to the astonishment in her voice. He then smiled, recalling the message Mrs. Hardinge had given to the nurse to pass along. "Your mother, the nurse told me, said you're just as pretty as you were when we attended junior high school."

Connie Reardon faintly bowed her head while watching the road, which provided a sign warning of a low shoulder. "I don't think so," she said.

"Oh, I quite agree with your mother," he said, expecting some reaction.

"How long has it been, Eugene? How long since I last saw you?"

"Fifty years. Five decades. However one says it, it's

been a very long time."

His answer appeared to surprise her as she glanced from the road to him and back to the road. He was having a hard time diverting his eyes from her and, sensing this, she looked over at him again

"You must be wondering why I'm here."

"It's occurred to me."

"It's because I'm getting older, as are we all. Only in my family that means there's not likely to be many more years remaining. What I mean is, no Banishes and before the name change at Ellis Island, no Banaszeks ever survived beyond the age of seventy-five. At least none that I've ever been made aware of. With that history in mind and unable to believe that I can expect something different, it's occurred to me it would be a good idea to get some things straight in my life before it's too late."

"What kind of things?"

"People things, I guess you would call it. I wanted to know the men and women who have been important in my life, and so I've been thinking about that. I've been thinking about it a lot. Perhaps you'll find this hard to believe, Connie, but you're at the top of the list. Through the years I've never thought more about anybody than I have of you. During times when life was much less than what I hoped or wanted it to be, when I was saddened by an event or if I grew terribly depressed, I very often thought of you, and when I did there was always relief. You've appeared in my dreams, too, time after time after time—and everyone a good one—so that when I awoke in the morning and recalled them, I would smile to myself and look forward to the day. What I'm trying to say is this: you were a significance in my life and you still are."

Had he gushed? He probably had, there had been no rehearsal. But there was no taking back what he had said.

He would have to rely on her to understand, which is what she did.

While she had been the prettiest thing he had ever laid eyes on as a young boy growing up, he had noticed too how kind she could be, and that had not changed in Connie Reardon, despite the passing of a half century, including two divorces about which she would later divulge to her visitor a few details. By her eyes alone, Eugene could tell she greatly appreciated what he had said, however gushing, and that she was thankful for the recognition of her importance in another person's life.

Yet, but for the eyes, Connie Reardon did not respond to Eugene's heartfelt admission, and it was the kind of expression that often ached for one of similar content and emotion from the other person, a complex variation of the "I love you," "I love you too" dialogue. When Myra Fassett had expressed herself in the same manner, Eugene assured himself his fellow high school graduate was not expecting him to say he had frequently thought of her over the years. And for comparable reasons he did not now expect Connie Reardon to express the identical sentiment for him. After all, it was a long, long time ago, their years at W. Stewart Junior High School, and the year difference in their ages had prohibited them from being classmates and consequently shortchanged their lives of the many day-to-day memories other youngsters of a similar relationship would have. No, Eugene had never deceived himself into thinking she was in love with him all those fifty years of days and nights. But neither had he allowed himself to consider the possibility that she had not thought of him at all during her adult life, that he had never once made an entrance in a daydream or otherwise.

The nursing home was a long, single-story, orange-brick building surrounded by an array of bushes and dozens of oak trees, customarily pruned for shade. They stood collectively away at a distance where squirrels and rabbits and various birds moved about without the constant worry of human interruption. Eugene and Connie Reardon entered together under the repetitive notes of an invisible warbler and their movement as a couple was too fluid and natural for the little time they had spent together. Eugene, picking up on this himself, could not resist thinking of the two of them for the moment as husband and wife, made even more the realistic fantasy to him because they were performing an obligation common to couples—that of visiting others who were older and confined to an institution.

A middle-aged female attendant inside, recognizing Connie and smiling at Eugene, pointed to a set of doors at the rear that opened onto a patio. That's where they found Mrs. Reardon, the mother of Connie's ex.

Without deliberating, Connie felt for Eugene's wrist and took gentle hold, an action and a sensation he would play over often in his mind in the days ahead. "She may call you Rance," she said. "He has never come to see her and that bothers her very much, despite her dementia. When we're finished, maybe we can get something to eat. Then I'll fill you in a little."

The frail Mrs. Reardon had lost much of her height in her later years, and yet it was easy to single her out from the other women in the home and on the patio. Her brittle white hair remained clean and styled, and the dress she was wearing was unwrinkled, possibly even pressed, and fit her reasonably well at every dimension, unlike other nursing home patients about whom Eugene had heard stories who were forever donning the garments of their fellow residents and claiming them as their own. She delighted in seeing Connie and several times Eugene observed that she glanced at him, but she never once called him Rance, for which he was grateful. Connie Reardon gave up all of an hour of her time and she did not appear to want to cheat on it. Eugene, although he tried to politely listen, realized their entire exchange was meaningless and without direction, and he thought dying at seventy-five might not be so bad in some cases.

"Mom?" said Connie Reardon, bending over toward the woman so that her words might better be heard. "You haven't asked me who this is I brought along this week. This is someone you've never met. Do you want to meet him?"

Connie looked back over her shoulder and up at Eugene, and he saw the old woman raise her own head, with a smile from faraway capturing her face.

"This is Eugene, Mom. He and I went to school together. Junior high school. He was good-looking then, and isn't he still good looking?"

The old woman managed to produce a "Yes" or a croaking syllable close to that sound, but Eugene doubted it had anything to do with the question.

"I have to go now, Mom. Eugene and I are going to get ourselves something to eat, and then talk about those days in junior high school. I'll see you again next week, if not sooner, okay?"

The old woman, with smile still in place, repeated the single syllable. Connie kissed her, and Eugene managed to release a smile of his own.

They considered it a late lunch and drove to an Olive Garden located on the strip leading into St. Andrews. As they waited for their orders to be served, Connie Reardon sipped her water, then said, "Why don't you start, Eugene."

"About what I've been doing?"

"Or what you haven't," she said, smiling.

He knew one the of things he hadn't been doing, and that was actively searching for her, and he said as much, making sure it wasn't another instance of gush, which was certain to get old very quickly.

"Okay," he then said, and he went on to summarize the bulleted points of his life: the jobs, several trips around the states and the big one to the old Soviet Union when the aluminum company had sent him and six others, the only time he had been out of the country, except for a couple fishing trips to Canada when he was younger; the marriage to and his long life with Ginger, and finally the conclusion he was living alone over top a garage on the property belonging to his daughter and her husband. None of it seemed very exciting anymore, not even the trip behind the Iron Curtain; and the one event in his life others might have found oddly exciting, he had never told to friends or family, Ginger included, and he was not about to bring it up before Connie Reardon. The truth was, he still wanted to forget the terrible incident, and he often wondered why he continued to keep that bloody picture in the scrapbook, why he didn't rip it out and throw it away.

Connie Reardon's story began with her first marriage, of which she remembered the year and during which a daughter had been born. The husband, the youngest son of a golfing pro, was a spoiled brat who had verbally abused her, which she declared was nonetheless endurable. What was not endurable was his crossing the line into physical abuse. He had struck her only once, she told Eugene, but even once she would not allow. She took her baby and left him before the week was out and filed for divorce.

"Two years later, Eugene, I married Rance. He became a mistake of another kind. I had always thought we were okay and that we loved each other, but now I'm certain he was unfaithful all along. Yet it wasn't until we turned fifty I discovered this for real. I learned he was having an affair with a woman more than half his age. I filed, which turned out to be a long process in this case. But three years later he wanted to reconcile and we did. Foolish me, I believed him when he said he had made a mistake that he deeply regretted, and of course I was lonely. As things turned out, Eugene, I was the one who made the terrible mistake. He once again had taken up with some woman who could have been his daughter."

"You're divorced from him now?"

"Four years."

Something didn't seem right. It had to do with these visits to an ex-mother-in-law.

"What Rance did to me I forgave him for, and because I set the precedent, so to speak, I suppose he thinks I could forgive him a second time. But what he has done to his mother is inexcusable and not deserving of forgiveness."

"Are you sure you want to make any of this my business?" Eugene said softly. It had occurred to him that none of it really was.

"Can you believe he continues to call, wanting to again reconcile? Can you imagine what he must really think of me? I know this isn't any of your concern and you probably would rather not hear it, but what I remember about you best, Eugene, is that you were a patient boy and you didn't mind listening. It does me good to sound all of this out once in a while, only not in front of Allan, who comes to visit frequently and who's divorced himself. Allan never could stand Rance. He disliked him from the start. I don't know the things you may have discovered about yourself as you've grown older, but I've realized how gullible I was and how I trusted too much in others. It's a serious fault, and that's the reason it does me good to say these things out loud."

"Then I'm your man," he said with the proper smile.

"I visit his mother because I can't often visit mine, but also because she's a good person and we got along well before old age robbed her of her memory. And I feel sorry for her because of what her son has done to her. Rance not only doesn't ever stop to see her, he also schemed to get her money, her home, and everything else she owned of any value. She was worth a good deal, Eugene. But her care is at the expense of the state. He plotted exactly how long was needed to keep his mother out of the home so the state could not sue him legally to gain her money. Then he placed her in the home almost to the day that he was clear."

Yet the old woman had looked nice, Eugene thought as he listened, and he was about to ask if Connie was paying for the perm and the dress, but the annoying computation along with the surfacing of a long submerged memory demanded to break through to his consciousness; and finally they did, so that from then on he heard only small parts of what his first love was saying. Instead, beginning at that moment and continuing into the days and nights to follow, both the indisputable math and the unexpected revelation that would emerge from that memory tortured him with what might have been.

THIRTEEN

The math aspect was understandable to Eugene, as it would have been for almost anyone. Connie Hardinge had married immediately after graduation from high school, and in the optimistic mind of his romantic youth, she and her husband would raise a family. They would take the kids and vacation at the beach. Their children would ride the roller coasters at Kennywood and mother and father would watch and listen to their screams. They would visit the grandparents and the grandparents would visit them. In other words, she was happy, she'd be married forever. In other words, she was gone. The thought of divorce in less than two years had not once crossed Eugene's undeveloped mind.

The revelation about himself, however, this was not so readily packaged. Much to the contrary, he had to imagine himself as an observer to ponder its origin. And once he did, he recognized that it traced back to the slow breakup of the Banish family and to his father in particular.

The explosive quarrels that had erupted between Mr. and Mrs. Banish before Eugene was a teenager would soon become routine so that all three of the children expected there would always be another. As the youngest, Eugene remained in the house and pressed his hands against his ears as though he wanted to pop his brains the same as others popped a pimple. The older boy had his friends and when the mother and father raised their voices, this son left the house and did not return until after midnight. The firstborn of the family stayed behind. Her room, however, was on the far side of the house and the altercations were muffled. Even so, she was aware of the words that came shrieking like missiles from the tongues of both adults and the psychological incisions they made to her siblings and herself.

On each occasion, after the argument wore itself out, Mr. Banish left the house for the garage at the back of the property. Inside, undergoing restoration, sat a 1937 Chevrolet Cabriolet. Mrs. Banish, if she wasn't already there, bolted to the bedroom and closed the door. Inside, she laid herself across the bed and wept. Eugene, having removed his hands from his head, couldn't help but hear her poignant chords. But they were too loud and drawn out for him to feel a satisfactory measure of sympathy. Hadn't he shut himself away after his little cat was crushed under the wheels of a car and cried quietly and to himself? He hadn't been asking anyone to feel sorry for him. It was the kitten he had wanted the others to feel for. His mother's crying was always overplayed, manufactured. She'd wanted her little boy to feel sorry for her and Eugene could not. Much to the contrary, he resented the emotional ploy, and each time it happened he left the house for the garage.

His father employed his son's presence in a different manner. He used it to take in several deep breaths and to calm himself. Soon he smiled at Eugene and, if he hadn't already taken hold of some tool to work on the Chevy, he did so then. All those times Eugene stood in place and watched his father work on the classic automobile. But following an argument when he was finally in his teens, his father, without looking at him, had asked, "Do you know the meaning of the word 'virtue'?"

At first, Eugene wasn't sure the question had been addressed to him and he looked behind him at the garage door.

"Did you hear what I said?" And his father spelled out the word. "V-i-r-t-u-e. Virtue."

"It's, it's a good thing." Eugene remembered that he had stammered in his reply. "It's something in your personality and it's … it's good."

"You were very young when I trailered home the skeleton to this ol' Chevy. Do you remember what it looked like?"

"It was all rust," said Eugene. "Many things were missing."

"You do remember it. Well, at first a number of people told me that I was crazy and had wasted my money buying it. They said it would require too much work. They said I would never restore it.

"But you're almost done, aren't you?"

"That's right, I'm almost done. Its ragtop is all that's left to repair. A little bit of stitching and the car will be completely restored to how it looked coming off the assembly line."

"They were wrong then."

"They were, son, and many have acknowledged that. Now they say that I own the virtue of persistence, which they never realized. Some have slapped me on the back and told me I'm a committed man. I have what others say is a stick-to-it-ive-ness, I don't ever give up."

"That's good, isn't it?" said Eugene.

"I like to think so," said his father. "I certainly like to think so."

And yet, as the man walked away to the rear of the garage, Eugene was sure he heard him mutter these additional words, "But it's also a flaw."

At 13 no one would have expected any boy his age to be a critical thinker, and so the phrase, which his father had not intended for his son to hear, did not prep Eugene for anything at that time in his life or in the future. Still, the young mind, like all young minds, had an abundance of vacant cells and the words were kept together and stored in a few of them. And there they would remain until his reconnection with Connie Hardinge. Then, almost like a dark murky thing at the bottom of a well that is slow to float to the surface, their meaning came clear at the appropriate time. His father, much too late in life, Eugene realized, lamented the commitment to his mother. His stick-to-it-ive-ness, his persistence, this virtue others had offered as a compliment had undone him, and Eugene the Man now understood that his father that day in the garage regretted that he had not abandoned his mother.

Yet that is not the entire meaning, is it? Eugene asked himself. And the formulation alone of this question caused him to realize that he was like his father and the same flaw had passed to him. Were it not, he understood that he would have separated from Ginger long ago and went searching for Connie. And if he had, he just might have discovered the infidelity of her husband. If he had, he just might have saved her from years of misery. If he had, they might have married.

FOURTEEN

"Four days, Eugene! Four fucking days!"

"Riddell! Your language! We're at the table."

The killing of Brownie was already several weeks in the past. Eugene had spoken barely a word to his son-in-law during that time and he had persuaded himself that he should start eating dinner alone in his apartment above the garage rather than continue to suffer this awkward discomfort.

"Old man, your little girl wants me to clean up my language. Well, you can help. You can tell Paulette and me about this visit to your friend. Or do you plan on sitting there like a goddamn mute until your air runs out? You know what I think, Sweetie? You want to know why your father here is refusing to speak to us? He'd like us to believe it was because I did away with the dog. But that's not it, is it, Eugene? That's not it at all."

"No, son, that's exactly it."

"Well now. Lookee here." Riddell grinned behind his words, which oozed from his mouth like thick tar. "I thinks me finally got us a rise, Paulette."

Eugene glared at his son-in-law, knowing the younger man enjoyed assuming the role of a baiter. After a few seconds he turned away, looked to his daughter, and said, "What I expect your husband was about to say is that I went to see a man for whom I had feelings. Am I right,

Riddell? You were intending to have a little—"

"—Hon? Were you?"

"My God, if you don't got a screw missing."

"But I will tell you this," said Eugene, continuing to address Paulette. "Thanks to your husband's greedy hands when I first moved into your home, one of the tires blew out along a dangerous stretch of road. I had wanted to replace his castoffs before leaving, but I didn't find the time. I was lucky it didn't cost me." This story was a fabrication intended to cut short the couple's questioning.

Eugene shoved the plate away from himself and rose to his feet. "This rendezvous—or whatever you want to call it—at the dinner table every evening, it's laughable. I won't be joining the pair of you any longer. Frankly, Riddell, you disgust me. And yes, Paulette, you're my daughter, but I might as well tell you that I'm not altogether thrilled with you either. You could have said something to your husband that afternoon and maybe that wonderful little dog would still be here today."

Riddell slammed his fork to the table, cutting off Paulette who was about to speak. He shot to his feet and extended an arm, pointing it to the outside. "You hear me, Eugene, and hear me good! I put a second floor on that garage out there. I put it on special for you, and you know that for a fact! Now this is how you repay my generosity? You insult me?"

Eugene pushed his face toward Riddell. "You had Lila finish off the garage because you intend to rent it out. That's what you said, son. And next week when I finally close on my house with her friend, I'll write out a check in your name. The amount should more than make us square. Now excuse me, as I want to get the hell away from here."

Cooking for himself would not be a problem, though the two of them were probably thinking otherwise, he figured, were likely chuckling to make themselves feel better, convinced he would return to their table sooner than later. The old man would have difficulty boiling water, let alone frying up an egg or a pork chop. They could not have known that in the recent years before her death, Ginger had withheld food in place of sex, the latter her punishment for her husband in their younger years. But it had scant negative effect on him. To the contrary, he discovered he was not a bad cook, and in fact preferred his preparation of numerous dishes to hers. What's more, if his daughter and Riddell were assuming he would hate shopping for food, now that such an activity would be necessary, they again would be wrong. After discovering early in their marriage that his wife would drive several miles to redeem a twenty-five cent coupon for an item available at a competitive price in a neighborhood market, he had begun to perform a share of the grocery and household shopping himself.

But even if his daughter and her husband were correct in their assumptions, it would not have made Eugene apologize and rejoin them. For neither did they know he was on the greatest high after finding and reconnecting with Connie Hardinge, his junior high school sweetheart, what others likely would have described in earlier days as a sweet but laughable puppy love, but to himself a young girl whom he could never get out of his system. And although the paradoxical virtue of commitment inherited from his father would continue to upset him for some time, he nonetheless realized that was *then* and this was *now*. And *now* meant both he and Connie were alone.

To begin, he wrote her. The first, a thank-you note for her hospitality. He expressed how truly wonderful it had been to see her after the passage of so much time. He was careful not to gush. He signed it, *Affectionately, Eugene*. In the fall she had a birthday and he remembered it as he had every year throughout every decade in the past, only this time, knowing her address, he jotted down a few words inside a card, asked a couple simple questions hoping she might respond, signed it, *With Love and Affection*, and sent it off. Then the holidays arrived and he mailed her a Christmas card, one he had selected at a gift shop showing a man and a woman in different homes staring out a window at a frozen pond, again with a few words and a question or two. Twice he called and they chatted. Once, when she had said that she would be driving down on the morrow to visit her mother, they made plans to have lunch, only she cancelled before hanging up, telling him she had forgotten something she had sworn to do with her mother.

It was not a quick realization. At first, it did not resemble even denial. He simply did not think about why she did not write back, or send a card, or telephone. When finally he did, then came the denial, and he made excuses for her. But they were lame and he could not construct new ones, and the denial soon hammered itself into the awful realization that she would never call, never write. All the questions concerning him she wanted answers for, all these had already been asked. She had asked them during their reunion in St. Andrews. There was nothing more about him she desired to know.

And, suddenly, he was alone.

This moment, when it arrived, was one of stifling silence and yet it occurred on a day in June with a tremendous thunderstorm breaking overhead. He stood beneath the roof of the landing Lila Shrum had built for him the previous year with his back against the second story, as the wind swept the torrential rain in sheets from rear to front. Thunderous explosions convulsed the dark roily air in every direction and a bolt of lightning directly in his line of vision, expressing its magnificent power, blew the bark off a tree on the slope above the house and set the trunk on fire. He was not deliberately tempting fate by remaining out of doors. He was not feeling sorry for himself. He was merely coming to realize how truly alone he now was and in some way marveling how such a state of life had stolen up on him.

All those years with Ginger he had experienced a different kind of aloneness, but it was not his wife who was the cause. He simply had realized long ago something fundamental about himself: he was a man who was not in need of people the way most others are. Their physical presence, he required that, certainly; he could not have lived in total isolation as a recluse. In part, it was the reason he had left his house to join his daughter and her husband in theirs. The communication of others, too, he sought, though seldom with himself. Forever had he enjoyed the role of eavesdropper, reason enough why he had numbered only a handful of friends then, and now none at all.

A year after the killing of Brownie, nothing had changed in the feelings he harbored for his daughter and her husband. He spurned them both, reluctant as he was to use the word "hate" with his own flesh-and-blood, but he felt betrayed, and there could be no forgiveness because neither of them sought forgiveness. He saw them, and they stared at him, and a phrase was on occasion passed between the parties, but those from Eugene might just as well have been primitive grunts to himself and the surrounding air.

The result was a new kind of aloneness, which gained its attention through a persistent ache—Eugene was hurting inside. When he studied his figure in the mirror, usually at night when the only sound was the occasional drifting and pathetic howl from a dog confined at the shelter amid the pines, he hoped he might see the diminished halftone, like those that he had observed in others, which would have signaled a dishonesty with himself, that he was perhaps engineering this feeling of aloneness in order to attract the sympathies of others. To his dismay, the reversed image was sharp and clear and fully saturated of the light his person reflected. The undeniable truth was, he was by himself. And what that meant was there would be no one with whom he could talk out things, not a single soul to whom he might unburden himself and ask for advice. More than ever would he now have to keep his own counsel. In the past, although he had always felt the need to do the same, at least there had been Ginger, who believed in their marriage and whom he could usually trust to listen, despite having little to say in response. All the same, she had acknowledged his dark moments and tried to prod him out of them. Back then, there also had been his sister Aletha, and she, too, patiently heard out her younger brother when required, but in time Eugene ceased to make any deeply personal admission to her because she had kept with the religiously straight-and-narrow of their upbringing and her replies were stringently illustrative of this, whereas he himself, despite accompanying his wife and child to church year after year, had known since he was in his late teens that organized religion, with its many rituals and various ornaments and collared men, did not resonate with him, it never had, perhaps not even as a child when father and mother had held their son's tiny hands. Try as he had in later years, he remained unable to believe that God was in all the churches that claimed He was; unable to understand why an Almighty Power would give a damn about his praise and the praise of others; unable to see the church as anything but a combination of Field of Dreams and Roach Motel. His jokes then and now were unchanged: *Build it and He would come.* And *Once God checked in, He would never check out.*

● ● ●

The idea of a companion dog came to mind on a Saturday morning while he was shaving and ruminating on a story in the local paper's weekend edition of twenty-four abused animals that had been recovered from a puppy mill. That same day, he drove out to the shelter amid the pines to select an animal to take back to the apartment. The shelter's young female director walked alongside and attempted to dissuade him from his pick, a collie-setter type.

"I don't like to put the life of any animal above another," the woman said to him, "but I also don't want their owners to be disappointed."

"Why would this poor creature disappoint me?" Eugene asked behind a questioning smile.

"Sir, this dog is old."

"As am I."

"But, sir, do you see how she has trouble walking? How her back legs fail to go where she wants them to go? That is going to worsen, and soon. And once that happens, this poor thing will not be able to walk at all, and you will be forced to euthanize."

He was about to ask if that was soon to happen anyway, but the answer was obvious. "Nevertheless," he said to the young woman, "this is the dog I would like to take home with me. Let's go back inside your office and fill out the papers."

When he drifted down the driveway a half hour later, Riddell was replacing the yellow insect bulb in the porch light fixture of the house and Eugene saw him glance his way. The dog, which had been lying on its side in the back seat, raised its head when the car slowed.

Eugene got out and opened the rear door on the side

opposite the house. Although he doubted the dog could bolt, he nevertheless attached a leash to its collar.

"Okay, girl. Here's your new home for the time you have left. Let's pray it's a lot."

"Whatcha got there?" Riddell hollered over.

Out of the corner of his eye, Eugene could see that his son-in-law had already set aside the bulb and was walking his way. He tried to hustle the old dog up the steps, but it wasn't going to work.

"What's with the mutt?" Riddell asked suspiciously as he strode up to the garage. "You looking after someone's pet while they're away on vacation? Tell me that's the case. I'll go along with that."

"This is my dog," Eugene declared.

"Your dog! I thought I made it clear at some point I don't want no animals tossing their cookies on my rugs inside the apartment."

The dog attempted unsuccessfully to seat itself on the steps. It uttered a whine to signal it was not able to stand much longer. Eugene reached out and scratched its head.

"You're not about to give a damn what I say, are you?" A smirk soon settled into Riddell's bony features as Eugene maintained a reticence. "Aren't you afraid I might up and shoot this dog like I did the other? Although judging by its looks, that would be a waste of a bullet. Where'd you get hold of this mongrel, anyway?" Riddell shook his head in scorn. "Wait'll your little girl hears her old man brought home a cripple. You're something else, you know that? You're something else."

Riddell swung away, laughing, but swung back after a few steps.

"Bear this in mind. If that bag o' bones you got there destroys the apartment in any way, it's coming out of you."

Turning his back on his son-in-law, Eugene urged the

dog up the remaining steps and into the apartment.

In the immediate days to follow, he congratulated himself on making the decision to get a canine companion. He talked to the animal, much as he had talked to Brownie, and he fed it some of whatever he had prepared for himself, practicing what he had once advised his daughter to do if she wanted to lose weight. Fill your plate the same as you always do, he had told her, and then shovel off half to Brownie. The old dog devoured the remnants of steak and eggs, salami, ham-off-the-bone, cheeses Swiss and Provolone, cookies and cake, and often lapped a small bowl of milk afterwards to wash it all down.

He could just hear his son-in-law: "You feed it all that stuff, naturally it's going to stick around. But that's all it is. Don't get to thinking the mutt thinks you're something special, because you ain't." Like Riddell would remain with his daughter if Paulette didn't put a meal on the table at least five days a week.

Unfortunately, within the month the dog was dead. Eugene assumed a stroke or a heart seizure. Each night the animal, with his assistance, had started off at the foot of the bed, but by morning, after too much tossing about by its new master, it was somewhere on the floor and that's where Eugene found it. He knew at once it would not wake up, and cradled it in his arms. The movement of the limp muscles caused the bladder to relax, and a pool of urine flooded the carpet in the apartment's bedroom.

When Riddell, returning home from work, learned the news of the dog's death from Paulette, he laughed. Whenever he saw Eugene, he made it a point to laugh harder. Paulette didn't think it right and voiced her objection.

"You mind your own business," he replied harshly. "Your old man's been acting like a goddamn clown for more than a year. I've been telling some of the guys at the terminal about what a jerk he's become and they find it funny too. He deserves to be laughed at."

"He's still my father."

"Well, that's your problem, isn't it?"

"Now that's unnecessary. You say you're sorry for that."

"Right, woman. At this late date we'll start in on something new."

"Don't you dare make fun of me when I ask you something, Riddell. I've never asked you for anything."

The second dog, about the size and age of the first, might have cancer, the shelter's director warned Eugene.

"Are you sure you want this dog, Mr. Banish? You could be burying him just as quickly as you did the last, and I hate to see that happen."

The dog's coat was a threatening black-and-brown amalgam of hues, not the kind of animal that was often seen in the Valley. It was the eyes that told Eugene where he had seen this kind of dog. The eyes were a startling green, and yet as beguiling as they were to gaze at as a whole, it was the pupils of a lighter, stranger emerald green that were hypnotic. This was the kind of wild canine he had seen when Ginger and he, early in their marriage and on vacation, had traveled south into Kentucky and Tennessee. The trip to a thoroughbred horse farm, a bourbon distillery, and a walk through Mammoth Cave had been fun for both of them and he was glad the dog could act as a reminder of such a pleasant memory of a time so long ago.

"Yes," he answered the director. "This is the dog I want."

FIFTEEN

As the chief dispatcher for Hollowell Cartage, Inc., Riddell garnered three weeks of paid vacation away from the terminal. One he reserved for the Christmas holidays in the event Junior and his family decided to leave Oregon and visit, an annual reminder from Paulette that she hoped would someday become a reality. The remaining two weeks he took in late summer.

"So, Honey, what do you have planned for this first day of your vacation?" Paulette asked. "A beautiful one is shaping up." She stood in front of the window above the kitchen sink, swabbing a metal pan that had failed to dry overnight in the rack.

"I'm putting the boat in. Thought I'd run up to the lake at Crooked Creek this morning and fish for the day. Want to come?"

"I don't think so."

"You don't like that lake, do you?"

"I don't like any water where I can't see the bottom."

"You're not alone," he said. "If I run into more than one or two other fishermen while I'm up there, it's only because it's an absolutely perfect day. All right, so you have no interest in joining me. Only my guess is something else is floating about inside that female brain of yours. So out with it."

"Riddell, why don't you ask my father to go along?"

"You're not serious."

"It won't hurt to ask."

"What makes you think he'll trouble himself to even answer the invite? He looks at me nowadays like he wishes I were dead and it was just the two of you living here."

"He's wearing down, Hon. He's been speaking to me the past couple of weeks."

"Sometimes, you know, it looks to me like you're wishing the same."

"Hon, he can't hold conversations with just an animal all the time. He needs to talk with people, real people. Ask him, won't you? And stop with this ridiculous idea about how he looks and how I look and the rest of what you said."

The hitch was on Paulette's blue minivan, but before hooking up, Riddell climbed into the boat, a sixteen-foot aluminum runabout with the steering mechanism and ignition upfront. He went aft and squeezed the black rubber bulb on the red fuel tank, then retraced his steps forward and flicked the key. The outboard motor turned but would not start.

Eugene, with the green-eyed dog beside him, stuck his head through the garage's side entrance.

"You shouldn't do that," he cautioned.

"Do what?" Riddell responded absently, going aft to squeeze the bulb several more times.

"Start a boat motor outside of water."

"I do this every year. Think it makes more sense to haul this thing out to a launch, only to find it doesn't run? Truth is, the thing should have been in the water months ago, only I've been too busy sending out trucks all over the goddamn country."

Riddell tried the key a second time and the motor fired amid sputtering. Eugene entered the garage and positioned himself at the side of the transom. He saved Riddell a few steps by reaching in and squeezing the bulb yet again. Riddell turned the key and this time the motor fired and caught. He permitted it to run for a fast count of five before switching it off.

He then regarded Eugene for a few seconds.

"Maybe Paulette is right," he said under breath. "Look, I'm heading up to Crooked Creek this morning to throw a line out and catch a few crappies, maybe even a bass or two if they'll take a popper. Probably drink a couple of beers while doing it. You want to join me? I've got extra poles. Bring your hound, too, if you want."

"You're not worried he'll scratch your cushions?"

"So you saying you'll go?"

"Tell me, Riddell. Why is it you haven't any friends who'll fish with you?"

Riddell shook his head and laughed to the air. "Go to hell, Eugene. Asking you was your offspring's idea. I'd just as soon fish alone."

Riddell turned away and climbed out of the boat, and the two men soon ignored each other without effort. Eugene went back outside and watched the dog relieve itself in several spots. After sliding behind the wheel of the van, Riddell backed the vehicle out of the center bay and around against the boat trailer's tongue, then jumped out, quickly made the connection, and crossed and secured the safety chains. He was all set. For a moment he almost said, "Last chance," but was glad he checked himself.

As he was about to get into the van again and drive off, a tall woman appeared at the entrance to the driveway. Dressed in a breezy summer outfit with an undulating golden skirt that might have suggested an easygoing nature, she depressed the same consideration with shoulder-length hair styled to brush the facial flesh on all sides and around the corners as if her countenance was unsure it should be seen.

"What the hell is this?" Riddell grumbled to himself. When the woman was close enough, he raised a hand and shouted, "WE GAVE AT THE OFFICE!"

Either the woman didn't understand his words, or she chose to ignore them. She continued to walk down the driveway, finally stopping within a few feet of the men. She regarded Riddell for a moment before turning to Eugene.

"Mr. Banish?"

"That's me," he said and smiled at the woman. "My son-in-law was just about to go fishing. We can talk upstairs."

The woman appeared surprised. "You know who I am?"

Yes, he could see plainly the little girl in the adult, and without his consciously willing it, the thought occurred to him that her unexpected presence was, in some strange mystical way, the reason he had never removed that disturbing news photo from the scrapbook.

"I certainly do," he said.

Riddell remained standing beside the driver's door of the van, tapping a finger on the roof and waiting on some explanation from his father-in-law as to who the woman was, but instead Eugene extended a hand to the staircase and she preceded him up toward the landing.

"Where's your car?" he inquired.

"Your neighbors in Arlion said you were living with your daughter. They knew the name of the street, but they couldn't recall the last name of her husband. I simply parked on the shoulder and started knocking on doors and ringing bells."

He slapped his leg, summoning the dog to follow. "Well, it worked," he said. "You found me."

They reached the last riser and, as they stepped inside the upstairs apartment and he closed the door behind them, a bizarre and sudden change took hold of Eugene that he could never have predicted. The urge to talk to this woman was gone, the same urge that had been strong and eager mere seconds ago. Much the opposite, something unknown was warning him not to talk. He lingered beside the door and peeped around the curtain on its window at his son-in-law below who was beginning to stir again. He watched Riddell at last toss a final glance to the second floor of the garage and then get back inside the van.

"You can leave in just a second," he said awkwardly to the woman. "My son-in-law is heading out the driveway and as soon as he's out of sight, you can go."

The woman shrank from the unexpected confusion. "Mr. Banish, are you certain you know who I am? My name is Barbara…"

Eugene opened the door and let it swing wide. Details of the incident were already coming back to him without his willing them.

"I thought you said we could talk."

He barely shook his head.

"Mr. Banish?"

"I'M SORRY!" he shouted, and the thunder of his voice, he realized, was uncalled for and he swiftly regained control. "I'm sorry," he said softly. "I wanted to. Or I thought I wanted to. But now, out of nowhere, something is making me more than a little reluctant and I'm not sure that I can. Please don't ask me to explain because I can't explain it to myself. And I'm trying to."

The yellowed news photo came flashing to his mind as it had time and again across the years, and he thought he ought to rip it from the scrapbook that very moment, tear it out and crumple the fucking thing into a hundred brittle pieces. Be done with it, once and for all. But the reason for the delay of doing so, if he'd never known the reason before today, he saw it now as his eyes gathered in all of the crippled, beseeching face of the woman who stood before him.

She turned away and walked deliberately to the opposite side of the room and waited. It was a small act of determination, not stubbornness.

"Why did you come here?" he asked.

"I want to know what happened."

"Haven't you ever asked your father?"

"I did, and he told me all he knew. It wasn't much."

"It should be enough."

"Mr. Banish, what happened, happened to me."

"SOME OF IT HAPPENED TO ME!" Once again the voice was too loud for the circumstances, and he frowned instantly out of embarrassment for himself because of his anger and selfish response. He surrendered and shut the door. "Forgive me. Go ahead and sit."

"No no," she said, imploringly. "You're right, and I'm the one who should apologize. It happened to both of us. I understand what you're saying, Mr. Banish. I really do."

"Why now, after almost forty years?"

"Because it's not something I can forget, and I've tried. God knows I've tried."

He could easily understand that. He had been unable to forget it either.

"Mr. Banish, I've been through three husbands, all of them good, responsible men. Educated men who were not insensitive. I no longer believe it was their fault the marriage failed. I think it's me and it's connected to all the horrible things that took place on that day. I'm just trying to figure out what is going on inside me that I don't understand. What's ruining my marriages? That's all I'm trying to do here."

She had grown into a very beautiful woman. Not for a second did Eugene doubt her word.

The dog, which had disappeared into the kitchen after they had entered the apartment, now showed itself. It set its eyes on Eugene.

"Give me a moment," he said. "I have to give my Ring-a-Ding a little something in his bowl."

"Ring-a-Ding?" she repeated with a strained, but honest, smile.

"It wasn't me who named him, I assure you. But he's too old for a change. So I just call him Ringo, which is apparently close enough, because he responds."

The woman trailed him into the kitchen. From the refrigerator he removed a can of dog food already opened, plus some ham slices from a deli package.

"Barbara Lennox," he said. "Your father's name was Orlando, your mother's Maria."

"Mary," said the woman.

"Mary," said Eugene, nodding. "That's right."

"My father didn't tell me much because he said he couldn't. He said you were afraid to talk."

"I was afraid of the law. I didn't trust it."

"That's what he said."

"Let's go back into the other room. Ringo's unlike other dogs. He'll spend ten seconds or less wolfing down what I gave him and another five minutes making certain he has removed even the smallest morsel attached to the bottom and side of the dish. At some point in his life I have to assume the poor boy was starving."

A shadow crossed the curtained window on the door to the landing as they returned to the front room. Both glanced in its direction before taking a chair.

"Would you like me to start from the beginning?"

The woman's eyes all at once flooded at his question and observing her silently cry and not even remotely expecting this kind of emotion, Eugene realized in all the years since he had rescued this woman from death, he had behaved the same as he had with his thoughts of Connie Hardinge. His thoughts always had been much more about himself. This woman had been hurting all this time, decades, and she was still hurting.

"I don't know that what I have to tell will help you understand your marriages," he said. "All I can do is tell you what I remember happening and how I felt at the time."

"That's all I'm asking," the woman said, wiping her eyes.

Both could hear the bowl bullied around the tile on the kitchen floor as the dog worked its every corner. It was an oddly assuaging squeal of a sound to each of them in light of what they were about to bring up from the past.

"I was driving by," Eugene began, leaning forward in the chair with his hands clasped together, as though his subconscious mind knew they would be needed if the memory was to be fully wrung out. "Driving around, really. Bored, as I often was during that period of my life. My eyes glanced down the street to the Willow-Edgecliff intersection at the very moment you were getting dragged off your bicycle. It was a distance, and I reacted by thinking that what I saw wasn't what I saw.

"I can't say I knew what it was, but before reaching the next intersection I realized that car had to be followed, and so I turned around. You were already out of sight by then and I flew down that road in the direction of the river, but even when it crossed the railroad tracks, his car was nowhere to be seen, and I began to think I had made a mistake, that I was just being foolish. That something other than a kidnapping had occurred. Only I had passed your bicycle upturned alongside the shoulder and couldn't convince myself otherwise. Seventy miles an hour I must have been rushing down that narrow winding road and then along the river and then up the other side, and it was a piece before I came upon you. It was growing dark, too, and I remember becoming angry with you and your parents as well, even talking out loud to myself in the car. What the hell were you doing out on your bicycle at dusk? Did your parents even give the slightest damn if an automobile struck you because the driver was unable to pick you out on the bike? Later, I realized these were arguments my mind was creating to protect itself and me. To get my body to stop and go back. To forget about what I was thinking, it was likely all a mistake. Then, when I drew up closer, I couldn't see anything of you. All I saw was your kidnapper who appeared to be keeping an eye on me in his mirror, and out of frustration at myself and, I suppose, my inflated thinking that I could be a hero, I floored the gas pedal and flew around him without even looking to see if you were inside.

"Only I couldn't force myself to keep going, especially when his headlights diminished and disappeared completely. That's when I stopped the car and tried to think about what I was doing. Was I being a fool? Was I still acting like a kid? I was already in my twenties, about to get married, but I wasn't too sure about myself, or about anything, really. All I knew is I would definitely feel like a fool, and worse, if I read about what was happening in the next day's newspaper and saw your picture. Finally, I backed the car around and went searching for you. His car wasn't anywhere to be seen. But I remembered a high school friend of mine had told me of a dirt path just off the point where the road again flattened out high above the river. Where he'd said you could dare to take a car if it hadn't been raining. He'd boasted that he'd taken several of his dates there.

"I found the path, it wasn't difficult, and in the distance was the dim glow of the headlights. I decided it would be safer if I walked. I tried hard not to give away my presence. And I was becoming afraid.

"Both of you were outside the car when I came up on its driver's side. He had your clothes removed and was doing things, and I could see how utterly terrified you were. Neither of you had any idea I was near. The window on his car was partly down and I reached in and removed the key. At the same time I saw the gun and grabbed it. The key I laid on the ground on the inside of a rear tire. I had thought about throwing it into the brush, but feared he might hear the sound, and I remember thinking he would never think to look under the car.

"It seemed he finished quickly, but I don't know because time was nowhere then and it was getting darker by the minute, and he was already pulling a knife. And that's when you saw me...."

Eugene paused in his delivery. He stared at his guest who was not looking back at him, but seemingly into the depths of herself. What next was on his lips he couldn't say, he didn't want to say it, and how could it help this woman, anyway? He remembered when he had taken real notice of the little girl's face, as terrified and frightened and violated as it was, he realized it was colored, not so very much, but colored all the same; and he knew immediately what had prompted the unstaging of the knife so prematurely by her attacker. Had her skin been darker, Eugene knew nothing would have happened to Barbara Lennox on that evening; she would have returned home on her bicycle and done what little girls do. But as it was, the man had released himself in her mouth and was now about to slit her throat, while promising himself not to make the same mistake again.

The woman raised her head because of the unexpected silence and her eyes sought Eugene's, who was moved to set aside his thoughts and go on with the story. "I put the gun to his head and he pulled away from you with the knife in his hand. Then he turned to look at me. His eyes were as wide as any eyes I had ever seen. I don't need to describe him, do I?"

"Don't."

"I didn't want to kill him," said Eugene. "No, that isn't really being truthful. I did want to kill him. I really did. Only I was afraid if I did, in the end it might get turned all crazy and I would be the one in trouble and not regarded as some hero or good Samaritan. I didn't trust the law, you see. So I told you to collect your clothes from his car. You did, and afterwards we began backing our way out of the woods to the road.

"He looked at his car, I remember, but he didn't go near it. He must have figured if I had his gun, I had the key as well. What he did do, he started walking after us. I told him to stop or else I would shoot. *'Pull the trigger,'* is what he then said—it was almost a plea—and he started to babble. He began saying things like, *'Do you think I want to do this sort of thing? I need help. Take me in and turn me over to the police. I'll do this again if you let me go. I need help. I've wanted this to happen. I've wanted someone to catch me.'* He was continuing to hold the knife at his side, and I told him to get rid of it. He didn't hesitate. He flung it into the woods. *'There,'* he said. *'Now you have to take me in.'*

"I didn't know what to do, but I did know I wasn't going to take any chances. I ordered him to get down flat on his stomach and said that he would have to crawl to the road, like he probably had seen pictures of soldiers who crawl under wire and gunfire. That's what I told him he would have to do, and if he didn't, if he gave any sign of doing anything other than what I told him, any sign at all, I would kill him. I ordered him to keep his mouth shut, too.

"Well, he didn't say a thing to any of that. He took some time to think on it, then he finally got down on his stomach and started to crawl through the brush and dirt. But it wasn't long before he began to complain, and that was when I realized I had taken a chance I shouldn't have. By this time I was scared out of my wits, and my body was shaking, trembling throughout, I couldn't control it; and he could see my fear. Anyone could have. I knew, too, if my concentration strayed from him for even an instant, he would make a break for it and rush me. And if he succeeded, then both you and I would die. He would take the gun and kill us both. I screamed at him to stay quiet and to continue crawling, and if he didn't, if he said one word or raised his head again, I would shoot. He must have calculated I was too frightened to do what I said. But it was really the opposite. I was too frightened not to do it. Really, I didn't care about his life. I cared only about yours and mine."

"Is that when you shot him?"

Eugene paused again before nodding slowly. He looked her in the eyes. "Yes. That's when I shot him."

The dog had ceased bossing around its plastic food dish and was standing in the doorway to the outer room, watching them.

"I didn't know whether I had killed him or not. I took your hand in mine and the two of us then ran as fast as we could to my car parked about a hundred yards away. After that, he must have crawled the remaining distance because the police found him close beside the road, dead, according to the next day's paper. I asked you where you lived and you told me. I then delivered you to your mom and dad. I told them what you already knew before you came here today. I gave my name to your father in trust. If what happened were to come back at me and I was arrested and charged, I wanted his help. Your father understood my fears and respected them, and he wasn't wanting to put you through anything more. Your mother was in agreement.... I never asked. How is he?"

"Daddy died some time ago."

"And your mother?"

"I lost her, too."

"I'm sorry," he said and got to his feet.

How much had she recalled on her own, he wondered. In recent years, at the same time he asked himself the reason why he was reluctant to destroy the picture from the *Star-Enterprise*, he would often wish that more of the man's face could be seen; but in fact, if he pushed his memory of the terrible event, as he had just done, there continued to remain more than he ever wanted to see; more, too, than he wanted to hear. In his recollection of sights and sounds from that evening, there really was no diminishment of details. It seemed the memories of his life had assigned themselves to be the opponent in a zero-sum contest with the realities of his life. Had his memory undergone the usual attrition, a fading not so different from what was currently occurring to his vision, the integrity of the man's plea as he had attempted to negotiate with Eugene might have been afforded a hearing. But as it were, the man, both a pedophile and a racist, was dead while this woman and himself were finishing out what remained of their lives.

SIXTEEN

Two hundred feet down the road, after leaving Eugene and the woman in the gold skirt in the upstairs apartment, Riddell brought the minivan with the boat in tow to a stop. He had forgotten to take along a bottle from the six-pack of two-cycle engine oil in the garage to mix with the gasoline he would be purchasing for the old Evinrude. Rather than deal with the frustration of wrestling the short trailer backward such a distance—annoying even to an experienced big-rig operator, and Riddell had been one before becoming the company dispatcher, hauling as far north and west as Montana and as far south as the Huntsville, Alabama PPG—he returned to the house on foot. Arriving at the top of the driveway, he spotted Paulette on the landing and she looked to him to be eavesdropping on whatever was going on inside. He quickly dismissed the idea of re-entering the garage, instead deciding to pick up the oil at the same time he bought the gas on his way to the lake at Crooked Creek, but he did not turn aside. Rather, he watched and, as his wife moved from one ear to the other, he laughed to himself, saying under his breath, "I told you someday you were going to wear out that ear."

The familiar remark had originated at a time when Ginger Banish was alive and well and either of the couples would often visit the home of the other. During these visits there had been moments when Paulette and Riddell were in one room, Eugene and his wife in another, and the young bride would project her right ear into the hallway or press it against the wall to learn if her parents were saying things about her husband and herself they wouldn't say openly. In many ways the older couple had been a secretive pair, and some form of covert operation, albeit a seemingly primitive one, had passed to their daughter. Riddell, watching his wife in her absorbent pose, could be counted on to always say, "Girlie, you'll wear out that ear!"

Paulette, too, had remembered her husband's droll warning while standing on the landing of her father's apartment and it was the only thing laughable, she told herself. Except her other ear hadn't performed a whole lot better, and maybe that was laughable, too. Of course, it was possible there was nothing wrong with her hearing. She'd once heard Riddell pitch a driver who was asking about local contractors, "With Lila Shrum you'll get more for your money." So perhaps the floor above the garage, door included, was heavily insulated, and that was the reason she had to duck under and scooch from one side to the other to use the left ear instead of the right. But she hadn't been able to duck but a few inches because of her swollen knees, which were continuously under threat of collapse from the extra weight above, and when through the window she had seen her shadow flit across the wall inside the room beyond the entrance door, she knew she would be thoroughly embarrassed, with nothing to say, if her father and the unknown woman were to part the curtain further and look out.

If Riddell had not confessed that he had been a spectator standing at the top of the driveway watching her, Paulette was sure she would have said nothing to her husband, at least not any time soon. However, he had confessed, and now she could see that he wanted details.

"So whatever were you expecting to hear?" he asked.

She threw out her hands, as she didn't have an answer. In fact, no sooner had she descended the landing she cursed herself for having climbed the steps at all. Why hadn't she stayed inside her own home and minded her own business? And yet if, a year ago, her father had invited Lila inside a room and shut the door behind them, she would have done the same. Let him take a woman his own age into his apartment, not someone from another generation. She owed that much to her mother.

"You want to know what your problem is, girlie? You're too much of a soapster."

"What is that supposed to mean?" she said.

"Real people, Sweetie, walk into a room without an invitation. They're aware their entrance by itself will change things and certain things won't happen. Do you remember when Riddell, Jr., was a teenager and he had his party here? Remember how I crashed it? Didn't that put a damper on all the groping and who knows what else!"

"In front of his friends. Yes, I remember. That was wrong of you, Riddell."

"Like hell! Ask the old man of each of the girls who were here that night and see how wrong they think it was. Too bad somebody didn't walk in on our daughter. Things in that department might be entirely different today and perhaps she would come around."

Paulette waved a hand of resignation in the air as there would never be an understanding on what had happened to their daughter. She deliberately returned to the original subject. "And so what about soapsters? What do they do?"

"Same as you. Soapsters look for dirt. Walking into a room, they're more than aware, would spoil the chance."

"Well, I found some, there's no doubt about that."

"Now hold on there a minute." Riddell placed a hand on his wife's arm. "Did I hear my woman correctly? Are you saying you found some dirt on your old man? Is that what you're telling me?" Riddell grew suddenly buoyed and, as what he considered to be a laughable moment came to mind, he took a step toward his wife. "That black woman is his daughter, am I right? You do realize she was black, don't you?"

Although meant only to be a snappy reply, Riddell's words eagerly erupted inside himself as a rash of tiny thought-processing blisters: *black she was, but very light in color—Eugene's genetic contribution; the ages seemed right; and each had recognized the other.*

He slapped his hands together playfully. "That's it, isn't it? Your old man fathered a child with a black woman. Was this before or after he was married to your mother?"

"Stop enjoying this. This isn't funny."

"Just tell me I'm right."

"You're not. And I'm not sure I should tell you what I heard."

"Say again?"

"Don't get angry. I just don't know if I should tell you this."

Riddell tossed his head to one side in the fashion of a gangster and pretended to roughen his voice. "Don't make me twist your ear, Sweetie."

"Riddell! I mean it! This isn't funny."

"Why don't I be the judge of that?"

"I don't know," said Paulette, no less unsure now she should tell her husband the alarming news than she had been minutes earlier.

"This isn't the time to begin keeping secrets from each other," he said.

Paulette looked ashamed for her husband. "Please.

Don't even try to convince me you've never kept anything to yourself. I'm the one who confides. It's rarely been the other way around."

It was time to remain silent in order that his wife could come out with the story, and so Riddell said nothing more. Instead, he stared at Paulette, moving and dipping his head emotionally to maintain eye contact and to make sure she understood he was waiting patiently. Paulette, still in turmoil, shook her head at herself, and it continued to shake as she revealed the skeleton from her father's closet.

"I think my father shot and killed a man a long time ago."

Unsure whether his wife was turning the tables to have a little fun with him, Riddell waited until her eyes were raised to meet his.

"You're serious, aren't you?"

"It had something to do with that woman when she was a young girl. There was mention of an overturned bicycle."

"What else did you hear?"

"Thanks to that dog, nothing much. It kept shoving its dish around. Every time one of them said a word, the dish went sliding across the floor, making a racket."

"Nothing at all?"

"I heard the word 'gun.' And, I believe my father was in his car and chased the man."

"Road rage, maybe," said Riddell, thoughtfully. "Before it was even an expression. Perhaps Eugene saw this driver strike the girl on her bicycle and he went flying after him. Then it got out of hand, with your father ending up shooting the guy."

"My father has never liked guns, Riddell."

"That could explain it. If this occurred before you happened on the scene, who knows what kind of oats your old man was sowing."

"I don't think it was road rage, Hon."

"Then there's only one other possibility that comes to mind. And if that's the case, Sweetie, you should quit looking so worried. The victim got what he deserved and your old man's a hero."

Paulette screwed up her eyes. "What are you saying? That woman was maybe molested when she was a child and my father rescued her? Is that what you're getting at?"

"Can you think of anything else?"

"No. Not really."

"What about the man he killed? Did you catch a name or anything?"

"I didn't hear a name. But the next time he leaves the apartment, I'm heading over there to look at his scrapbook. There's a clipping inside I've often wondered about. It's a picture of a man ripped from the newspaper and he's gravely injured, maybe even dead."

"Let me know when you do. I'll go along," he said. "It's been a while since I've been through every corner of the place, and I want to see if either of his dogs has crapped up the rugs or been chewing on the cabinets. I also plan on taking his car keys, by the way. Your ol' man needs to see a doctor. If the doctor says it's okay for him to keep on driving, I'll give them back. Did you know he ran into the mailbox at the top of the drive?"

"How do you know it was my father?"

"Who else would do it? The mailman?"

"Maybe," said Paulette.

"Bullshit! I'm doing your old man a favor."

SEVENTEEN

Two days of rain followed the visit from the Lennox woman. Although Paulette spied from her window during the day and Riddell during the evening, Eugene was not to be seen except when he opened the door to let the dog in and out. When out, the animal made its way slowly down to the stream at the far corner of the property. Paulette observed it took such a distance for the dog to fully arrange its bowels for release, and then she would be forced by revulsion to look away as the decrepit animal dropped its ordure, not in a single spot, but in several, all the while walking in a semi-hunched position, reminding her of a tiny Godzilla on the move into a nearby metropolis destined for destruction. Thank God, the dog did where it did, and not on the section of lawn, she thought; although had she considered further, she would have realized neither slice of property had much experience with human footsteps, certainly not her own.

In the evening on the third day after the Lennox woman's visit, Eugene descended with the dog from the garage apartment, and old beast and older man walked up the driveway together. Riddell, on watch duty, left the one window for another and saw the two were taking a constitutional along the road above.

"Paulette!" Riddell called out. "Your old man is stepping out for a while. I'm heading over to the garage to look for his keys."

"Give me a second. I'll come with you."

Not one to wait on others, his wife included, Riddell reached the staircase to the apartment with Paulette twenty paces behind. Inside, he found the key case on a stand beside the door. He removed the key to the Plymouth and slipped it into a pocket. Paulette, upon entering, immediately opened one drawer and cabinet door after another in search of the scrapbook. She located the collection of old newspaper clippings and photos in little time.

"I don't think I'll even mention I have the key," Riddell announced. "For a day or so anyway. Just to see what he does."

"It's not here," said Paulette. "This is the page where it was and it's not here anymore. He must have gotten rid of it after that woman went away."

Riddell came over and glanced at the page in the tattered scrapbook. It was obvious from the two different hues of cream in the old paper that something rectangular had once been attached.

"Do you remember seeing the photo?" she asked him with odd urgency.

"Can't say I do, Sweetie."

"Now why all of a sudden would he throw it away?"

"Paulette? Just where are you going with this? I see you getting all worked up, and I'm not sure why. What is it? What's on your mind?"

"The picture of that dead man was in this book for as long as I can remember. Just a picture out of the newspaper. No caption, no name, no nothing. Now after this woman's visit he just up and tosses it in the garbage. That gives me an idea...."

She moved in the direction of the kitchen in order to

inspect Eugene's trash, but Riddell stepped in her path.

"What's the matter?"

"Sweetie, what are you doing? Are you thinking of calling the cops on your old man, or something? What's going on? I mean, at first you didn't want me, your husband, to know anything about this. Now you're becoming all agitated, like you have to do something with this information."

Paulette stared at him without answering.

"Sweetie, he's your father. He's family."

"I'm pretty sure my father killed a man and the only people who have known about it are himself and this woman. And maybe her parents. I heard mention of them."

"Well, so what? The only explanation we came up with makes your old man a hero. And even if that's not the case, even if he murdered someone in cold blood, you turn him in and you'll be screwing up your own life, not just his. You'll be screwing up mine, too, in a way, and I don't take too kindly to that from anyone, my spouse included. So let it go. You hear what I'm telling you? Let it go!"

"I wonder if my mother knew."

"You don't ever mention this to anyone, you hear? Not to the cops. Not to Eugene himself—don't go interrogating him. Not even to me. I don't want to hear anything about it ever again. If Eugene killed a man, he must have had a good reason. And if he never chose to let others in on it … well, he must have had a goddamn good reason for that as well."

"All right," said Paulette. She was somewhat, but not altogether, relieved Riddell was putting his foot down.

"All right what?"

"You're right, Hon. I'll let it go."

"You're not putting me on? Not just saying so because you want me to quit?"

"No. I'll let it go."

"Good. You know what your problem is, don't you? You paid too much attention in your goddamn civics class."

Paulette issued a half smile in response.

"So we're really clear?"

She bunched her lips and nodded.

"Then come along with me. Let's see what shape these rugs are in." He offered a hand, which she accepted, and pulled her around the upstairs apartment. They found the soiled spot where the first dog had died and released its urine.

"I knew it," he said wearily. "I just knew it. What am I going to do with that old man of yours, Sweetie? As he gets older, you and I both know he'll only get worse."

EIGHTEEN

Often enough in a two-party relationship, the actual fool is the one who has convinced himself it's the other person who's the fool, and Eugene was certain that Riddell was regarding his aging father-in-law as a fool. *Else why did he remove a single key instead of the entire ring?* If Riddell had done the latter, Eugene would have concluded he misplaced his keys and inquired of his son-in-law if he had seen them lying about anywhere on the property. As it were, he was sure Riddell had slipped the car key from the ring—there was no way it could detach on its own. In view of this, Eugene made no attempt to drive during the next two days. Instead, he waited for Riddell to approach. And on day three, while standing outside with Marshall and the dog, an approach came. Only from Paulette, not her husband.

"Dad, why don't you and Marshall go and get yourselves an ice cream cone or a sundae?"

"Where?"

"Hazlett's, of course. They've great ice cream."

"That's a three-mile walk, Paulette. I don't think Marshall would be anymore in favor of it than I would."

The child grimaced at Eugene, then smiled. The little kid was full of mercurial expressions that often substituted for speech, and during his two years' of visits to the Parker house, Eugene had developed a real fondness for him.

"I wasn't suggesting that you walk," said Paulette, frowning.

Riddell emerged from the house, aimed in their direction. Eugene waited until he was near.

"Riddell, let me ask you. Do you think I should drive the car with Marshall as a passenger? That's what your wife is recommending."

"Sure. Why not? Take the car," urged Riddell.

"Hold on now, what's this all about? Why did you have your wife come out here and suggest that I take Marshall for an ice cream treat? Normally, neither one of you do anything but scowl when I get behind the wheel. Now you not only want me on the road, but you also want to put Pippa Goodwin's child at risk."

Riddell and Paulette exchanged glances.

"What's going on?"

Finally, Riddell said, "We haven't seen you out of the apartment."

"And what? You're worried about my welfare?" asked Eugene, grinning. "Is that what you're telling me?"

"I don't know why I bother with you," said Riddell. "But yes, we've been worried. You're sixty-five years old."

"And we have a right to worry," added Paulette.

Eugene widened the grin, knowing it would make his son-in-law uncomfortable about what his wife's father might know or not know about the current moment.

"Why haven't you been out?" Riddell asked. "Why haven't we seen you go out and return in your car? Isn't it running? Did you lose your keys, or what?"

"The car's running just fine, son. And no, I did not lose the keys."

"So?'

Time for the tall-tale, thought Eugene. But before speaking, he stared hard at the ground as a pretense that he was troubled and undecided. "Very well," he finally said, bringing his head up. "If you must know, there's a good reason I haven't been driving my car. There's a bomb attached and in all honesty I don't think it's for me."

Riddell hesitated, and a look of befuddlement captured his drawn features. Paulette's own shrank with concern.

"What kind of craziness are you talking now, old man?"

"Just what I said. I'm thinking it might be for you, the bomb. Probably a surprise from one of your drivers who's seen you operating my car on occasion and thought it was your own. Or maybe one of Hollowell's brokers who's disgruntled because you save all the best-paying loads for the company trucks. Or maybe your employer discovered you're not the avid anti-abortionist you want him to think you are. Riddell, is that the reason you attended his church? I've long wanted to ask you that? Was that just to get yourself off the road and into the dispatcher's office? And then when he became too old to attend church himself, you stopped going as well?"

"Just stick to the car!"

Eugene laughed again, and Riddell cast a glance toward the driveway at his father-in-law's automobile

"If you don't believe me—and it appears you don't—start it up. The keys might already be in it. Only let the rest of us step away before you do." He took Marshall's hand and removed the boy and himself to a safe distance.

Riddell stared hard at his wife's father to see if there was any crack in his demeanor. Eugene seemed serious about his claim, at the same time he was making fun of Riddell.

"Why haven't you called the police?"

"Why don't you?"

"I don't want them to think I'm a goddamn asshole in

the event this is bullshit."

"Same here," echoed Eugene. "What I mean is, I could be wrong. I don't think so, but it's possible."

"So where is this so-called bomb?" Riddell asked, his tone giving away the faintest suggestion he was almost ready to buy Eugene's story.

"Underneath," said Eugene, and he withdrew Marshall and himself yet a few more steps. He called the dog over to reinforce his ruse, and it was noticed by Riddell. "You'll need to crawl under from the front."

Riddell sidled over to the car.

"What makes you think what you're seeing is a bomb anyway?"

Eugene offered a scornfully dismissive laugh. "It ain't original equipment, I can tell you that."

"You be careful, Honey," Paulette said.

Riddell cleared some small debris from the driveway in front of the car, then got down on his back and snaked himself underneath the chassis.

"I don't see anything," he said after a while.

"You're not looking hard enough."

"Be careful, Riddell."

"I still don't see what you're talking about." Another thirty seconds followed and Riddell wormed himself out, only to find a grinning Eugene just a few feet away.

"You miserable sonovabitch! I ought to smack you silly."

Riddell got to his feet and brushed himself free of numerous pebbles that clung to his clothes.

"Where's the key to my car?" demanded Eugene.

"Dad," Paulette intervened, "Riddell took away your key because he's worried about you. He wants you to see a doctor."

"To determine if I can see well enough to drive?"

"That's it, ol' man. There's no mystery here to unravel. If the doc says its okay, I hand the key back. But if he doesn't… well then, you'll just have to find yourself some other means to get around."

As Riddell started to walk back toward the house, Eugene shouted, "So get the key, Riddell. Marshall's expecting ice cream. You can drive."

Riddell couldn't keep himself from turning back in Eugene's direction. "You got to be kidding. Have your daughter take you."

"Hon, I've got a house to clean!"

"Drive them. It won't take you long."

"Riddell!"

"He's your father. You take him."

"But the ice cream was your idea!"

"Do as I say and take 'em down to Hazlett's. Besides, I've got to get back to the terminal."

NINETEEN

If there was to be any conversation between his daughter and himself on the way to the dairy store, Eugene understood he would have to initiate it. It was obvious Riddell had embarrassed Paulette with his "Do as I say" treatment. During the early years of their marriage, she occasionally had stood up to her husband, but it seemed with an empty nest and the addition of each new pound those occasions became less frequent, and Eugene imagined she now worried Riddell might leave her to look for another woman.

Breaking the front-seat silence—Marshall was intermittently humming and chattering to himself in the back—Eugene chose a subject altogether new even though he was eager to ask if her husband had always been so gullible.

"You probably don't remember, Paulette, but when you were just a child, Hazlett's was the Golden Horn Creamery. Do you remember that? Your mother and I used to take you there for milkshakes. They had the best milkshakes around."

Paulette leveled her attention away from the road to her father.

"Don't worry, I'll visit the doctor," he said.

"Why did you pull that trick on Riddell?" she asked. "Why did you embarrass him like you did?"

"My daughter, I believe, might have it backwards," he answered while looking straight ahead. "He could have been straight up with me from the beginning, you know. I might not have surrendered the key to the Plymouth, but I could have been talked into getting the old eyes checked out."

"Riddell believes you wish he wasn't around," she said. 'He thinks you might even wish him dead."

Eugene glanced out the side window and chuckled in a dismissive manner. "If he's planning on putting a bullet in that old dog of mine like he did to Brownie, then he might be on to something."

The response caused her to slow the car and as the semi behind them began to pass, she failed to notice her drift across the centerline. The driver of the truck gave a blast on his air horn to avert a collision and the woman with him threw up a finger at Paulette.

Eugene, faintly grinning, again asked after the incident was over, "Anyway, do you remember the Golden Horn Creamery? That's what I'm going to talk about whether it's agreeable to you or not. Of course, after it closed and before Hazlett's opened, there were several other businesses, which didn't sell ice cream, that occupied the same space."

"I don't remember the name," said Paulette, grudgingly.

"Come to think of it, Golden Horn Creamery actually occupied two, maybe even three commercial spaces at the time in the Glade Plaza. That's what that little shopping center was called when I was growing up. Everything was 'glade' back then, and 'plaza' was popular, too. There was Glade News and Tobacco, which was no wider than half an alleyway, I swear; the Glade Hodgepodge store whose owner once accused me in front of your grandmother and grandfather of stealing from him; the Glade Star market where your Uncle Val stocked shelves when he was a high school senior; plus Glade Shoe Repair. Golden Horn Creamery may have been the only store there that didn't have 'Glade' in its name. Do you know the elementary school I attended was named Gladeview? There was woodland all about in those days before the condos were built, and that was what the developers were referring to."

Paulette looked again at her father, but this time for only a second or two.

"However, the one thing about Golden Horn Creamery I will never forget," Eugene continued, now shaking a finger to show how emphatic he was about this particular memory, "is its ceiling."

"Its ceiling! What about its ceiling?"

"It was covered with thousands of those paper wrappers that protect straws."

Paulette glanced at him with a wrinkled brow.

"Ah, now you're taking an interest. All of us kids, you see, when we got our milkshakes, would tear off one end of the wrapper and dip the other end in the shake. Then we would point the straw toward the ceiling like a missile ready for launch and blow off the wrapper. The dab of milkshake made the wrapper heavy enough on that end so it went sailing straight up, and it would stick wherever it hit. Then the wrapper would dry and it would hang there forever. There were thousands of them that hung from the ceiling by the time your mother had you."

"I don't remember the milkshakes either."

"What about the straws on the ceiling? Do you remember them?"

"How would I remember them if I can't remember the milkshakes?"

"We kids had some good times back then. Simple times, but good ones. There was a ballfield and a basketball court behind the elementary school. Before they were covered with the apartments and condos you see now, we played each sport there every day of the summer, and when we finished we all hopped aboard our bikes and pedaled to the Glade Hodgepodge store."

"Where everyone stole, what? Candy bars and gum?"

"Not everyone, Paulette, and certainly not your father. The owner was a little bit like your husband when it came to kids. He thought he was really tight with them, thought he had their confidence, as they would tell him jokes and then he would tell them his. Most of my friends would laugh at his jokes at the same time they were performing the five-finger discount. He was blind to what was happening right under his nose. He was my first real-life example of a fool."

Paulette thought maybe her husband was being called a fool.

"Why did he accuse you? Didn't he like you? Did you pull some dirty trick on him?"

"Get off it, girl. That man never liked me because I watched him more than a few times flirting with his female employee who was younger and much prettier than his wife, and he knew I saw him. Only he gave me more credit than I deserved at the time. It didn't occur to me until many years later that what he was actually doing was putting a move on the woman. But here's what I wanted to say. When we arrived on our bikes at the store, a number of us would buy a big bottle of chilled mint ginger ale. Quarts, as we didn't have liters back then. I loved the stuff. Still do. And do you know, to this day the Valley remains the only place you'll find it. If anyone wants mint ginger ale, they'll have to come to the Valley."

Paulette swung the car onto the pavement fronting the Neighborhood Shopping Mart, its newest name, and before

Eugene could point to a vacant slot in front of the ice cream parlor and next to a black SUV, she slipped into a heavily oil-stained one in front of All-Rite Cleaners, two storefronts away.

"You're not coming in?"

"Marshall and I will wait in the car."

"I think Marshall might want to come in."

"He can wait in the car with me."

"I WANT TO GO IN!" screamed Marshall.

"Marshall, hush up!" said Eugene sternly, who then turned his eyes toward Hazlett's, and as he did, he saw someone whom he recognized walking toward its entrance from the giant SUV. It was the manager of Sparkleman's Market. The man named Jerry.

"Marshall, tell Eugene what kind of ice cream you want," said Paulette, and slowly Eugene realized she was keeping the boy—and maybe herself—from running into Jerry.

"Who is he?"

Paulette secretly signed so Marshall would not notice.

"You don't like him?"

"No, I don't much care for him," she muttered. "He's always thought he is too good for her, but it's really the other way around."

"Oh," said Eugene, with sudden understanding.

"About the only good thing I can say about him is he keeps up with the child support, and yet not always on time. He drags it out and plays enough games to keep her worried. He's the kind of person who can see an advantage and will work it for all it's worth. He can be charming, too."

"I see," said Eugene. "Okay, what flavor of ice cream would you like? It's my treat."

"Whatever their flavor of the day is for frozen yogurt."

"Marshall!" Eugene raised his voice to include some

fun and pep. "You're staying in the car with Paulette. So just tell me what kind of ice cream you want and I'll be back with two giant scoops of it before you can say C3PO frontwards and backwards."

Marshall was about to complain, but Eugene put a finger to the boy's lips. "Just the flavor, young man."

Inside the ice cream shop, Jerry was already waiting on his order, which required some time on a pair of mixers. The woman behind the counter took Eugene's request for three waffle cones, filled it quickly, and stepped to the register to ring up the sale. Eugene had said nothing to the man who was the manager at Sparkleman's and the father of Marshall, but there was a moment when he believed Jerry's memory of him might have been triggered. He thanked the clerk and went back outside, his concentration directed to holding all three cones together and upright until he got to the car. Still, at one point he noticed another familiar face. This one had raised itself inside the monster SUV. It belonged to Dara, the young woman who had cheated him out of his money on two occasions and who mistakenly had thought he was father to Riddell. And the same woman Jerry had fired.

Guess she swapped her live-in for her boss, he thought with equal amounts of humor and curiosity.

TWENTY

The physician's office was on the third floor of the old Mellon Bank building, a gray stone edifice recently sandblasted, in the center of downtown Kensington, a town whose border was contiguous with Arlion, and it was Paulette again who drew the assignment of transporting Eugene. But on this occasion she offered no resistance because Riddell had said he had a hundred trucks to get out on the road and loaded.

"Some big orders come in at Ludlum and PPG," he had announced. "I'll be at it all day, Sweetie."

Paulette had hoped her father would call the practice of a specialist, an ophthalmologist, but Eugene had his reasons for making an appointment with familiar Dr. Mohr, a straight shooter of a man only a few years his junior. It was Dr. Mohr who had assumed the practice of retiring Dr. Patton, which had included the entire Banish family as patient; and Eugene, following his first visit decades ago to the new doctor for a back that was killing him in its lumbar region, soon learned what the family practitioner was all about.

"Here's a pamphlet showing several exercises I want you to do when you return home, Mr. Banish. I want you to do them every day, and I'll see you again in a week."

"Exercises," Eugene could recall himself saying, with an inflection just short of incredible.

"You're getting yourself a potbelly, and you're too young," said Dr. Mohr. "Toughen up those muscles in your abdomen and the back will take care of itself."

"What about the pain?"

"What about it?"

"Can you write me a prescription?"

"Of course. I have a license, you know."

Eugene remembered the response had stymied him.

"Will you?"

"I don't have to," said Dr. Mohr, who removed a small packet of pills from a nearby shelf. "I can give you these. They're free samples."

Eugene had held out his hand.

"Not until you do the exercises. After that, if there's still discomfort, I'll write you something or give you these. Mr. Banish, I'm afraid if you start taking medication for this condition, you'll be back at my office every time it hurts. I'll have to start charging you rent. You came to me for medical advice, and my advice is to get yourself in better shape. Now if my prescription is wrong, then we'll travel your route."

Eugene had gone home and lain on the carpet, done the exercises under the scrutiny and occasional good-natured laughter of Ginger and his teenage daughter, and within days the pain completely disappeared. He had continued to do them ever since, year after year, although now only once a week instead of every day. Dr. Mohr was a no-nonsense doctor and Eugene liked and respected him. He was sure he would receive an honest evaluation regarding his vision.

Aware her father did not want her to tag along into the doctor's office, Paulette said she would do some shopping and meet him at a nearby luncheonette in an hour and a half. Eugene went up in the elevator, alone, and down the hall of the third floor, virtually unchanged over several decades. None of the doors to any of the offices was solid, yet neither could a person see through to the other side, as each contained a huge pane of beaded glass inside an age-darkened mahogany frame. All the corridors remained poorly lit when contrasted with contemporary standards, but this atmosphere was not unpleasant. To the contrary, they conveyed a feeling that the doctors and lawyers, who were hidden behind the many doors that opened off the warm dark corridors, would offer their services before issuing a paper form or requesting payment.

Inside the front room, he found two women and a teenager waiting on the doctor. He selected a *National Geographic* from the magazine rack and settled into a chair, but no sooner had he opened the periodical, Dr. Mohr's head appeared in the doorway to another room and summoned him before the others, who had apparently arrived early for a later appointment. It was another reason for Eugene's appreciation: the doc had always made himself visible; he didn't shunt every small interaction with patients off to his nurse or receptionist and thereby give the appearance he was special and untouchable except for a few precious minutes.

"It's good to see you, Eugene. How is everything?"

"I'm living above the garage belonging to my daughter and her husband," he answered.

The doctor released a humorous grin of old-male fraternity, and Eugene was not required to say anything more concerning his life without a wife.

"You want your eyes checked, you said on the phone. Are they giving you trouble?"

"While I'm here, ears too, if you don't mind. My son-in-law thinks I shouldn't be driving. I made a mistake and once complained that my vision seemed to be on the wane, and he hasn't forgotten. Then, recently someone drove into his mailbox and he convinced himself it was me."

Dr. Mohr nodded. "And the ears, what about them?"

"I seem to be experiencing the same sort of thing in the audio department."

"How do *you* feel about your driving?"

"I can still handle it, especially the daytime."

"All right then, let's have a look. But understand, Eugene, I can only test your vision and hearing the same as I test those of the kids at school. If I believe something more is required, I'll refer you elsewhere."

"Eye chart and a buzz in the ears I think is all that's needed."

"Do you ever wear corrective lenses?" inquired a squinting Dr. Mohr. "Most everyone your age can't avoid it."

"I have reading glasses. But unless the print is the size of an ear mite, they remain on the dresser, collecting dust."

"Take a seat over here," said Dr. Mohr, and Eugene set himself on a cushioned white stool.

Over the next several minutes, Eugene identified the many letters of different sizes on the Snellen wall chart, saw the numbers in the Ishihara color plates to prove he was not color deficient, and pointed to one ear or the other, never once shaking his head to indicate he heard nothing of the minimized tones that sounded in the earphones.

"You're remarkable," Dr. Mohr said when they finished. "In both departments. I see no reason why you can't continue to operate a motor vehicle. What about your reflexes?"

"My son-in-law isn't questioning them," replied Eugene who already was making signs to leave and head for the luncheonette to break the news to his daughter. "Anything else?"

"Sit back down. I'm not through with you."

"I'm not here for a physical, Doc."

"Sit."

Eugene returned to the stool and the doctor moved a chair opposite.

"I'm not going to give you a physical because as you know, there are other patients waiting. But it would be a good idea if you made an appointment for one in the not-too-distant future. What I want to know is why YOU think your eyesight and hearing are failing."

"I don't know," said Eugene unconvincingly, sounding to himself like Marshall.

The doctor held up a hand to put a stop at once to his patient's reluctance.

"There's too much disparity, Eugene. Your eyes' visual acuity and your hearing certainly aren't perfect, but they are still much too good at your age for you to think they're failing. What's going on?"

Eugene raised his head a degree and regarded this man who was looking straight at him and showing no intention of turning away in the very near future.

"Out with it. Describe to me what it is that you see and hear."

"Very well. I see and hear with a filter."

"A filter? What sort of filter?"

"A filter. Actually, with the eyes it's more like a screen. A lot of dots appear and move around. But it's not always uniform, and the densities vary."

"Are they there this moment, the screen and filter, as you're staring at and listening to me?"

No, in fact, they weren't. Not the one and not the other. But Eugene had known this would be the case before entering the room. That the density was unstable and could be thick or thin was made clear to him one day when he ran into a supervisor from his working days; and before this, because the variations had not shown up with sufficient differentials, he hadn't taken notice. Everyone who had worked under this supervisor and had been subjected to his contentious outbreaks and humiliations regarded him as a person whose first concern was always to cover himself in the event of trouble. A CYA-man is what they dubbed him, a man who would distort the truth whenever necessary, and ultimately it seemed there was never an occasion when it wasn't necessary, so in the end the man achieved the deserving reputation of a compulsive liar. Accordingly, when the supervisor had hailed Eugene on the sidewalk, his former employee had given no indication of recognition. The truth was, Eugene could neither see nor hear the man, at least not very much in either case. It was as if an instant fog had materialized within a sector of space two feet wide and six feet high. Only after the supervisor had announced himself did Eugene realize who was standing before him.

"You're saying neither the visual nor audio filter are in place as you talk with me."

Eugene nodded.

The doctor looked puzzled. "Is there anything else?"

Eugene's face betrayed his thought.

"What is it?"

"What about those patients waiting in the other room?"

"They're fellow Americans," said Dr. Mohr, wryly. "A little time-out will do them good."

"Well, you're going to think I'm crazy."

"Maybe you are."

"Thanks."

"Let's go."

"Okay, the reason the screen and filter are absent when I'm listening to you is this: you aren't lying to me."

Dr. Mohr swung his head a full ninety degrees to the left and gazed at a spot on the wall where inside an aluminum frame was a detailed drawing of human intestines, remained there for at least a count of three, then swung back toward his patient.

"And when someone else is the object of your audio and visual attention, they appear? Is that what you're implying?"

"With some, yes. More dots in the eyes and less audio making it to the—what do you call that?—tympanic membrane."

Dr. Mohr made a sound that Eugene took to be a grunt.

"So if someone is really giving you a line—"

"—If they're lying or twisting the facts or doing anything that isn't true to the topic under discussion, I neither see nor hear much of those intentions. What I mean is, their lies and deceit are made immediately clear to me in both sight and sound, no matter how clever they may regard themselves in the practice. Doc, it's as if those things are just naturally stripped away. Of course, it still requires my attention. If my head is somewhere else, I can be fooled."

The doctor blinked and Eugene wasn't sure he was making himself understood.

"Let me give an example that relates to you. Do you recall how you talked to Ginger and me after getting back her tests? At first you considered that she might not want to know that she was dying and had very little time remaining? Well, if my vision and hearing then were like they are today, those subtle inflections punctuating your voice at that time, those certain configurations added to the muscles in your face.... It's not that I would have seen through them. I merely would not have seen or heard them at all. You voice and expression would have appeared to me in its most unadulterated form."

Dr. Mohr stared at his patient.

"So, do you think I'm crazy?"

"Hell, don't you?"

Both men laughed.

"You're aware most people lose some of their hearing as they age and many people see spots floating around before their eyes. You know that, do you not?"

Eugene nodded.

"All right. Then how have you explained this to yourself?"

"First, let me ask, have you heard of such a thing before?"

"Never," said Dr. Mohr, almost too quickly for Eugene's confidence.

"Then you will conclude I'm loony bin material."

"Let's hear it."

"I'm one in a billion. Maybe a trillion. Or perhaps I'm the first human throughout the history of Man this has happened to. The spots appear and float about in just the right places to block out the signs of deceit, and the ears tune in only to those notes that carry the truth. I'm a Ripley Believe-It-Or-Not entry awaiting discovery."

"That could be," said Dr. Mohr with an expression Eugene was unable to interpret.

"Doc?"

"As the lottery slogan goes, 'Hey! You never know!'"

"But you're not letting me leave your office without something else to think about."

"No, you're right about that. And I'll be frank. Many people, when they reach your age, have had enough of their fellow man's bullshit, and overtime they acquired the necessary skills to cut through it and find the truth. Many also begin hearing only what they want to hear, putting on the brakes to anything that passes through their minds that doesn't fit nicely with everything else that's collected on their intellectual shelf over time. And whenever they respond and whatever they say, they regard it as truth. My mother is getting like that, and I know I won't be able to curtail anything she says, short of putting a pillow over the divine woman's head, because she's been a wonderful mother throughout my entire life. Now I don't understand exactly what is going on with your vision and your hearing, but it could be you are one of the very best of aging people who can cut through the so-called 'malarkey'. And that's all I have to say on the subject. So good luck, Eugene. And don't forget to get in here in the very near future for a checkup. Say hello to your daughter, too."

TWENTY-ONE

While in his pre-teens, before the onset of the family's disintegration, Eugene overheard his father speak about a ringing in the ears that he was afraid would drive him crazy. For months the youngest child spied on his father for signs of insanity, but Mr. Banish remained the man he always had been, neither stoical nor wildly out of control. One day Eugene asked his father questions concerning the ringing, including, was it there inside his head every day?

"Every *second* of every day," his father had replied.

Eugene, capable of imagining how horrible such an incessant condition must be, said, "That would make me really nuts. Why doesn't it make you nuts, Dad?"

"I'm sure it will," his father had said, "if my children intend to remind me of it."

This brief exchange from a long time ago with his father flashed to mind only because Eugene recognized the opposite had happened at the doctor's office. Forced to focus his attention on his vision and hearing by Dr. Mohr and made to talk about them, Eugene understood such a reminder had been necessary if he were to make the most of his failing senses, which, if he were honest with himself, were more strange gifts than afflictions. Although he agreed with Dr. Mohr and felt he likely was improving at "cutting through the malarkey," now that he was much older and presumably wiser, he knew also that an oddity of time and the world was in play.

The doctor's free-and-clear evaluation produced in Eugene a feeling of near jubilation, and it was a similar feeling shared by Paulette who understood immediately at the luncheonette that she need not be so apprehensive anymore when her father slid behind the wheel of his car. With enthusiasm she relayed the news to Riddell the same day. They were in their kitchen and Eugene stood off to the side waiting for the return of his car key.

"Look at him," Riddell said to his wife. "The last time we saw that idiotic grin I was sliding out from under his Plymouth."

"Son!" groaned Eugene. "Do you really think I'm pulling something over on you? Give me the key. You've had it long enough."

"Call Mohr," Riddell said, nodding at his wife to pick up the phone. "I want to hear it from the good doctor himself."

"He's not going to speak with you," Eugene said.

"I'm not a cop. I won't be asking for your medical records," said Riddell sarcastically.

At first Paulette was reluctant, except the expression on her husband's face was a familiar one that foretold events would not proceed until he was satisfied. After punching in the number and identifying herself, she surrendered the phone.

"I want to speak with Dr. Mohr," Riddell said while posting his eyes on Eugene as if the old man were a murder suspect and he a detective. "...No, it's about my father-in-law, Eugene Banish."

Seconds later Riddell asked for the report. When he replaced the phone on the wall, Eugene held out a hand.

"The key, son."

"What else is going on?"

Eugene gimmeed his fingers at Riddell, who only repeated his question.

"Riddell," said Paulette, "didn't Dr. Mohr tell you that Daddy's eyesight and hearing are okay for him to drive? Dad, you weren't lying to me, were you?"

"You're beginning to upset your wife," said Eugene. "Why not hand over the key, and I'll be on my way."

"What else is going on?" Riddell asked a third time.

"Enough of this!" said Paulette, finding both men exasperating. "Dad, were you lying to me? Tell the truth."

"Of course not!" exclaimed Eugene.

"Riddell?"

"Mohr said his eyes and ears are near optimum for driving during the day. But he said also that something else was going on, only he wouldn't say what it is. He said it's up to your father whether he wants to make us aware of it."

"Dr. Mohr's a wise man," said Eugene.

"What's he talking about, Dad?"

"It's none of your business and it's going to stay that way. Now once more, son, let me have the key to my car and I'll get out of your hair."

This should have been the end of the discussion, and appearances suggested it was. Riddell at last slipped his hand into a pocket and withdrew his own ring of keys that included the one to the Plymouth. Even so, he did not readily detach the item, but instead stared for a long moment at his father-in-law. And Eugene, staring back, as he waited for the key to be handed over, observed Riddell's countenance had partially faded. Suddenly, there were not quite so many parts per million forming the tight flesh. But Riddell said not another word, and while Eugene's beneficent devolution of his senses alerted their owner of some new development in his son-in-law deserving of further observation, it could not read minds.

TWENTY-TWO

With Dr. Mohr's assurance that his vision and hearing were more reliable than what was expected for a person his age, Eugene started driving more. Even so, he did not travel far, usually not outside a thirty-mile radius, and seldom would he cross the river or enter the tunnels to the more constricted suburbs of Pittsburgh. But he did drive to places where the population was in moderate abundance. It was true he had resumed a discourse with his daughter and her husband during the past year, but certain things, like trust and openness, had been lost and he did not believe they could ever be recovered. And the companionship of a dog continued to be a blessing, but all the same he felt the need to get away from the apartment above the garage and include himself in a gathering of people.

His favorite hangout soon became the luncheonette in Kensington. Meeting up at the old eating establishment with his daughter following the visit to the doctor had brought back a pleasant recollection from his days as a shortstop in the Twin City Midget League. Ray's Luncheonette had been painted on the window in the old days, and on one occasion when the team it sponsored beat up on the 7th Street Sportsmen, Eugene's ball club, owner Ray had invited both winners and losers to the lunchroom at the conclusion of the game for free soda pop and ice cream. Currently, it was known as Gino's and, while sitting there with Paulette in one of its red booths—new ones, although of similar style—Eugene had observed that it had a steady flow of patrons, many of them obviously regulars, as they were always at ease and friendly. Even the more important observation to him was that Gino, a short ruddy-faced man with thinning air, had no objection to a customer nursing his beverage.

Usually, Eugene visited the luncheonette in the early afternoon, ordered a sandwich, then read a newspaper, or sometimes a book from the local library, which he had begun also to visit on a schedule. Others began to recognize his face and would often stop and say a few words, including Gino himself who could be counted on to deliver the coffee if his waitresses were otherwise occupied.

"What do you think of this year's upcoming election?" Gino once asked him after providing a refill. "To me, they all look and sound like a bunch of liars, and not just the men. The women, too."

"You may be right," said Eugene, who had yet to consider himself enough of a loyal customer to respond to the man by using his name.

"When they come on the TV with all their commercials, I stare at them hard, and what I see is their mouths moving a mile a minute, and on both sides."

Eugene would have liked to confirm the man's observation, but viewing the face of a person on a television screen produced the usual image and not what he had come to expect.

On another afternoon, after the lunch crowd had dwindled, Lila Shrum walked into the eatery, delighting both the woman and himself. Neither had seen the other since the completion of the apartment over the garage, although at the closing on the Cape Cod, he had inquired of the buyer about Lila and was told both she and her construction business were doing well.

"So what brings you to Gino's, Eugene?"

"Please, Lila, sit down. Join me."

"I haven't seen you in here ever before."

"What I'm doing is simply getting myself out and about," he said.

"That's good to hear. We all need to get out and about once in a while."

"More to the point, I recently received a clean bill on my visionary and auditory health. In other words, the ol' man before you can still see and hear. Which, by the way, doesn't sit too well with Riddell. He thinks I shouldn't be getting behind the wheel of a car. As for Gino's, I discovered it's a pleasant place to pass some time. What about you?"

She nodded to the outside. "I'm remodeling an older home up on Church Hill." She called out to Gino to bring her a bowl of the day's soup and a grilled cheese sandwich.

"You're not a grazer?" said Eugene.

"You mean do I eat salads? Never was fond of vegetables as a child, and that hasn't changed."

Eugene smiled.

"So how is everything with my cousin and your daughter?" she asked as a waitress delivered her a cup of coffee.

A quizzical expression came over Eugene.

"What? You never knew Riddell and I are cousins?"

"No, I didn't," he said, showing surprise.

"I thought you did. Yes, Riddell and I are first cousins. I have three sisters and a brother, and we're all close in age, but I was the only one Riddell ever liked when we were growing up."

"Why was that?"

"Good question."

"You don't know?"

"No, I really don't. He just liked me better than my siblings. Maybe he hated vegetables too. I don't remember."

She inspected the cream pitcher, then poured some of its contents into her cup and raised the drink to her lips.

"WHERE'S YOUR FRIEND TODAY?" Gino called out from where he was standing in front of the grill.

"SHE'S BUSY, GINO," Lila answered over her shoulder. Then to Eugene, "He means Pippa. We became friends out at your place. On the days she's not working we often have lunch together. She brings Marshall with her and he behaves pretty well in here. ISN'T THAT RIGHT, GINO? PIPPA'S SON MARSHALL IS A GOOD BOY?"

"A NICE BOY," shouted Gino while flipping the cheese sandwich to its other side for browning.

"Pippa Goodwin aware you two are related?"

"Oh, I know she can't stand Riddell. That was obvious the first time we met."

"She told you what happened then."

"You're referring to the little dog? Certainly not one of his finer moments."

"I was surprised when she and Marshall continued with their visits after that happened."

"There wasn't much choice. Her mother can watch the boy only twice a week, and Pippa doesn't earn enough to pay a sitter. Besides, I don't think she blames Paulette."

"Truth be told, I'm glad she didn't pull away. I've come to be quite fond of the little feller."

"Then you should know that it's over. She's enrolling Marshall in school as we speak."

"Well, that no doubt should make it easier on her."

"On the one end, yes. On the other, there's a new development. Marshall's father is remarrying and threatening to return to court in order to gain custody of his son."

Eugene let the words sink in and the earlier trip to the creamery with his daughter came to mind. He raised a finger for emphasis. "Inform Pippa that I might be able to help," he said. "I think I know this woman his daddy is marrying."

"She's an ex-employee of his."

"Just who I figured," he said, nodding. "He fired her. She was stealing from customers and she stole from me and I'm the one who got her fired. But it wouldn't surprise me if she's now working at one of the chains and running the same scam, only this time with the approval of her spouse-to-be."

Lila smiled an appreciation of the information. "Hey! I'll be sure to let Pippa know."

Over the next few minutes the luncheonette became pleasantly quiet as the pair were the sole customers remaining. Outside its windows traffic noise had dissolved to almost nothing. Gino disappeared into a backroom, followed by the waitress. Lila finished the bowl of soup and was halfway through the cheese sandwich. She glanced at the clock above the counter.

"Apologies, Eugene, as I've a meeting with the homeowner on the half hour."

"Well, don't let me keep you."

"How is your old dog doing, I meant to ask?"

"Ringo? He's fine. Why the question?"

"What?"

"Why the question? Your face suggests you've more than a friendly reason for wanting to know."

Lila Shrum grinned at Eugene and even shuddered because of his uncanny instant read of her. She said. "It's just Riddell has been talking about you and your old dogs down at work. Pippa's overheard him."

"What does he say?"

"I guess he's getting off on your bringing home animals that are on their last legs."

Eugene reacted with a faint upward nod punctuated by a smirk, and Lila understood he wasn't intending to speak directly to what she had just told him.

"So why are you bringing dogs home that are not in the best of health?" she pressed.

"Companionship. It gets lonely in that upstairs apartment."

"I imagine it does. But you could have gotten yourself a pup, or a dog that's only a few years old."

"If you're finished. I'll walk you out."

Lila stared at him a moment, understanding that he was deliberately ignoring her remark. As an act of acquiescence she took the last bite of her sandwich and washed it down with the coffee. Eugene picked up both her check and his own.

"You're treating?"

"Soup and sandwich I can afford," he said.

He moved to rise from the booth but she put a hand to his wrist, restraining him.

"You know, Eugene, if you had said to me that you brought home those old dogs because they had been abandoned after serving their masters so faithfully, and you felt sorry for them—"

"—That was part of the reason," he said.

"I'm sure it was. But let me go on."

He nodded grudgingly.

"Thank you…. I think the real reason for those old dogs is that you want to make as certain as possible that they die before you do. I don't think you want to die first and leave an animal's fate to my cousin."

"You're going to be late for your meeting," he said.

Lila pursed her lips and her expression became that of

study. Finally, she released his wrist and smiled in surrender. "All right. It's still too early in the day to press the matter, so I won't."

She slid herself from the booth and stood. She smiled again even as she retained her expression of study. Then bending forward, she planted a respectful kiss upon his cheek. "Eugene? You watch out for Riddell."

And while her words were a surprise to Eugene, it seemed to him they had surprised herself as well.

TWENTY-THREE

Paulette was returning to the house after toting a bag of trash to the garbage can in the garage when the big diesel truck bobtailed to a stop at the top of the driveway. She watched the driver in the faded gold cap and pleated blue vest toss a rolled-up something out the window, then climb down from the cab with a plastic jug in hand. Once on the ground, he picked up the rolled-up something, threw it over a shoulder, and ambled down the driveway while the black truck continued to rumble like a giant steady hammer next to the Parker mailbox.

"Riddell's at work," she said.

"Yeah, I know," said the truck driver. "He asked me to drop off this rug. I thought too, with all the friendly bitchin' he's been doing, that the stuff in this bottle might shut him up."

The man was grinning and laughing all the time he talked and so Paulette knew he was not being really critical of her husband. Still, she didn't understand what the man was delivering for Riddell.

"Is he a worrywart in your own home?"

"I'm afraid you lost me before you started," she said with a grin of befuddlement.

"It's your father," said the trucker. "Riddell's been going on, it seems like forever, about how your old man brings home these sickly dogs and they do their business on the rug. Some of the guys have now been turning the fun on Riddell and saying any man who's so obsessed about a rug might have a touch of the fairy in him."

"Oooh," said Paulette, wincing.

"Ooh is right. Riddell, he don't like that. He don't like that one bit. Anyway, I thought I could help him out and put an end to this rug jibber-jabber. You tell him the stuff in this bottle is some kind of super-duper detergent enzyme that's supposed to remove any stain and animal odor. I've used it after our terrier Spud had a few accidents, and it works. But if it doesn't for Riddell, then maybe he can replace that portion of the rug with what's in the roll. I had him describe the pattern and passed it onto my wife who works at Discount Carpet and Linoleum down on 4th Street in Kensington. This is nothing but a remnant they would throw away. And if it doesn't match up, then Riddell can throw it away hisself. Where do you want me to put these things?"

"Just set them inside the garage. I'll tell him."

When Riddell returned home from his job as a dispatcher late in the afternoon, he noticed immediately the Plymouth was missing from the driveway.

"Where's your ol' man?" he inquired of his wife.

"I saw him coming down the steps toting a bag of books. He must have gone to the library."

"Then fix me a bite. I want to run over there and take care of this rug business before he returns."

"Riddell, why...?"

"Why what?"

Paulette hesitated from uncertainty. She realized her question would be a senseless pursuit. Of course the carpet revealed some discoloration, but the spot itself wasn't overly large and the stain was faint. Moreover, there was no lingering smell. It was clear her father had done his best to clean up the rug. What was more disturbing was how Riddell seemed to be regarding the rug as something special, as though it might be of Persian origin, when in fact they had installed the cheapest fiber they could find that wasn't embarrassingly ugly.

She slipped a plate from the cupboard and spooned on a generous portion of a stir-fry. As she placed it on the table in front of him along with a beer, she said, "Hon, is there something new going on with you regarding my father?"

Riddell picked up his fork and dug into the meal without answering.

"There was the Brownie thing," she went on, "but this is something else, and it seems to have developed ever since Dr. Mohr gave his approval for my father to drive the car."

Riddell paused with the fork in mid-air.

"Are you telling me it hasn't dawned on you what your old man did to the two of us? Am I having to spell it out?"

"What are you talking about, Hon? What did my father do to us?"

"He took us for a ride, Sweetie. Your old man played us."

Paulette's face tightened with both doubt and concern.

"Why is he continuing to live here, tell me that?" Riddell asked, suddenly too serious for her liking. "He's got money now that I've sold his house. He could live elsewhere. He could even buy himself another house, one more fitting for just one person. It's still not hitting you, is it? But he's *your* father, so maybe I'm wrong to expect it should. Eugene lied to us, Paulette, when he first complained about his vision. He was already afraid to live alone just a few months after your mother died, and so he came up with a plan whereby we would feel sorry for him and invite him to live here with us. Small wonder he didn't want to go to the doctor's to get tested. He knew there wasn't anything wrong."

"But, Hon, remember he was positively elated when the news was good."

"Sure, but who knows what the hell that was about."

"And Dr. Mohr told you that *something* is going on."

"Right! And we still don't know what that is, do we?"

"Riddell, he first turned us down, don't you remember? He said he didn't want to move out of his house and live with us."

"Yeah, that's what Eugene said, all right. But look at what he did."

Riddell resumed forking the stir-fry beef and vegetables into his mouth. Paulette, studying her husband, weighed a thought.

"Hon, I don't want us to get into an argument over this, but are you wanting my father to leave here?"

"We can make inquiries," said Riddell around a swallow.

"Inquiries? Are you meaning a home?"

"He won't go to a home. Not yet. But if it's the dogs that are now soiling the rugs, in a few years your ol' man will be doing the same."

"Oh, Riddell!" she cried, rejecting the remark as utter silliness.

"Sweetie, I'd think you would be a little shocked! You're old man isn't going to stay healthy forever, and in time he'll be pissing on the rugs and the furniture, the same as the dogs. If we're lucky, that's all it'll be."

Paulette, still standing, reached down and put a hand on the table. "Well, if that's how you feel, maybe we should encourage Dad to move elsewhere. Ever since Brownie died, the atmosphere around here has been more strained than I like, and what you're saying isn't any improvement. I don't want to live like this. Maybe we should make inquiries."

"Good! If you have any ideas, don't keep them to yourself. But forget about your Aunt Aletha and Val. I already called each of them from the terminal earlier this week." Here, recalling these conversations, Riddell laughed out loud and almost choked on a mouthful of food. "Aletha is apparently already too old to come to the phone. I spoke with her oldest, and judging from his tone, I imagine your aunt has begun doing some squirting of her own in his lovely Somerset castle. Now as for Val, he never did like me—I've always known that—and seeing he and your father have not been the friendliest of brothers, our conversation barely approached the minute mark before the old bastard hung up." Riddell laughed again before returning to his food, which he now consumed without further interruption from his wife.

Once finished, he got up from the table and carried his empty plate and beer bottle to the sink. Paulette, upset, had disappeared downstairs.

"I'm heading over," he called down the staircase. "Are you coming?"

"I don't know," he heard her reply over Pat Zajac, but he could tell from the displeasure contained in her voice that she would be staying back.

He left through the front door of the house and paused on the small landing of worn creosoted ties. The evening air was rapidly cooling as the fall sun was setting. Most of the leaves were at their peak of color while the larches at the side were just starting to lose the green in their needles, and some of the maples to the west and south were still picking up the illustrious backlighting of the sun at their crowns. He glanced toward the creek fronting the north side of his property and a couple on horseback waved to him, but he pretended not to see them, though in fact he always saw them and wondered why they insisted on carving out a portion of their trail on his land. He had let it go each time he noticed them, observing if they were widening the trail and eroding the bank, and should that ever be the case, then he would be sure to have a word.

He stepped down off the landing and sauntered the hundred feet to the garage. He found the plastic jug and the carpet remnant just inside the first bay, gathered them up along with a sponge and a handful of rags from an old milk canister, and mounted the staircase to Eugene's apartment. As he expected, the door was unlocked. Eugene had left a light on and the dog was stretched out beneath its glow. It stirred upon Riddell's presence and issued a throaty warning.

He paused to regard the dog with the strangely alluring eyes.

"Go on. Turn that greeting of yours into something real. I'll take that fucking lamp you're lying under and put it to use on that stupid canine skull of yours. By the time I'm finished, your head'll resemble a goddamn gravel pit." He lowered himself and leaned in the dog's direction, like a third-base coach trying to get his message to the runner at second. "Doggie piss or doggie brains," he whispered to it, "it makes no difference to me. I clean up one, I'll clean up the other."

The animal offered not the slightest sign of capitulation and sustained its sonorous growl. Riddell was forced to realize it had no fear of him and broke his connection with its eyes. He next moved into the bedroom and set the things he was carrying alongside the soiled spot on the carpet. He started to open the plastic bottle, but stopped and instead unrolled the carpet remnant.

"Close, but not close enough," he said aloud. He

quickly re-rolled the unusable remnant and flipped it toward the bedroom door, then uncapped the bottle and generously poured its contents over the discolored spot, spreading the liquid with the sponge. Afterwards, he searched the directions on the bottle's label to determine how long the enzyme was to set before he could soak it back up, along with the stain.

"Ten minutes…. Shit!"

He next reappeared in the front room and the dog's eyes tracked him.

"I've got to waste some time. Where's the ol' man's scrapbook?"

The growl sounded, grew more guttural.

"You're tempting me."

Riddell thought for a moment and soon remembered where Paulette had found Eugene's scrapbook the last time the two of them had entered the apartment without her father's knowledge. He withdrew the deteriorating collection of memorabilia from the drawer with a natural callousness.

"Hey," he addressed the dog. "Is your mug in here? How 'bout your filthy cousin who left the souvenir in the other room?"

He went to the end of the book and thumbed backwards a few pages.

"Doesn't look like it. So maybe one day I'll slip a picture in here of our old cocker. That'll surprise the old man, won't it?"

Almost methodically, Riddell sifted through the rest of the book, putting aside those pages he had seen at a previous time. Eventually, he came upon one that interested him, becoming so thoroughly engrossed that he failed to hear Eugene's return in the car and his footsteps on the outside staircase.

"What are you doing?" Eugene demanded upon entering the small upstairs apartment.

"Looks like this hound of yours don't hear so well," mused Riddell, unashamed and unapologetic. "'Course, he could be playing 'stupid.' He's got himself a good teacher."

"Whatever it is you're blabbering about, I don't care. I just want to know why you're here in the apartment when I'm not."

Riddell tossed his head in the direction of the bedroom. "I'm cleaning up the mess on my rug. The one from your other dog."

"I already did that," said Eugene. "I did it a long time ago."

"You did a half-assed job."

"Are you finished?"

"I imagine the ten minutes are up."

Putting down a bag of books on the sofa, Eugene stepped closer to Riddell and saw the picture in the scrapbook.

"What's this? Why do you have my scrapbook out?"

"This Paulette's grandmother, Eugene? The one at the wedding?"

"That's my grandmother," Eugene corrected him.

"Is that right?" said Riddell. "She ever live with you?"

"After Grandpa died, she moved in with us, yes. Why you asking?"

"Bet that was a joy. Where'd she sleep, in your room?"

"I didn't have a room in those days. Val and I shared a garret."

"So where *did* the old lady sleep?"

"She shared Aletha's room downstairs."

"Ho ho!" Riddell said, widening his eyes. "Was Aletha thrilled with that arrangement?"

"Son, why don't you finish what you started, then get

the hell out."

Riddell looked up at his father-in-law, thumbed to the page of the missing picture but decided it was best to leave the matter untouched as he had directed his wife to do. He closed the scrapbook and pushed it to Eugene at gut level. He got up from the chair.

"You actually don't know why you were looking at my scrapbook, do you?" said Eugene, curiously. "But when you do, make sure you come and see me. That way, I'll know too."

"Right, Eugene. You and me, we'll share some secrets."

Riddell disappeared into the bedroom and picked up the sponge and rags. He started soaking up the liquefied stain. When he finished, he asked Eugene standing in the doorway, what he thought.

"Doesn't look a bit different."

"We're in agreement there."

"That's because you're not doing it right. Did you read the directions?"

Riddell brought the label on the jug up to eye level.

"The final step is to soak it all up with a cloth dampened with water, not with the sponge and rags you used to spread the stuff," Eugene instructed him. "Do it a couple of times for best results."

"You have a bucket?"

"Under the sink. You should learn to read labels, son."

Eugene turned away and went back into the front room. He doubted the stain would look any better now than when he had attempted to remove it, which had been soon after it appeared. He replaced the scrapbook in its drawer before attending to the dog and petting it.

"Is he bothering you?" he said to the animal.

Riddell, in the other room filling the bucket with water, overheard the remark. *Yeah, he's bothering me. He and you both, old man!*

Before sitting on the sofa and removing the fresh set of library books from the bag, Eugene switched on the stereo and inserted a CD. The first song was an instrumental featuring a blend of saxophones.

"What the hell is that?" Riddell shouted from the doorway.

"'*Velvet Waters*' by the Megatrons."

"You mean 'Megatons,' don't you?"

"No, I meant what I said. This came out way back when I was still in high school."

"Big on the charts, was it?"

"I don't remember," said Eugene. "I just liked it." He favored an ear to the recording, smiling in spite of the strained atmosphere. "And wait till you hear the next one! *'Near to You'* by Wilbert Harrison. A great rock-and-roll tune from the early years. I used to have it on an old forty-five until a school buddy borrowed it and gave it to his girlfriend. I never got it back. Can you believe I discovered this CD compilation of hits out of the past by accident when I was shopping at—."

"—Your music sucks. Shut it off."

Eugene lost the smile, reached down without hesitation and switched off the music. Riddell was again on his knees, working the sponge on the carpet when Eugene appeared in the doorway and leaned against the jamb.

"Nothing much is about to enter that postage-stamp world of yours, is it, son? For a moment I thought music might help us reconnect since it has a history of bringing people together when all else fails. But I suppose there had to be an exception."

Riddell ignored Eugene's words and continued to work the sponge. Once done, he again clambered to his feet and collected the rags and roll of carpet. "You can empty

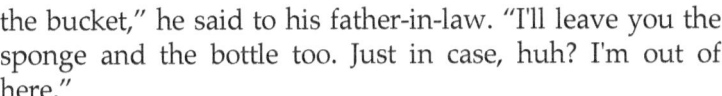

the bucket," he said to his father-in-law. "I'll leave you the sponge and the bottle too. Just in case, huh? I'm out of here."

Brushing past Eugene toward the apartment door, he could not resist, for his father-in-law's benefit, directing a forefinger at the dog, then briefly kicking the barrel upward.

"He's one miserable human being," Eugene remarked to the dog after Riddell was gone.

Removing his jacket, he settled himself on the sofa. He took up each of the volumes and showed either its cover or spine to the dog, often commenting about what he already knew about the story inside or how some critic felt about the book. The dog rose and padded over to Eugene's legs. He reached down, petted the old animal, and ran the hand over the familiar places.

"Maybe they misdiagnosed you," he said to it. "Maybe those lumps aren't anything but a bunch of harmless sebaceous cysts, like the one on my back. Hey, there would have been a name for you: Lipoma. Meet my dog Lipoma."

Eugene winked at the dog as it gazed up at him, then followed with a vigorous rub of affection.

TWENTY-FOUR

Proprietor Gino's grumbling at the luncheonette regarding the slate of political candidates running for office around the region had prompted Eugene, in a moment of rare advanced-age boredom a week before the November election, to attend a debate involving the two men and one woman who were seeking the office of mayor in his current community of residence. The affair had been held at an elementary school auditorium and when he stepped out of the building and into the damp and chilly autumn air at the end of the evening, the concept of *living a lie* was strong on his mind. The oldest of these candidates had been prominent for two decades in the politics of his former community of Arlion, and many of the things this man said to the audience Eugene had recognized to be false for most of his own lifetime. Yet there appeared to be no signs missing facially and inflectionally to reveal that the candidate was lying. The aging politician had reminded him of a TV actor who once played a used car salesman in an episode of *In the Heat of the Night*, and when suspected of murder and asked to take a polygraph, whispered to his accomplice, *"What do I care? I lie all day, every day."*

Although living a lie was not a new idea to Eugene, it was something in two and a half years he had not connected to his declining, yet astute, visual and auditory senses. And however intricately expressed the deception might be at its commencement, if the lie were ever absorbed by its promoter, Eugene understood there could be no detection unless the other party knew the truth beforehand, as had been the case with himself when listening to the veteran pol.

About Lila he did not know the truth and he even wondered why he was feeling concern. Yet, after their meeting at the luncheonette, he felt with an increasing swell of certainty she was living a lie that had relevance to his daughter's husband. But to her credit, she had not reached the point of total absorption, else Eugene understood he would have suspected nothing. Why had she denied giving the reason she was Riddell's favorite of all the cousins? Why, at the end of their lunch, had she warned him to "watch out" for Riddell?

"Watch out for what, Ringo? And another thing. Why was my son-in-law staring at the picture of my grandmother the other day?"

Before the political debate, Eugene had hardly pondered the significance of Lila's denial and her goodbye admonition at the luncheonette. Likewise, he had thought little of Riddell's viewing of his scrapbook. But for reasons he wasn't entirely sure of, he now wanted answers to these questions and he realized they would not be proffered by his canine companion.

To get the answers he first approached his son-in-law; however, his experience at subtle interrogation quickly unveiled its limitations, especially in light of the extinguished trust in the relationship of the two men, and he was reluctant to probe too hard out of worry he would alert Riddell to Lila's part in the matter, and there was something that cautioned him against doing so. Next, he considered getting in touch with Lila herself, driving up to the street lined with the many old churches, and pressing the subject. But he liked the woman too much and did not wish to place her in an uncomfortable position where she might be forced to equivocate to him in a location where God was presumably housed in abundance. Finally, weeks later, the matter still of interest, after Riddell had driven off to work under a light snowfall, he came down from the apartment, crossed the crunching gravel to the house, and entered its kitchen.

"I'm out of coffee," he responded, a meaningless fabrication to his daughter's obvious expression questioning his unexpected presence.

"Sit down, Dad. I'll pour you a cup."

Eugene ran a hand through his hair, which he had recently noted was finally and rather rapidly turning gray, before saying, "You never told me Lila and Riddell are cousins."

"That's what's on your mind this morning?"

"Yes. You never told me."

"Why would I? You knew that already."

"No, I didn't. I would have remembered."

Paulette bunched her lips in a manner to indicate his denial was ridiculous, set down a mug of coffee before him, then went into the adjoining room. From a cabinet under an end table next to the sofa, she removed her treasured wedding album. She brought the thick book back to the kitchen and placed it in front of her father. She flipped through a dozen of the stiff panels until she found the photo she was after and planted a forefinger on the woman.

"That's Lila?" said Eugene.

"That's Lila. She was at the wedding and I can't believe you didn't have the chance to ...," but she never finished the thought. Instead, her tone changed to one of less certainty as she said, "Well, maybe the two of you were never introduced. I forgot for the moment that she had come only to the church, not to the reception."

"Why was that?"

"Other commitments. Riddell was happy that she at least made it to the ceremony. She's Riddell's favorite of all the cousins, you understand."

"Is that right?" Eugene said in a voice that masked his desire to learn the answer. "What's the reason for that?"

Paulette, assuming an expression of not really knowing, said, "I suppose when they were children, they simply got along and played together without a lot of squabbling and fighting that's so typical of many youngsters. Riddell thinks of her as a sister. Once she overcame the objections of her husband about starting her construction business, Riddell supported her at every opportunity. He's sent a lot of work her way."

"Is she married in this picture?"

"Yes, but her husband wasn't able to make even the ceremony."

Paulette took the book away and restored it to its hiding place in the adjoining room. Eugene sipped at his coffee, ruminating.

"The other cousins, were they...?"

"No!" Paulette said. "We invited them, but Riddell had known ahead of time they wouldn't show up. Would you like something with your coffee, Dad? I've got some day-old Danish. I can soften it in the microwave."

Eugene waved off the pastry. If his memory were serving correctly, many of his son-in-law's relatives chose not to attend the wedding. Most of those at the ceremony and reception had been from the bride's side, the Banish side.

"They were jealous, and still are," Paulette added as an afterthought. "Riddell worked hard to get himself a good job, while none of them ever did amount to anything."

After his daughter, there was really no one else for Eugene to question. Riddell's parents were dead, his aunts and uncles resided in other parts of the state, and although there was an older brother plus a stepbrother, Eugene couldn't recall either of them ever paying more than a single visit, and that was already ages ago. And those other cousins, Lila's siblings, he knew not a thing about any of them. As a result, he could only set the matter aside, all the more so when he received a call from Pippa Goodwin's attorney, who wanted to hear with his own ears what his client had passed to him.

And so a week before the start of the winter holidays, Eugene drove into Kensington and spoke out in Family Court on behalf of Pippa Goodwin and her son Marshall. There he informed the judge of the thieving habits of Jerry's second wife, Dara. The visit was a reminder of his lack of trust in the law, still with him at his advanced age, and of the unsettling possibility that, in some convoluted way, it might result in the judge's belief that he had conned the cashier during that troublesome event a few years earlier, that he was really the thief, not the new bride. To one of the questions asked him, Eugene made certain he added what the new bride's late grandmother had conveyed to him, that other market customers had suffered the same experience at checkout time with Dara. That statement of hearsay, permissible in this family court, had drawn the greatest interest of the judge and slapped the proverbial clamp on any attempt to lie by the father. If Jerry wasn't thinking about killing Eugene because of his interference, it was a consideration altogether too evident in the glower directed his way by Dara.

Pippa was greatly relieved, and outside the courtroom she expressed her gratitude to Eugene. Both she and her lawyer had known her chance for retaining custody of

Marshall would have been severely diminished, were it not for his remarks.

Pippa Goodwin's victory over custody of her son served as the first of several good things that in the months ahead would happen for the woman. Following her return to work after the New Year's celebrations, her employer informed her that she would begin working full-time. She learned, too, that her hourly rate would nearly double, plus some benefits would now be hers that weren't possible before. In February a friend in the finance office from one of the local banks called about a repossessed car with low mileage that was reasonably priced for resale. In March she began dating again.

One rainy evening in early spring, Eugene left his apartment, climbed into the Plymouth, and went out to the local library as he'd been doing in recent months. While there, he watched Pippa and her son enter and seat themselves in the children's section on the opposite end of the building at one of the undersized tables. He strolled over to say hello after they had been to the shelves.

"Hey, look at the little scholar."

"He's started asking about books," Pippa replied in a whisper. Marshall was tracing his fingers around the illustration of a crocodile.

"Hi, Marshall."

"Grrrrrr...," said the boy.

"I don't believe that's the sound a crocodile makes," Eugene said as he rubbed the child's head. "Everything okay, Pippa?"

"Everything's just fine."

"Happy to hear it," he said. And then it occurred to him that, because she was employed by the same outfit as Riddell, she might be of some help in answering his questions. "Pippa, would you mind at all if I sit with you a while?"

"Oh please do, Mr. Banish. If you can."

He settled himself as best he could into one of the Lilliputian chairs and stretched out his legs to make himself as comfortable as was possible. He kept his voice respectfully low.

"Now I know that you aren't fond of my son-in-law," he said, "and you needn't say anything to that. But I've heard that Riddell talks about me down at the terminal."

"Uh-huh. He does it often, too. I've told Paulette about it because you're her father, and I think Riddell is out of line."

"Does he ever talk about Lila?"

"Oh, sure, but it's just the opposite, what he says about her. Riddell's very positive about Lila. If there's a driver who's considering building a deck or an addition onto a house, Riddell's always there to bring up Lila's name and recommend her work."

"Does he ever say anything else about her? Like something about the two of them when they were growing up?"

"Not that I've heard."

"Hmm." It was a syllable of disappointment.

"Not everyone listens to Riddell, Mr. Banish. Some of the men don't like him."

"Really? What's the reason for that?"

"Well, because of what he says about you and some others. There's a few who laugh when he talks, but because most of the men don't say much back at him, I imagine he thinks everyone is in agreement. The only time he really stops talking is when Joe Nemerov is in the room."

Eugene smiled out of a curious ignorance. "Who's that?"

"Everyone says he's one of the best truck mechanics

around. He's past retirement, but he still comes in and works twenty hours a week. If he makes an appearance when Riddell is running you down, Riddell shuts up real fast."

Eugene was amused. "Do you know why that is? Why Riddell clams up?"

"Someone said Joe was a neighbor to the family a long, long time ago and he probably knows some embarrassing secrets."

And on that, Eugene's search for answers instinctively resumed. Although he had never heard the name Joe Nemerov, it brought to mind that his son-in-law, at one time or another, had mentioned the names of every other employee who worked at the trucking terminal. Why had he not talked about Nemerov? Eugene did not press Pippa any further regarding the matter that evening. On the following day he discovered the retired mechanic's home address in the phone book and, before sunset, drove out to Nemerov's residence.

Nemerov lived in a small, single-story house on an isolated hill that overlooked a section of the Allegheny River north of the bridge. The structure was in slow decay as evident in the peeling white paint and the minute shifts from square at each of the corners. To one side was a collection of rusted automobile and truck parts, but Eugene observed there was order to the display, both in their contribution to the appearance of the property and in their stacking. The yard was orderly too, and around the walkway Nemerov or someone had done some meticulous edging which had endured the winter, plus there were groomed shrubs at the front of the house to the left and right of a small wood plank porch.

In contrast was Nemerov himself who Eugene saw climbing up from a whitewashed shed on the slope to the river. He was short and carried around an enormous potbelly. His eyes were bunched top and bottom by tiny fists of fat. His beard, though shaven, looked coarse all the same. His flesh was dark, oily, and he walked by moving each thick leg in a small arc to get it from back to front. He wore a heavily pebbled river driver's shirt and a crushed billed cap of really old leather.

"See a shovel?"

Eugene smiled at the sound of the voice, an affable crabbiness its prominent feature.

"I'm missing a shovel. Look around. You see it?"

Eugene did as asked, but was forced to shake his head. He introduced himself.

"Can't say I hear a bell going off."

"Riddell Parker's father-in-law."

"I find that shovel," Nemerov said with a glint in his eye, "you might want to borrow it."

"How's that?" asked Eugene.

"Give that son-in-law of yours a good crack in the head."

Eugene smiled again. This Nemerov was a likeable fellow.

"Aaaa, it'll show."

Eugene trailed Nemerov onto the porch and into the house, which signaled to him immediately that the truck mechanic was not married and probably had never been. The interior so obviously had been menaced a very long time by only a man.

Nemerov went into his kitchen and Eugene continued to follow. "You want something to drink? There's beer. I got whiskey, too. Cheap stuff."

"No thanks," said Eugene.

"Have a seat," Nemerov said, and Eugene slid a chair out from under the kitchen table. Nemerov kept the crushed cap on his head and Eugene wondered if it was ever removed. "You here wanting to know what that boy says about you at the terminal?"

"Not exactly," answered Eugene.

"You should."

"I think I know"

"Then why the visit?"

"I've heard Riddell shuts up when you're around."

"And you want to know what's behind that." Nemerov lifted a finger and scratched the part of his ear brushed by the old leather cap.

"I'm just curious. But if telling me goes against your principles...."

"My principles?" Nemerov grinned with amusement. "If I didn't believe it was true, telling you, or anyone, would be against my principles. Your son-in-law, when he was a teenager, murdered his grandmother." Nemerov watched his guest for a reaction, and when there was none, he said, "No surprise there?"

Eugene moved his head in some awkward fashion, which he could not have described to himself.

"But why should it, huh? I heard you were on hand when he shot his own little innocent pooch."

It wasn't Brownie he was thinking about; it was the picture of his grandmother pasted in the scrapbook and Riddell's study of it.

"When the boy started out as a driver and I recognized who he was, I was never sure it was anything but a rumor, something that just grew and got out of hand. But the longer he stayed with us, and then when he stopped with the driving altogether and Mr. Hollowell moved him to company dispatcher ... well, the more he talked of just about anything at the terminal, the more he started to convince me the thing hadn't been rumor at all. What I'm saying is, I got to know some of what makes your son-in-law tick, and I don't think it's too fucking good."

All this time Nemerov had been standing while Eugene sat. Now he pulled out a chair for himself.

"My folks lived on the same street as Riddell's. Four doors down. This was across the river way up in West Deer, which wasn't flooded with folks back then as it is nowadays. There wasn't much of anything in the township and there certainly was no nursing home around. It was his mother's mother who came to live with them after the grandfather died and the old woman could no longer take care of herself, and her children were all worried about her burning down her own home with herself in it and maybe even take a house or two of her neighbors along for the ride. Riddell was a teenager then, fifteen, sixteen years old. He wasn't driving yet, I know that. The grandmother was in her eighties and she stayed with them a year. A week before Christmas she died in her bed. Or in Riddell's bed, I should say. He had to give it up. That was the word on the block…. I know where that goddamn shovel is!"

Eugene chose not to respond, hoping that Nemerov would resume with his story about Riddell's family.

Nemerov crunched his eyelids in secretive fashion. "You aren't wondering just a tit why I want that shovel? You didn't smell anything driving in?"

"Like something dead, you mean?"

"Shit is what I mean. Some asshole with a camper drove down here and emptied his holding tank just off the road in the bushes. Must have figured nobody lives here and no one would smell it." He pushed his chair back and stood. "I'm getting that shovel now before I forget where it is. Come on. We'll cover up that crap together."

They went back outside and Eugene walked next to Nemerov who entered a field of mostly weeds. The shovel was about a hundred yards inside.

"What's it doing out here?" Eugene asked, curious.

"Fellow I drink with wanted some dogwoods. They're scattered around and I dug up a few smaller ones, but left the shovel behind. That was last fall. I just forgot about it."

From there they walked back past the old house and up the dirt road on which Eugene had driven in. At the first bend Eugene could detect the rank smell of new sewage. Nemerov went straight to the spot. Toilet paper and human feces, drenched with urine, comprised a small dump.

"What kind of man does this?" he asked.

"Coming out here where he figured no one was living, he probably thought he was being considerate."

Nemerov looked briefly at his visitor as though Eugene were crazy. "Yeah?"

"All right. Maybe 'considerate' is giving him too much credit."

"Yeah, maybe." Nemerov jammed the shovel into the earth and began digging a pit next to the sewage. "It was my old man that told me about Riddell and what he done. I don't remember where he first heard it. Anyway, the rumor was the old lady didn't just die in her sleep. On the block the word was the teenage son Riddell had put a cushion over the old woman's head and smothered her."

"What made the neighborhood think that?"

"I never found out. No one seemed to really know. Yet I had me an idea. It was just one of those things that got started, but it hung around for years. Of course, I didn't live with my folks then, but I came over often to help out the old man with some odd job needing an extra pair of hands. Every time I did, this was brought up, if not by my folks themselves, then by one of the neighbors I got to shooting the shit with, like I'm doing with you. You know, autopsies on old people who died in bed, they weren't done in those days. They probably aren't done much today either, but they weren't done at all back then. Leastways, I never heard of it. Dead old people were just planted in the ground, so there wasn't a way to put the rumor to rest or prove that it wasn't a rumor at all, but was instead the goddamn truth."

When the hole was wide enough and more than a foot deep, Nemerov used the shovel to scrape the sewage into its bottom. The stench was instantly amplified from being stirred, and Eugene stepped backwards.

"You said you had an idea of your own."

"Yeah, that's right. Grandma was a trial, see. One mean old woman. She was always doing things that would embarrass her daughter and family. Once, when I was over, I caught her taking a dump outside. She knew I was there too. I believe she was doing it on purpose. I guess you could also say she was plain nuts, but to me there was some thinking to it. Anyway, that's the reason Riddell tightens up like a stretched rope when I'm around. That's because he knows what happened. And he knows that I know."

Nemerov stopped talking and covered up the hole containing the sewage. It took most of a minute.

"Another job well done!" he said with levity. "Now, Eugene, how 'bout you and me go back to the house and have a shot to celebrate. Any time a man can bury shit in this life, no matter the kind, I say a drink is in order."

TWENTY-FIVE

Nemerov went into the kitchen and fished out a bottle of Kessler's from a bottom cupboard to the right of the sink. There was a bug that came out with it and he let it scurry quickly inside an opening under another cabinet.

"How do you take yours?"

"Straight up. Only not too much."

"You're not a drinker?"

"When my wife Ginger was alive, I was. I could rest assured she was counting, which I didn't appreciate. But without her around, I've stayed away from the hard sauce almost completely, sticking mostly with the suds. Now, with what you related to me about my son-in-law, I'm thinking it might be a horrendous mistake for me to ever lose control."

Nemerov glanced from the counter, where he was pouring the drinks, to Eugene. "For all I said, it's still a fucking rumor."

"Didn't sound like you think so."

Nemerov delivered the whiskey to the table and sat down opposite Eugene. He raised his glass a few inches off the surface to signify a toast. "Here's to old age."

Eugene regarded his host with an expression of doubt before saying with emphasis, "To *healthy* old age!"

"When you're a youngster," Nemerov said wistfully inside the crabby voice, "you're expected to live. But after you reach our age, the expectation takes a dive the other direction. With each year passing there's more of a rush, especially if we begin to drool and fart too often. Of course, none of the family with less experience wants to admit it. Your folks still alive, Eugene?"

"Dad passed on back in the 70s. My mother May died a few years before my wife."

"My youngest brother suspects they killed our mother, you know. At the home. There's five of us children, but we all worked. Spouses, too, so we couldn't take her in at the time. So what we did was, we each kicked in and found Mom a nice home. Best of the bunch in this area. We went there as a family to inspect the place and saw that it was clean and orderly, and the food looked good too. Plus the younger fellows who worked there, they had themselves haircuts and not so many tattoos. Nothing crazy going on that we could see, in other words. Ralphie—that's the youngest—says he knows why. They take in a few old-timers who turn out to be troublemakers, he says they soon get rid of them."

"Your mother was a troublemaker?" Eugene joked.

"Ralphie's serious. And I can't say he's full of it."

"What's his reason?"

"Our mother was diagnosed with dementia. When we placed her in the home, she wasn't too far gone. I mean we were able to laugh at some of the crazy things she did, like making chile and dropping in a banana. However, before the year was out, the dementia turned into something altogether wild. Eugene, the last time I saw the poor woman alive, I didn't recognize my own mother who'd raised me. A nurse pointed her out sitting at a table in the dining hall and I laughed, told her she was crazy. The woman she'd pointed at resembled some wild creature out of the jungles of Borneo. Chocolate pudding smeared all

over her face, globs in her hair, and she took the rest of it and flung it at another nurse, cursing as she did. Like I'd never once heard her curse."

Eugene shook his head.

"It's our oldest sister who took care of things and went to see Mom at least once a week, and she learned from the doctor and a nurse at the home that Mom was in a lot of pain, and they were giving her morphine to ease it. Three months later, Abby got the call. Mom died in her sleep."

"And your brother figures, what? They gave her a little more morphine than needed?"

"That's what Ralphie thinks, you guessed it. He thinks that kind of thing happens in these homes a lot more than anyone would suspect. Once the person's dead, it's just a transfer from old home to funeral home, with no stop at the coroner's."

Eugene pondered the contention Nemerov offered. He'd heard it before, with respect to hospitals.

"What would you have done if it was your mother and you believed they'd given her a drug overdose to end her life? Our mother was 89 years old, Eugene. We were supposed to ask for an autopsy? Have her cut up into pieces and examined for signs of murder?"

"I don't know what I would have done," Eugene said.

"No one is about to have their old man or woman sliced open if they died in their sleep. If they'd put a bullet in our mother, or stabbed her, or strangled her with a cord from the curtains, then sure, my family would have raised hell. Anyway, Ralphie didn't begin to think as he did until after she was laid to rest. You want something to eat?"

"No thanks."

"Well I hope you don't mind, but I got to get something inside this pouch of mine," Nemerov said, patting his big stomach. "I don't, and you'll be looking around for a dog that's growling, and I ain't got none."

He rose from the table and stepped to the refrigerator. He removed a covered green dish from a lower shelf and placed it inside the oven. Eugene measured what remained in his glass.

"I need to be leaving soon," he said.

"How do you like being on your own?" Nemerov asked as he turned the oven's dial to a warming temperature.

"You mean do I miss my wife?"

"I'm sure you miss her. But what's it like?"

"Honestly, I don't know. What I mean is, I still can't describe it even to myself. But I can say that it's not like I feel single again."

"I gotcha," said Nemerov as he returned to the table and his drink, but he did not sit down.

Eugene was thankful his host was not attempting to detain him. He raised himself from his chair, glass in hand. "You never married?"

"Waited too long on one, so she married someone else." Nemerov sipped at his whiskey as he watched his guest give a quick encompassing glance around the room. "But I haven't always lived alone. Did your son-in-law ever mention Bezzy?"

"Never heard that name."

"I thought he might, but I must have shut him up about that as well. Many times Bezzy came by the terminal to pick me up so we could go and have a few beers. Riddell the next day would poke his fun at my friend. You see, Bezzy couldn't talk like you and me. I was the only person who could understand what he was saying. If he was here now, you'd be looking at me for help. It was all marbles and mumble that tumbled out of his mouth. All the same, Bezzy was talking and I always knew what he was saying."

"He lived here with you?"

"Yeah, we lived here together since the mid-eighties. He died five years ago. I think he grew tired of no one understanding him but me. He was a misfit and I suppose I am too. It's just that I know how to fix a diesel engine."

A swig remained in Eugene's glass, and he raised it in a toast. "Well here's to you and your memory of Bezzy," he said. He finished off the contents and set the glass on the table.

Nemerov went over to the door and held it open. As Eugene approached, he said to his guest, "It's a blessing you're not living under the same roof with Riddell. He won't be wanting to put a pillow over your head like he did his grandmother. Listen, Eugene, if I pick up anything down at the terminal that proves I'm wrong about that, I'll be sure to let you know. You take it easy now. It was fun talking with you."

"Same on this end," Eugene said, and he offered a hand just as a cat scrambled onto the porch and into the house.

"Must be he's hungry," said Nemerov, nodding toward the animal. "'Cause he ain't never been much of a hunter."

As the Plymouth made its way from the slope overlooking the river and back to the main road, the sun was deep below the horizon and the sky was rapidly darkening. Many yards beyond the spot where Nemerov had buried the camper's discharge, the nauseating miasma was continuing to drift like an invisible cloud, and it seeped through the car's vents and into Eugene's nose. Even when he stopped at Sparkleman's to purchase a few items for the next morning's breakfast, it was there.

And so too was Jerry, the store manager and Pippa Goodwin's ex-husband. As Eugene entered the store, the young man glanced at him from the elevated platform of the front cubicle. Eugene disregarded him at the same time he made an observation that the independent market had become dingy, even dirty. Its appearance hinted that the business might soon be closing its doors. And should that occur, he might not have to run into Jerry and Dara ever again, which, as far as he was concerned, would be no loss.

Several minutes later, after leaving Sparkleman's and while approaching the driveway to the Parker property, he saw a brilliant light strafe the trees above the creek at the distant corner. Rolling the car to a stop beside the garage, he could see his son-in-law standing on the cresosoted ties at the front of the house. In Riddell's right hand positioned next to his temple was a high-candlepower spotlight.

Eugene got out of the car and stood beside it. From inside the apartment the dog Ringo sounded a welcoming bark.

"What is it?" he yelled, but Riddell did not answer.

He moved away from the car to a point where he could see the focus of the light. Inside the illuminated circle were a man and a woman on horseback, and the light tracked their horses' every hoof beat. The pair guided their mounts along the bed of the creek on the more open side that was Parker property, then crossed at a shallow onto their own land. Riddell continued to stand on the timbers and maintain the brilliant light on the riders' backs as they made their way up the hill. Twice Eugene watched them as they swung halfway around in their saddles to peer into the light, and once as they turned to look at each other, the man shook his head. Finally, the man tired of the annoying game and kicked hard at his mount, which collected itself into a full gallop and gobbled up the hill toward a barn. The woman, however, did not. She turned both her horse and self completely around and stared into the light and at

Riddell for several seconds.

The door to the house opened and Eugene watched his daughter poke out her head.

"Riddell, don't you think that's enough? They're going to think you have a screw loose."

Ignoring his wife, Riddell nevertheless removed the light from the rider. Yet he did not switch it off, and Eugene found himself the new interest of his son-in-law. The light blinded him, and he held a hand out front to shield his eyes.

"Turn that damn thing off!" he shouted.

Riddell moved the powerful light off Eugene's person and onto the Plymouth. Then the dog barked a second and third time from inside the apartment, and Riddell transferred the light to the top floor of the garage.

"What are you doing, son? Just what in the hell are you doing?"

Riddell lowered the high-powered light and finally switched it off. Remaining silent, he spun about, walked off the ties, and disappeared inside the house. Eugene could see that his daughter, continuing to stand in the frame of the open door, was looking his way.

TWENTY-SIX

Each Saturday morning, before 7:30, a brown Ford, riding low on its rear axle, momentarily idled at the top of the Parkers' driveway. The usually unshaven man at the wheel extended his arm through an open window and slipped two copies of the weekend-edition *Star-Enterprise* into a yellow tube. Often, Paulette was already up and retrieved them, although she no longer delivered her father's copy to his doorstep on the garage's second floor as she once had, but set it folded on the third step from the bottom. When the newspaper wasn't on the staircase, Eugene went to the tube himself and separated his own while leaving the other. This was the case the next morning, a warm morning with the sun already bright, and Eugene and the dog were about to climb the stairs back to the apartment when his daughter emerged from the house and made her way along the shade trees that bordered the space separating the two dwellings.

"Good morning, Dad."

"Good Morning."

When her father didn't move, Paulette paused in her mission. "Are you wanting something?"

"What was that about last night?" he asked.

"You mean Riddell and that light?"

"Was there something other I missed?"

Paulette took in a deep breath, too deep for the early hour. "No, you didn't miss a thing. And I don't know what it was about, other than Riddell worries their horses are destroying the bank on our property."

"Are they? Have you been down there yourself to have a look?"

Paulette hesitated at the question. "Let me get our paper out of the box," she said.

She hurried her weight up the grade to where the driveway met the road while Eugene waited with the dog. She stood to the side of the mailbox as a red Explorer with a conspicuous light bar atop the roof ran past, claiming most of the narrow pavement. Eugene watched his daughter briefly wave to the young woman behind the steering wheel, but she was barely offered a response.

"You asked if I had a look myself at the bank," she said when she came back down with the newspaper in hand. "The answer is no, I haven't. But from the house everything at the creek looks like it always has. I think they just enjoy riding their horses. It's only that when Riddell gets something in his head, he just worries it to no end."

Eugene smiled discreetly at the assessment of his son-in-law. He said, "Have you ever invited them over?"

"Who? You mean the horse couple?"

"Yes. Have you and your husband ever asked them over?"

"You mean for dinner?"

"For coffee. For a drink. Just to meet them."

"This isn't that kind of neighborhood. You've been here long enough to know that."

Eugene faintly inclined his head to show he did. It was a neighborhood quite different from what his own had been in Arlion where people talked with each other, sometimes for hours.

"Riddell will be getting up soon. He plans to wash the cars this morning. Do you want to come over for breakfast?"

"The coffee's already on," he replied. "I'll pass."

Still, he didn't move, so Paulette didn't either.

He shook the folded paper at her, but the action got rid of nothing. "I was thinking about a fellow I used to work with, is all," he said in explanation. He gripped the railing and raised a foot to the first board.

Paulette expanded her eyes their widest to show that she was listening.

"Okay, he once witnessed a hit-and-run," he went on with some reluctance. "Only he didn't say a word about it to anyone until months afterwards. He'd known the driver's wife. She was special to him and he didn't want to cause her any hardship. Yet I've often wondered how a person could sit on a thing like that."

Paulette first reacted with an honestly blank expression as it seemed her father's words were a strange non sequitur. She had no idea what he was going on about.

She was about to tell him that she was baffled when from out of nowhere a thought crossed her mind that what her father was speaking of in such a roundabout way was his killing of a man decades ago—the newspaper photo that had been in the scrapbook and the subject of the conversation she'd overheard between him and the woman in the gold skirt. She'd honored her words to Riddell not to ask questions. But was it possible that her father was now trying to broach the subject to her in some crazy way?

"Dad, is there something bothering you? Do you have something that you want to get off your chest?"

She could not have known that what Eugene was actually wondering about involved what Joe Nemerov had said to him the evening before. Wasn't he now in a similar position to that man who had witnessed the hit-and-run? That's what he was mulling over. Paulette waited behind a curious face and Eugene looked back at his daughter and asked himself once more, what was he to do? It was of some relief there was no real evidence, that the claim Riddell had deliberately killed his grandmother was only an allegation. And yet Nemerov had not struck him as a man who would lie or make up stories. The truth was, he believed the old mechanic. He believed that his son-in-law had committed murder while a teenager, and he didn't know if he should convey the same to his only child who was married to the man.

"Dad?"

With a deceptive grin he waved the paper in the air as a sign their morning discussion was over. "Gotta see how the Bucs did in the second game of their doubleheader on the coast," he said with an overstressed exuberance. Then he started up the steps again, the dog in front.

Yet at the landing he paused to glance below and saw that Paulette still had not moved and was continuing to look up at him. He flashed a perfunctory smile at her before turning away. Once inside the apartment, though, a new and disturbing notion began to settle in his mind. He wondered if Paulette herself might not be in danger from Riddell. Was there perhaps a suffocating pillow in her future?

TWENTY-SEVEN

While Eugene and his daughter had been talking outside, inside the house Riddell had risen and slipped into his weekend clothes. He stood in the kitchen at the coffee maker, pouring himself a mug, when Paulette returned.

"What were you two jabbering on about?" he wanted to know while holding out his free hand for the morning paper.

"Nothing much."

He grinned sideways. "Nothing much always take that long?"

"Very well then! You and your spotlight. That's what we were talking about. Dad asked what was going on last night with you and that ridiculous light."

Riddell raised the mug and carefully sipped its contents. "You know, Paulette? Sometimes I think you're *still* more of a daddy's girl than you are my wife."

"He is my father, Riddell."

"Yeah, we've been through that. Give here with the paper."

She reached out and presented the newspaper to him and he went over to the kitchen table and seated himself.

A short while later she heard him mutter, "Huh."

"What are you huh-ing about?"

"Remember a screwball everyone called 'The Humper.' Before we were married and I had the bike."

"'Humper'?"

"Yeah. His name was actually Humphrey. He and I rode together a few times. But he drank too much and I didn't want to hang around and be the one to someday scrape his hide up off the pavement."

"What happened?"

"What do you think? He's dead. Made the front page. I'm surprised he's been riding all these years. But it all came due. A pickup ran a light. He was clipped in Illinois while on his way home from a rally."

Riddell moved his eyes to the obituary list at the bottom of the front page where each of the deceased's name was followed with the age.

"I'll be damned. The Humper had a few years on me. I'd always thought it was the other way around because most of the time he behaved like some screwball kid."

Paulette turned aside and removed the milk, butter, and a carton of eggs from the refrigerator and set them on the counter.

Eleven names appeared in the newpaper's list of regional deaths that Saturday morning and besides the one belonging to a fellow motorcyclist out of his past, Riddell soon recognized another. He opened the daily paper to the page carrying the obituaries and began to read its paragraphs.

"She wasn't very old," Paulette remarked. She held an egg in her hand and was peering over his shoulder, reading, too. "Did you know her, Riddell? Was she from work?"

He glanced back at her but avoided an answer to her question by saying nothing.

"She took her own life," said Paulette. "How sad."

Riddell hesitated, then swung around and looked up quizzically at his wife. "Suicide? What the hell makes you say that?"

She pointed a finger of the hand holding the egg at the paper. "It says her age there, which isn't all that old. And the notice doesn't list a cause anywhere. It also says she was preceded in death by her mother and father. And it doesn't say that she is survived by a husband, or even a child. In other words, the poor woman was alone."

Riddell continued to give serious regard to his wife and her explanation of the black woman's death. Finally, he grinned out of some kind of bizarre appreciation, afterwards lending his attention again to the obituary.

"Eggs all right, Hon?"

"Sure," he muttered. "Over-easy."

● ● ●

On the front page of that same Saturday morning edition of the *Star-Enterprise* yet another familiar name had appeared. It alphabetized above the motorcyclist Humphrey. And while it meant nothing to Riddell, Eugene recognized it at once.

TWENTY-EIGHT

And on Monday Connie Reardon and Allan Hardinge, along with their siblings, buried their mother Elizabeth.

The gray hearse that carried the elderly woman and the ribbon of cars that followed passed in a caterpillar crawl in front of the Hollowell trucking firm. Several funerals a month passed there as the cemetery was near the end of the road, a perpetually crumbling two-mile strip of asphalt. In most instances, Riddell rarely took notice of any funeral procession. With the Hardinge procession, he was compelled to look because the cars had stalled for some reason, and within minutes four company trucks were bumper to bumper, unable to pull out of the terminal, slip between the nearest vehicles, and be on their way to plants across the river to get loaded. Since scheduling was at the heart of his job, he became irascible when something disrupted its predictability, and he was about to march out onto the broken pavement and insist to the drivers that they move their vehicles out of line and onto what little shoulder existed so that his rigs could make the wide turn they required, when the procession suddenly started to move again. Even so, the delay was on his mind later in the week.

"If you spy a hearse coming up the road, be sure and let me know at once," he'd said to his assistant on Thursday. "I've got to get out of here, and I don't want anything to delay me."

Normally a lethargic time for freight throughout the Valley, Thursday was also the one day each week that Paulette and Eugene disappeared from the property at about the same hour, although in different directions. Riddell, aware of their routine, drove out of the terminal's parking lot shortly before noon.

He arrived at his driveway fewer than thirty minutes later and drifted the car to a stop in front of the first bay of the garage. He shut off its engine, but did not immediately unlatch the door. For most of the next minute he remained seated behind the wheel, not moving a muscle. Finally he got out, stood, and rested one arm on the car's roof, listening. The air was still, marked only by the brief and low-pitched sounds rising off the distant bypass. From inside the second story of the garage came the vibrating hum of the motor for the overhead fan. He heard music too, faint classical notes. He stepped away from the car and peered at the house to confirm that his wife was not at home and hadn't made an exception of her habit to shut the front door and draw the blinds. All was as he anticipated.

Upstairs in the apartment was where he expected the dog would be as he knew his father-in-law never left the animal outside while away. Plus, it explained the playing of music. Eugene believed it served as company for the dog while he was gone. Riddell gazed up in the direction of the door, which was likely unlocked. Following that occasion when Eugene had walked in on him while he was studying the scrapbook, he thought his father-in-law might close up the place when empty. Checking later, he learned that was not the case. Not that it would have mattered because he'd kept the second key that had come with the lock.

All of which was the reason his first consideration to kill the dog had been antifreeze. The plan had been to carry up a bowl of the sweet but toxic liquid when Eugene was away and set it before the animal as though it were a peace offering. But death by that method, he'd eventually and wisely cautioned himself, would mean one, even two days of visible agony, and Eugene could become suspicious. Carbon monoxide poisoning, he'd concluded, was the better method. What's more, the ceiling fan would facilitate the drowsiness it brought on, since CO, he'd learned through a little encyclopedic reading, was a heavy gas that built its volume from the bottom up. The old man might just think the dog had succumbed to its many tumors.

He took a final look around him, included a glance up the driveway to assure himself that the mailman or pennysaver delivery person wasn't there watching him, then raised the door on the first bay. Sliding back behind the wheel of the car, he restarted the engine, and eased the vehicle inside. After removing his shoe from the gas pedal, he shifted the lever to neutral and set the parking brake. The engine idled nicely, dependably, not a hitch in its slow combustion despite the pinholes in its muffler and catalytic converter. Once outside again, he tugged down the door on the garage bay and walked past the line of big maples to the house.

TWENTY-NINE

Although Eugene did not attend the burial service for Elizabeth Hardinge, he had driven to the funeral home on Sunday night to pay his respects, and his expectations for the visit were uncomplicated. Condolences to Connie, and to Allan too, view the body, leave. All went as anticipated, except Allan intercepted him as he was signing the memorial guest book. Connie wanted to talk.

And so he waited near the vestibule, away from everyone. A few minutes later Connie appeared and pulled him into a vacant viewing room. There she informed him that she and her siblings were determined to settle their mother's estate before returning to their homes, all of which were a distance. This wouldn't take but a day or two. She then said that she had enjoyed his surprise visit to her home in St. Andrews and was hoping they might get together again. It was a pleasant development Eugene was not at all expecting and so he quickly offered to take her to dinner. She shook her head and said she did not want to eat out.

"Besides, you came to my home. I'd like to visit yours."

Embarrassed because there wasn't much to see at the above-garage apartment, he was forced to say the same. But when she repeated that she had no wish to eat out, he offered to do the cooking.

"That's more like it," she said. "I'll call and let you know when you can expect me."

Again, embarrassment because he'd surrendered his phone some time ago. The rare occasion someone needed to get in touch, he offered up his daughter's number.

"And what is it?"

His third expression of embarrassment brought an end to what he thought she must have interpreted as utter silliness.

"Okay, I'm not going to pretend I understand, Eugene. But these next few days, have you plans to go anywhere?"

He had none. What he meant was, he wasn't leaving town. He had a few local stops to his routine, but he was always back at the apartment within an hour or two.

"Then this is what I'll do," she'd said. And she explained just how they would get together.

Yet here it was Thursday, three days after the interment of her mother, and they had yet to meet up. It was a letdown, but he decided that something unexpected must have developed and she was already back in St. Andrews. He told himself he would wait another day or two before calling to find out what had gone wrong.

Pulling the Plymouth into the parking lot of the People's Library a short while later, he saw the school buses and was reminded of the flyer he'd noticed tacked to an announcement board inside the door on his previous outing. It informed the library's patrons that scores of elementary school-age children would be visiting once a week throughout the coming month.

He gathered the books for return from the front seat, opened his door, stepped out, and walked to the entrance. Inside, approaching the circulation desk, he saw that one of those children off the buses was Marshall Goodwin, who had sprouted more than a few inches since his first visit to the Parker household. The boy was scurrying like a fall squirrel from one bookshelf in the children's section to another and eventually to a table where he climbed onto a chair and shared his treasure with a classmate who had collected several magazines into a pile. The other students from the buses were equally busy, and there was an audible hubbub in the place that wasn't normally present.

"Busy little beavers, aren't they?"

"I'll say." Eugene recognized the young teacher who had come up beside him. She lived in Arlion, in his former neighborhood.

"You must know Marshall," she said. "I see you have your eye on him."

"My daughter used to sit him. Marshall and I became friends."

"I'll give him another five minutes," the teacher said with intentional wryness, and Eugene couldn't help but laugh. "You do know him," she said, grinning.

"I'm sure he's improved."

"Oh, he's not the headache some are," she answered, and comically appended her grin with arching eyes and a shaking head. "And no sooner said.... Excuse me."

The woman then hastened to a distant corner where two boys were slapping at each other with accelerating frequency, and a trio of barely older girls were giggling and moving out of sight behind a shelf filled with reference books. Another teacher at the opposite end of the room raised her voice so that everyone could hear: "We can all return to the buses!" she threatened. "Is that what you want?"

A reduction in the din came instantly from the entire group of children, which amused Eugene because he detected a minor chord of aggregate grumbling beneath it all. The sound reminded him of a feisty cartoon character from his youth named Yosemite Sam.

With quiet in place, he turned back to the circulation

desk and set down his books. Still, when he swung back, there was Marshall at the far side of the room, gaping at him. The boy waved and his right hand flapped vigorously in the air as though it were under the control of an external force. Eugene returned the wave before placing a silencing forefinger to his lips. Marshall in response stretched wide his eyes, shrank them, and shaped his mouth into a tiny venturi as though he and Eugene shared a secret. A teacher then edged up behind the boy and guided his shoulders in the direction of his work, which allowed Eugene to step away from the circulation desk and disappear amid the aisles.

Among the countless volumes sitting on the shelves at the rear of the room were hundreds with publication dates from decades past, which was why he always went to this section first. Many carried the titles of bestsellers before and shortly after he was married. He had read so few of them. Before Ginger entered his life, he had been a bored, unsatisfied young man and reading was neither a sedative for his hormones nor the fulfillment of any yearning. And after the wedding, orders at the aluminum plant had increased so quickly that he worked time-and-a-half, occasionally even double-time, to take advantage of the unexpected money, which he and Ginger were eager to have as newlyweds. It had left him little time to read, and certainly not enough. But he had always taken notice of what his wife was bringing home from the library, and many of the titles were these same books on the shelves before him.

He paused at a collection of novels by Leon Uris. He'd never read but one of the Jewish writer's many works, *Battle Cry*, and that was only because his father, whose brother died a Marine, had owned a copy. He slid a rebound *Exodus* from the shelf and another one of *Mila 18*. He began reading the opening parts of the latter when he heard the string of nonsense syllables issuing from the front of the library. They required several iterations before their familiarity from a few years back struck him, and then he listened to the teacher, the woman from Arlion who had spoken to him earlier, shout: "MARSHALL! STOP YOUR YELLING AND GET AWAY FROM THE WINDOW. GO BACK TO YOUR TABLE. GO BACK TO YOUR TABLE NOW!"

But Marshall did not return to his table and his voice only strengthened. Eugene shoved the Uris novels back onto the shelf and moved out from the aisle and into the main room. From there he could see the boy standing before the library's arching window with its trellis of thick wooden mullions and which extended from floor to ceiling. The boy was pointing to the outside and when he saw Eugene, the pointing finger became a jabbing finger and the garble turned to frantic. The scene reminded Eugene of that snowy morning soon after the two of them began spending time together. They were on the slope above his daughter's house and something down below had interested, perhaps troubled the boy, Eugene never could conclude which.

"Whatever is wrong with that child?" a gray-haired woman, standing in the doorway to an office behind the circulation desk, exclaimed. "Why is he pointing out the window like he is? There's nothing out there except an old oak tree. And it's just about dead."

Eugene stared at the woman who was staring back at him before looking again at Marshall, and then he realized that Pippa Goodwin's son was not pointing to a dying tree. In fact, he wasn't pointing to anything at all near the building. He was pointing in the direction of Eugene's apartment.

THIRTY

At the same time the deadly gas was collecting in the garage and expanding upward as an invisible cloud, Riddell was confronted by an unusual problem inside the house. There was nothing to occupy his time at the start of the afternoon, especially since Paulette was not around. First, he tramped downstairs and switched on the TV with the remote, aware that mostly soaps, banal westerns from decades past, and women talk shows were all there was to watch, yet he surfed the channels anyway before turning the unit off. He next tramped back upstairs, thinking he might be hungry. But after opening the refrigerator and peering inside for most of a minute, he realized he wasn't. He did, however, slide out a longneck bottle of Rolling Rock from the bottom shelf. He twisted the cap off where he stood and put the green container to his lips. There were, of course, things to do, items in need of repair as always, except they required use of the garage where he kept his tools and a workbench, *So scrap that idea,* he told himself. He took a second large swallow of the beer and stood in place, thinking some more. A moment later he set the bottle down on the countertop and started for the door, but quickly pivoted around and retrieved it. Still undecided on what he might do to amuse himself for the next hour or so, he nonetheless went out the front door to the tie landing. There he remained for a time and took several more hits off the bottle, quick nervous hits, one right after another, all the while gazing at his property. Eventually, he headed down toward the creek and the section that crossed a corner of his land where he often saw the neighbors and their horses.

About a hundred feet out from the water where the grass had grown high, thick, and weedy, his right foot slid out from under him after planting itself in shit. Up his arms flew for balance, as though shit were on them as well, and the beer sloshed out of the bottle onto his shirt. He swore a loud "Fuck!" to the air and his first thought on what he'd stepped in was a horse's dump until the odor of disturbance raked across his face and into his nostrils like a small bomb set off under his nose. The pile of shit wasn't that of a horse; it was the heady compliment of Eugene's dog, which he hoped now more than ever was dying sooner than later. He raised his foot to inspect the sole of the shoe, swore again, then scraped the maze of tread on cleaner grass, first back and forth about a dozen times, then in circles clockwise and counter-clockwise. The stinking ocherous excrement would not remove entirely. Presuming what remained would erode and disappear before he got back to the house, he gave up and resumed walking, but not without searching carefully in the ground cover ahead for any additional surprises. He made a successful job of this and reached the water's edge without a similar mishap.

Once there, he spun around to face the garage on the slope above and lent his hearing to the running motor. It was not to be heard, yet this was not a worry. The car had performed throughout its life without the threat of stalling, and in spite of the leaky catalytic converter and exhaust it remained to this day a quiet running machine that continued to pass the state inspections, although to be honest, he knew the station's owner who regarded many regulations as stupid and was not opposed to winking at the law for his friends. He raised the bottle high as if to toast the faithful car, then threw back a violent swig. This time the smell of the shit, still in the air, mixed with his taste buds. Another "Fuck" flew out of his mouth and he spat the beer at the earth around him as though it were the excrement itself. He inverted the bottle to pour out what beer was left, then tossed the empty container onto the opposite bank where the horses always came out.

Twenty yards ahead of where he stood a maze of hoof prints covered the bank. He saw them and moved forward into the muddy mess. For no reason that could be articulated, he began to tally their number, but soon gave up because there were too many and they were set upon each other like children's smudgy fingerprints on a glass tabletop. He could see that what vegetation had lined the bank was gone and that the rains had widened the creek by washing great amounts of soil downstream. He was busily trying to figure how many feet of his land had already been lost and how many he might further lose if he allowed the neighboring couple to continue doing as they had been doing when Paulette's minivan appeared in the driveway. The blue vehicle was lurching violently and he could hear the resulting abrupt jolts, one after another. Paulette parked it at the bottom, got out at once, and Riddell could see that his wife was shaken. She carried no packages and there weren't any grocery bags visible to him above the seats.

The curtains on the house windows remained closed and although he hadn't opened the blinds, he had unlocked the door. In silence he now watched his wife needlessly insert her key. Once she was inside he made his way up from the creek. After about a dozen steps he again came up short. This time horseshit was in fact the hidden surprise in wait of his feet—packed mounds of it resembling wet brown briquettes with hundreds of brilliantly bronze flies crawling over the surface. He stepped cautiously to avoid the noisome matter and continued to navigate carefully throughout the remaining high grass until he was back in what could be identified as lawn. From there he walked back to the house with a normal stride and went inside.

"Paulette?" he called out.

She emerged out of the kitchen. "Oh … so you're why the door was unlocked! What are you doing home? Don't you feel well?"

"What's happening with the van? I watched you pull in."

She threw up her hands and a look of disgust flooded her face. "The check light came on when I was only a mile down the road. However, I didn't notice any difference in how the van was running, so I just ignored it. Then, as I was about to enter the market's parking lot, oh my, the entire thing began to buck back and forth, back and forth, and the motor was acting like it was about to die. I thought, my God, if I have groceries—and especially ice cream, which was on my list—and I can't make it back…well, I just decided to turn around and come home. I can grocery shop on another day. It's not like our cupboards are bare."

"I'll have someone take a look," he said.

"I see my father hasn't returned from the library," she said. "Have you met the woman?"

"What woman?"

"I forget her name already, although there was something about her that told me I've seen her before."

"What woman?" he repeated.

"Just as I reached the top of the driveway when I was leaving to go shopping, a car stopped at the mailbox. A man and a woman, both older. They were looking to turn in. I thought right away, you know, Jehovah's Witnesses, as they show up at least once a year with their ridiculous pamphlets. Only the woman said she was here to see my father, she was a friend. I told her he had gone to the library, and she said he'd told her that might be the case, but that she could just wait inside and he'd be back in no time. So I said, 'Well, he lives above the garage and his door isn't normally locked. There's a dog inside, but he's old and he probably won't bother you if you don't bother him.' Then she turned to the man and said, 'So there you have it, Allan. Just drop me off and Eugene will bring me back.' Then I pulled out and they pulled in.... Riddell? You still in there?"

"What?"

"Did you hear everything I said?"

"Maybe I'll go over and introduce myself," he said absently, although an unexpected fear was fast settling inside him.

Paulette brightened like a switched-on lamp and rubbed her hands together in a devilish manner. "Want me to come along? We can grill her together. Find out who she is and if my father is up to anything."

"You don't want to do that to a stranger who's a friend of your father," he said inventively. "Besides, you didn't actually see her get out of the car and climb the steps. She might not even be there. She might have changed her mind."

"Okay, so go by yourself then. Since I can't do the shopping today, I might as well get started on the laundry."

"Now?"

"Just as soon as you move out of my way, Hon, I'm going into our room and gather up your dirty stuff."

"Relax," he said. "You just got home after a troublesome drive. I'll do it for you." He was desperately trying to gain control over the dread building rapidly inside himself, and collecting the laundry would give him the necessary time to decide what he should do.

He left on her smile of gratitude. When he returned to the laundry room with the soiled work clothes a few minutes later, he deposited them on the floor.

"What about the shirt you're wearing?" she asked, quickly separating the soiled laundry into piles.

"It's not dirty," he replied.

"I see you pulled out the tuck." She reached forward and grabbed the hem. "Is that beer I smell?"

"Always with the goddamn fingers!" he snapped. He ripped the material free of her hand and fled the room.

THIRTY-ONE

The voice inside him was screaming *"Hurry!"*

Either the ceiling fan had already drawn a lethal amount of the sleep-inducing gas into the upstairs living space to extinguish the lives of the woman and the dog, or it had not. Nothing he'd read had provided information or even a simple table on how rapidly the gas accumulated in a given volume of space. He had just figured it would take an hour, two at most, to flood the apartment and kill the dog. And if he were wrong and the dog remained alive, nothing would be lost. He could always come up with another plan. But a woman inside, that changed everything. That told him he could face a murder charge if she were dead. He hoped to God Almighty the CO that was now being pumped from the car's exhaust had yet to reach a level from which there was no return. He prayed the woman was still alive. But luck might be against him.

So you better think, Riddell!

The first consideration to come to mind as he'd pulled the dirty clothing from a hamper was to do nothing. Of course, this meant he would have to rely on Paulette and her father to assume the woman died of a heart attack or a stroke or something equally catastrophic like an aneurism. But if the dog also were dead, that meant complications. Then they might become suspicious. And Eugene in particular would begin to ask questions.

His second choice, if the woman were dead, was to slip the body out of the apartment and into the trunk of his car without Paulette's knowledge, drive to an isolated location out by Crooked Creek with its murky waters and surround of deep woods, and deposit the remains where they wouldn't be stumbled upon for some time, maybe never. In that case, the woman would be reported missing, the driver named Allan would inform the police he'd dropped her at the Parker residence, and the intensive questioning would begin.

And then there was the terribly messy solution that had come to mind unbidden as he pulled off several soiled items from the top shelf in his closet. It was as if the Devil himself were an intelligent designer. All the same, the solution had flashed too readily to his consciousness as he stared at the pistol. He could shoot the woman. Put a bullet in her, then grab her purse or anything of value and afterward toss it. Make it look like someone had followed her to the apartment in order to rob her. Except he had shot his cocker and that story had circulated to a great many people so that the police, once they learned of it, would want him to produce the weapon, if only to rule him out as the murderer, they would say. Consequently, he would have to lose the gun as well. Maybe sink it deep in the muck in the creek below the house.

Even as this thought, abhorrent as it was, ran through his mind, the scheming Devil would not relent and whispered to Riddell again when he arrived at the garage, causing him to glance back at the house where she was engaging the laundry. *"C'mon, son, you know one death won't allow for the revolver's disappearance."*

And yet, for all that, he argued, the cops still might discover from the autopsy that the woman had died of carbon monoxide poisoning and not a gunshot wound.

They might easily and correctly conclude no invasion of his home or the apartment above the garage had taken place.

As if the skull were working to expel the brain, his head gave a violent shudder in a futile attempt to shatter the disturbing thoughts of killing his wife and the woman.

There was nothing solid on which he could make a decision that would protect himself, and so he did what he could. He stepped quickly through the building's side entrance, yanked out the latch of the car door and reached in and shut off the ignition. A country silence, still prevalent in some areas of the Brells, crushed the scene, and a faint blue haze tinted the air beneath the floor above. He paused but a second before rattling up the panels of the bigger door behind the car, then raced to bays two and three and rolled up theirs as an invitation to the fresh air to make its way in.

Outside, there was the grinding of gravel as the Plymouth rumbled into the driveway, and several seconds after came a second car and one that he did not recognize because he was unaccustomed to seeing Lila in any vehicle but her pickup.

Eugene emerged hastily from the Plymouth and threw a glance as he did at the unfamiliar car pulling up behind him. "WHAT ARE YOU DOING, SON?" he shouted at Riddell who was now a few steps up the staircase,

"YOU'VE GOT A VISITOR!" Riddell responded with a shout of his own. He could see that his father-in-law was already taking note that all three doors on the garage were raised. A second question followed, but he chose not to answer and threw his attention at Lila who was now getting out of her car. Eugene also saw who it was and flung a hand in the air as his sole greeting to the woman.

"What's going on?" Lila inquired behind a bemused expression. "Neither one of you men appears particularly happy and it's a beautiful afternoon out here in the Brells.

Something going on that I should know about?"

"PAULETTE'S IN THE HOUSE!" Riddell barked.

Eugene was already brushing past him on the stairs.

"It's about that driver," Lila said, upping her voice. "The one you said was new and wants someone to build him an equipment shed? I've got a few questions."

Riddell stared at his cousin. Then turning aside abruptly, he scrambled after Eugene up the remaining steps and into the apartment.

There in the front room on the sofa Connie Reardon slouched and her body was motionless. Her eyes were shut, her mouth agape, and in her lap rested an open book. Eugene approached and touched her hand.

"Connie?"

He shook it when she failed to stir.

"Connie, it's Eugene. Wake up."

Riddell lingered at his father-in-law's back and his eyes searched the space surrounding them like a predatory creature's would. When they swung back, he saw his cousin was standing in the doorway.

Eugene turned about, too. "The dog is on the slope behind the house. He's just standing there next to a burned-out tree," she said. It was an offhand remark. Neither man had inquired of the animal's whereabouts.

She stepped across the threshold and her eyes swept the entire room before they settled on the woman. "What's wrong? What's going on?"

"She's not waking up," said Eugene.

Lila put a hand to Riddell's ribs to nudge him aside, slipped by, and knelt beside the sofa. She took hold of Connie Reardon's wrist and felt for a pulse. Next, she pressed a pair of fingers to a vein in the older woman's neck and positioned the backside of her hand under the woman's nose. Removing a cell phone from her belt with her other hand, she held it out to Riddell.

"Call 9-1-1, cousin, and get an ambulance out here." Then to Eugene, "Let's get her to the floor."

As Lila commenced CPR on Connie Reardon and while Riddell made the emergency call, an awful feeling not entirely out of nowhere unfurled itself inside Eugene that forced his reluctant disappearance from the apartment. He descended the steps before either of the others took notice and rushed into the first bay where Riddell's car was parked. He spread his hands on the vehicle's warm hood and kept them there, moving toward a severe inference. Outside, on the slope beyond the house and beside the lightning scarred tree stood the dog, silent and wary and looking back at the apartment and the bays underneath.

Eugene removed his hands from the car's hood and abandoned the garage. On the driveway he stopped and peered at his dog in the distance before remounting the staircase. Midway in his climb, he heard the resumption of the music, his favorite Chopin piece and the same selection that was concluding when he had walked in and seen Connie silent on the sofa. She had appreciated it like himself, he realized. She'd even programmed the player so that the waltz would repeat. As he made the landing before the door the first round of the siren from the ambulance now on its way reached his hearing.

Inside the apartment Lila continued her effort to resuscitate Connie Reardon while Eugene, acting on his reckoning, dashed about opening window after window to let in fresher air. Riddell, who had moved to the rear of the apartment, now exited the bedroom and in his hands he carried a pillow. He approached the two women. As he knelt behind the head of Connie, who lay on the rug, his cousin looked up at him. She put out a refraining, even alarming hand to his, it seemed to Eugene, but Riddell shoved it to the side and slid the pillow under Connie Reardon's motionless head.

The siren spiraled louder, then suddenly choked off as the rescue vehicle turned off the main highway and onto the road that led to the Parkers. It rolled down into the driveway seconds later and three paramedics got out. Two men and a younger woman, they mounted the stairs and entered the apartment where they took over the attempt from Lila Shrum to save Connie Reardon's life. The woman, while waiting for instructions from the other members of the team, asked, "Anything to tell us?"

Her question was directed at Riddell, which informed Eugene the young woman recognized his son-in-law as the property owner. Riddell nodded to his side so that she shifted her attention.

"Your wife?" she said to Eugene.

"It's not his wife," said Riddell.

"Can you tell us anything?"

"She was poisoned." The woman glanced back at Riddell, hoping for something more, when Eugene added, "Carbon monoxide."

"Sir?"

"My son-in-law left the car running inside the garage beneath us."

The oldest of the paramedics attending to Connie interrupted further questioning and ordered the woman to retrieve additional equipment from the ambulance.

Paulette was next to appear in the doorway. She looked alarmed. "Riddell, what's happening? I was putting the wash in the machine and—"

Riddell shook his head vigorously to shut her up and to rid the air of her question.

"She's back," the older paramedic suddenly said.

"Will she be all right?"

"For now, she's breathing," the man said to no one in particular. "But we need to get her to Salyer."

The paramedics huddled, and then at the same time she was delivered oxygen, Connie Reardon was removed from the apartment and into the ambulance.

"Go on. Get out of here," Lila urged Eugene.

THIRTY-TWO

"It's come to me, Hon."

"What has?"

"Why I mentioned at the house that I know that woman. Except I was under the impression she was dead."

With Riddell, Lila, and herself the only persons remaining inside the apartment, Paulette relaxed.

She began to explain—the winter phone call from a strange female, asking for Eugene; the picture of the girls in her father's scrapbook that had been cut from the newspaper many years ago; the day she had read the death notice of her favorite teacher, Mr. Enrico—only to be interrupted by Eugene who had returned and loomed in the apartment's entrance.

"It's a small ambulance. They won't allow riders," he responded to their curious faces. "I need you to move your car, Lila."

"Take it. The keys are in the ignition."

"Riddell. Drive Daddy to the hospital. That's okay with you, isn't it, Lila?"

Eugene slipped his focus from the two women and onto his son-in-law, who stood alone at the opposite corner of the room.

"You nearly killed her," he said to Riddell.

The words grabbed Paulette's attention and she glanced sharply at her father and then the others.

Bewilderment fleshed out her face and an irrepressible undercurrent of disconcerting silence swept through the room.

"Dadd-ee?"

"You want to explain why, Riddell? I'd like to know. I think everyone would."

Paulette, with tentative steps, sidled over to her father who was staring hard at her husband. She took his right hand in her own and stroked it as though he had taken leave of his senses.

"Dadd-ee?" she murmured again.

He jerked free of her grasp. "Your husband needs to answer my question."

"You drive him to Salyer," Riddell said to his wife. "And when you get there, see that they place him in a goddamn padded room." He assumed an expression of why-had-he-ever-bothered and moved from the corner and toward the door.

Eugene threw out a hand to prevent the exit and his fingers locked onto his son-in-law's shirt. Riddell whirled about to free himself, but the fist held fast and twisted. The shirt wrung to a thick knot and rose above the belt like a kitchen slicer.

"I SAID I WANT AN ANSWER!"

"You're losing what little sense you have, old man."

"Hon?"

"I had no idea that woman was here until your daughter said a car came by. For Chrissakes, Paulette had her figured as a goddamn Jehovah Witness."

"Hon?"

"Anyway, what do I care if you have some old flame in for a roll-around on the goddamn mattress? It keeps you out of my hair."

"Hon?"

"WHAT, PAULETTE? WHAT?"

"Hon, you have your gun tucked inside your pants. Your gun. It's hidden in your jeans."

Looming behind the leather belt was the dark wooden handgrip of the .22.

Eugene stared at it. Lila, too.

Riddell momentarily seized his father-in-law's hand, forcibly removed it, and wrenched down the shirt to again cover the pistol. "I'm fucking out of here!" he said and bolted from the room.

Once more Paulette searched the faces of her father and Lila, but she again found nothing in either to help explain what had just occurred. She trailed her husband out of the room, adding her own hurried footsteps down the exterior staircase.

"You should go, too" Lila said again to Eugene after his daughter's exit. "To the hospital. It's obvious you care a great deal for that woman."

Eugene, however, gave no sign that he was leaving. He squared himself and looked directly at Lila.

"When Riddell came out of the bedroom with the pillow... ," he began, but broke off because his son-in-law with the gun was pressing on his mind. He collected his thoughts and started again. "... When Riddell came out of the bedroom, Lila, I watched you put out a hand to stop him. You thought he was about to do something with the pillow."

"He was just intending to make her—"

"—You thought he was going to suffocate her, didn't you?"

"Eugene, what is it?"

"That's why you told me to be careful. 'Watch out for Riddell' Wasn't that your warning to me at Gino's? You saw your cousin murder his grandmother when you were kids, didn't you? And Riddell knew you saw him do it, but you didn't know what you were watching, and he made sure you never would."

"Murder his grandmother? Oh my."

"You never heard that?"

"It was the nastiest of rumors. Spread by some of his family's neighbors. They didn't like Riddell. They thought he was a sneak."

"Which of the neighbors told you that?"

"Riddell told me that."

"When you walked into the room and saw him looking all about the place, you knew at once that he was looking for the dog."

"You know he's never liked your dogs, Eugene. That shouldn't be any surprise."

"But you already suspected that he was up to something. You thought he was trying to kill my dog."

"I didn't say that."

"That's what you were thinking, wasn't it?"

"Eugene, are you leaving for the hospital? Or are you going to stand here and continue with this rambling psychoanalysis of me?"

"I'm not going anywhere. Not until I figure out why my son-in-law had a gun stuffed behind his belt."

He moved to the open doorway of the apartment and peered into the driveway below. Both the Plymouth and Lila's automobile, he could see, left insufficient space for Riddell to drive his own car around and off the property. He switched his gaze to the house and listened for any sounds that might be coming from the couple inside, but there were none.

"Something's wrong," he said. "I can feel it. I'm walking over to the house."

"Then I'll go with you," said Lila.

They descended the staircase and passed hurriedly under the big maples. When they stepped inside the split-level home and onto the slate landing dividing the floors, they were greeted by an ominous silence.

"I'll look downstairs," Lila said.

"I'm right here," Riddell announced from around the top of the staircase. He faded into view like a storm cloud and Eugene glanced at his son-in-law's midsection where the arch of the small revolver's handgrips was discernible.

"Where's my daughter?"

"She can't talk."

"If you've done something to her, Riddell …"

"You've a curious look to your face, cousin. Has this old man been been chewing on your ear?"

"Riddell, did you murder our grandmother?"

Riddell winced.

"Well, did you?"

"Is that what the hell it is?" He threw his attention back to Eugene and shook his head in disbelief. "You must have run into that gut of a grease monkey Nemerov. He's the only one I know who would bring that up. Any chance he told you about his dumb buddy Bezzy?"

"So Nemerov wasn't lying when he said you smothered your grandmother with a cushion?"

"That old lady's death was a long time ago," said Riddell. "And that tub of a Russki never knew a goddamn thing more than any of them neighbors we had in West Deer who were always wanting to stick a nose up someone's ass. And they're all dead. You're looking at the only person who knows what happened."

"What about me?" said Lila.

"What about you, cousin?"

Although her memories as a youngster were buried deep, Lila Shrum knew the truth, Eugene was sure of it. Yet he was forced to admit it was unlikely she could ever raise it to the surface.

"Well now, since we're having some kind of frank discussion here," Riddell went on, "has this old man told you, cousin, that he once killed a man? And I'm thinking it was in cold blood." He shifted his attention back to a startled Eugene. "Yeah, your little girl sometimes likes to stick her nose where it doesn't belong. See, she wandered up on your deck and overheard you talking to that woman who came by here the day I asked if you wanted to go fishing. Remember that...? What! Did you think I would just let it go? A younger woman shows up on the property with skin color different from yours, the two of you head upstairs to your apartment, and I'm supposed to conclude it's just another day at the Parkers? Fact is, Eugene, I thought she was a daughter from your days of whorin' around"

"She was a little girl and she was raped," explained Eugene. "I rescued her before she was killed. And I shot her abductor because I had to. She'll back me up on it. And if her parents were alive, they would do the same."

"Do you believe this old man?" Riddell addressed Lila. "He says he saved a little girl's life, and yet no one in the family knows of it. In fact, even the police don't know about it. And that's because he never reported the incident. And the reason he didn't report it is that he killed someone who wasn't trying to kill him and he knew he could wind up doing some serious time." He turned back to Eugene. "First off, old man, even if what you say is true about the woman who was here that day, you're right about her parents. They're six-feet under, mommy and daddy both, and so they won't be backing you up on anything. Secondly, their daughter won't be supporting your story either."

"Don't be too sure."

"Oh, I'm more than sure, Eugene. You see, Barbara Bogen killed herself. Took her own life. That black woman done committed suicide no more than a week ago. Yeah, go ahead, look confused. But that was the name she was using, which is the reason you overlooked her in the obits. You knew her by another name, didn't you?"

The news of the woman's death stunned Eugene. It was true, he had continued to think of her by her maiden name, Lennox, even though she had told him she had married three times.

"You knew this and didn't say anything?"

"Hey, I merely did what she did," said Riddell. "I knocked on some doors up and down the street and you could have done the same. If you had, you would have discovered that one of our wonderful neighbors pretended to give a damn and actually asked her who the hell she was. Anyway, that isn't what you need to think about at this hour. What you need to think about is this, Eugene. Of all the photos in that scrapbook of yours that's falling apart, there was only one that was missing a caption. And you and I know that's only because you blew away that individual and didn't want anyone looking at the book then or in the future to know who it was. You had your gun with you in the car and you used it to kill. Your daughter said you never liked guns, but that might not have been how things were before meeting that dude, whoever the hell he was."

"Paulette knows I never liked firearms. Not now. Not then."

A slow, calculated grin of self-satisfaction settled in Riddell's face

"Good. 'Cause, you see, just now I was fishing. You see, if you didn't kill him with a gun of your own, then you must have killed him with his. In fact, what I'm betting on is this. I'm betting you were so out of your goddamn wits that you dropped the gun right there at the scene. Now can you guess what that means...? No guess? Then let me spell it out for you. That means the cops have it. They have it to this day. Which means, too, they'll have a copy of Eugene Banish's fingerprints."

"What have you done to my daughter, Riddell?"

He moved to mount the remaining stairs but stopped as Riddell drew the pistol from inside his belt and pointed it at his chest.

"Easy, Eugene. I know it's been a long time since that episode in your life, but there's no one who's going to believe you. Think about it. The cops and everyone will say you could have been a hero. They'll say you could have had your picture and your name plastered all over the news. Anyone who had done what you claim you did, anyone who saved a little girl's life after she'd been raped and abused, what person wouldn't jump at the chance to be a hero and the envy of others. But you didn't make that jump and at this late date, they're not about to say any of that. All your story is going to get you today is confinement to a prison cell."

Eugene could feel the furrows in his brow begin to tighten.

"It's getting through, isn't it?"

"What is it you want?"

"Your daughter may need some convincing."

"I'm going to find her!" Eugene roared.

Once more he took a step up, only this time Riddell moved forward himself and the pistol swung so that it was leveled at Lila.

"Are you really threatening to shoot your favorite cousin?" Lila asked, incredulous. "Riddell, what have you done?"

"Talk to her, Eugene!" urged Riddell. "Talk to Paulette. Tell her to stay away from the police. Help her to make up a story. She's not all that bright in the imagination department. You're her father. You know that better than anyone. She can say she lost her footing and tumbled down the stairs. She's a lot overweight, so that isn't farfetched. She can say there were tools at the bottom and that she fell on them."

"What have you done to her? So help me, Riddell, if you've—"

"—If you don't want the police to learn that your fingerprints are on that gun, which they'll have to this day, you know that, then persuade her."

"Shut up, Riddell!" Lila shouted, her anger evident. "I've heard enough out of you. Eugene will do what you want. Now what?"

"Is she right, Eugene?"

"I said he'll do what you want," Lila repeated.

Eugene hesitated, then nodded.

"Good, I'll take your word. Now the two of you are going to walk out of here ahead of me and move your cars. That way, I can leave."

Riddell waved the gun and Eugene and Lila were marched outside, down the tie landing, and past the line of maples.

"Always the monkey with those goddamn fingers," they heard him mutter.

At the driveway Riddell ordered them to stop, and the respite endured longer than what Eugene would have expected so that he realized his son-in-law had not fully planned his departure.

"Before you leave, you haven't yet explained why you tried to kill my visitor."

"I already told you, old man. I had no idea she was in

the apartment! It was your mutt I was after. I figured on gassing it. That's what it was about—getting rid of your dog. I can't believe the filthy thing was outside all the time."

It was Connie who had left the dog out of the apartment, Eugene had concluded. Ringo likely had pressed her so that he could relieve himself. He was good about holding it and not letting go inside.

"Enough of this talking. Get in your cars," Riddell ordered. "Drift them down here to the third bay."

"What if she—?"

"—She was breathing when they carried her out. That's enough for me."

Eugene was about to speak again, but Lila pressed a hand to his arm. "We need to find Paulette," she said.

He surrendered to her restraint and they parted and walked to their respective cars. Once they had done as directed, Riddell backed his own out of the first bay.

THIRTY-THREE

After Riddell had raced off the property, they hurried back to the house and the silence again greeted them. Lila wasted no time in looking for Paulette and started to descend the stairs. Eugene reached out a hand to stop her.

"Forget it. She isn't down there," he said. "There's carpet in the basement." He did not explain Riddell's obsession to her puzzled expression.

Remaining on the upper floor, they then searched each of the rooms and soon discovered Paulette sprawled on the chessboard tile of the laundry room. She looked as much like an amorphous pool of rusty water as she did a human being. Blood flowed from a pair of savage rips across her hairline and a severe laceration at the side of her head. She hadn't been shot, which had been Eugene's first surmise. Even so, Riddell had come close to killing her. His son-in-law had slashed the steel barrel of the gun across her forehead, then raced it back the other way, carving out a smaller but deeper swath of flesh with the front sight. The welt and accompanying slice in the scalp could have been his attempt to finish her off, except he'd checked himself from striking her yet again, and Eugene considered that it was his and Lila's timely entry into the house that had prevented Riddell from going all the way.

"We have to get her to the hospital," said Lila. "Let's stand her up."

Each took hold of an arm and hoisted Paulette to her feet. Weak and unsteady and her added weight in recent years striving to pull her down again, she required Eugene's tight embrace. Lila dabbed her wounds with a clean towel she'd removed from the top of the dryer.

"I can manage," Eugene said, taking the cloth. "You get the car while I walk her to the front of the house. It's going to take a minute."

Lila left the room and with endless patience Eugene then maneuvered his daughter toward the front entrance.

"He wouldn't have done it," she whimpered

"Don't try to talk, Paulette. We're going to get you to the emergency room. After that, we'll worry about catching up with Riddell."

"He wouldn't have. He couldn't have."

With great difficulty he escorted his daughter down the carpeted stairs and onto the slate landing where he opened the door.

"Watch your step," he cautioned as they moved onto the ties. Blood was again flowing from her wounds and he blotted them with the towel.

Lila drew the car close to the bottom tie and hurriedly got out to help.

"Lean on me," she ordered Paulette. "There's more strength in these construction muscles than meets the eye. Give your daddy here a break."

She extended an arm around Paulette's body and carefully guided her to the car. Eugene held open the rear door.

"He wouldn't have done it. "

"Paulette. Listen to me! There's no excuse for what Riddell has done."

"Let's get her in," said Eugene.

Lila drove while Eugene kept watch on his daughter.

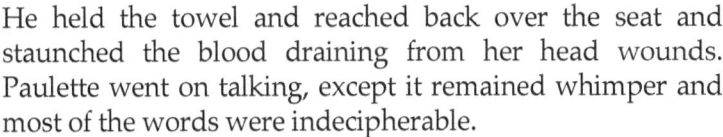

He held the towel and reached back over the seat and staunched the blood draining from her head wounds. Paulette went on talking, except it remained whimper and most of the words were indecipherable.

A mile into the trip when there was no vehicle coming at them, Lila briefly looked away from the road and at Eugene. "Is it true what Riddell said?" she asked.

"He said a lot of things."

"Did you kill a man in cold blood, Eugene? That's all I want to know."

"Nothing about it was cold," he said without hesitation. "I was a young man, and I was afraid. And shaking. Shaking that I couldn't stop. You've seen those paint mixers in the hardwood stores where they lock in a can and turn on the switch? It's not an exaggeration to say I resembled a thing like that. But this man who raped her and would have killed her, there wasn't a ripple coming off him."

"But why did you shoot him? Why didn't you just go to the police? You had a good description of him. You knew what his car was and all."

"I couldn't take the chance. I was afraid he might jump me and get the gun away and then kill the little girl and myself. And as for the police, I didn't trust the authorities. I was afraid that if they learned what I had done, it would somehow get all turned around and that I would be arrested and end up in jail. Her father understood this. But he also didn't want his little girl to go through anymore that what she already had. He didn't want the police asking her all kinds of questions. He didn't want the newspapers to find out and write about what happened to his young daughter. And being black, I don't believe he had a lot of trust in the authorities either. And while I didn't know then and there that I had killed her kidnapper, I learned the next day that in fact I had. And if he had any secrets in regard to other children that he had abused, they went to the grave with him. For that I am sorry because of the mothers and fathers who will never know a kind of closure. But that thought hadn't crossed my mind when all this was happening. I was simply satisfied to know that he would never do another horrible thing to another child. Don't ask me to make any more sense of it than I have because I can't."

"What of her abductor?"

"It turned out that he was some kind of higher-up at the same company where I worked, not that I'd ever laid eyes on him or even heard of him. Married, too, and he had a few children. There wasn't much written about the shooting, I can tell you, and I've often thought that was because some others in the company knew or at least had inklings of what he really was like. They probably were relieved to be rid of him."

Draped in the rear seat with the back of her hand against her head, Paulette stirred. Lila stretched to glance in the rearview mirror and Eugene swung around again in his seat.

"Is she going into shock?"

"I'm not sure," he said.

The incoherent phrases coming from his daughter continued.

Then, less than a mile from the emergency room of Salyer General Hospital, Eugene, still listening, began to consider for the first time that his daughter's words were possibly not so incoherent after all. Throughout the ride she repeated what she had said at the house when they found her, that Riddell "wouldn't have done it," and right along he had regarded it as nonsense, because his son-in-law had already done "it," had already attacked her. Like many other women whose spouses were abusers, he believed his daughter was in denial—nothing more than that. Only now, other claims were getting added.

"Riddell and I are close. I'd reached for the gun and as I did, I knew what he was thinking. That's why he turned angry. It shamed him that I knew. It shamed him terribly because he didn't want me to know. But Riddell loves me. He wouldn't have done it. It's just that he sometimes gets things in his head and they're crazy things and he doesn't want anyone knowing about them."

Eugene glanced at Lila to see if she was listening to his daughter's words, but the car was entering heavy traffic and her concentration was directed at the intersection and the other vehicles.

He turned back yet again and stared at his daughter in the rear seat. She hadn't been speaking to him or Lila. She hadn't been speaking to anyone at all other than an imagined third party. And on that thought his mind swept back to the cocker Brownie amid the pines, and there was Riddell squeezing the trigger on the small revolver. His mind reeled, next, to the crabby voice of Nemerov— *"I got to know some of what makes your son-in-law tick, and I don't think it's too fucking good."* And then onto Riddell's streak of gullibility, and even now a grin arranged itself on the face of Eugene as he recalled how his son-in-law had slid under the Plymouth to search for a bomb that didn't exist. And of course the obsession with the stained rug in the garage apartment, this too he remembered.

Under the direction of Eugene, the mind was working hard to discover the answer to a single question: why had Riddell hidden a gun on his person? What were his intentions? The answer refused to surface, but if Eugene was feeling stymied and at a dead end, the mind freed to act on its own without any rationale harbored no such reservation. It switched its focus before he realized and Paulette became the subject of attention.

It was her weight that first took center stage, a hundred pounds more than what she had carried down the aisle to the altar. This was followed by two children, who appeared as innocent, playful siblings and then were grown and gone and not returning even for the occasional visit children are obliged to make; and then her mother who lost all her weight to an aggressive cancer of the pancreas and she too was gone. And now Eugene took control again of his thinking as he fathomed what was next, and this was that his daughter understood that Riddell was all she had because even her father was likely to be dead before the passing of another ten years. Yet, why hadn't Riddell known the same? Why had he thought Paulette would attempt to have him arrested and jailed for his attack on her? So far she wasn't in denial, even, about what had taken place. What she was denying was something that had not happened. And as Lila made a final turn that took them onto the hospital grounds, Riddell's obscenity of a plan started to reveal itself. First, Eugene reproduced from memory the face of his son-in-law when Riddell claimed it was Ringo the dog that he had intended to kill. And as best he could, he reproduced the tone of his words that had accompanied the statement. In neither of these duplications did Riddell appear to be lying. Truth was evident too when Riddell said he hadn't known that Connie was in the apartment until Paulette mentioned it. But it was at that moment when the realization and panic struck him like a hammer that he might have already killed the woman, and he knew immediately that he would have to pay for his crime; knew he would be arrested, thrown in jail, and made to stand trial where a jury would find him guilty, and he wasn't going to let that happen, no. His plan, then, had been to shoot Connie with the .22 while she was dying or after she was already dead. Except a single murder—something else he understood—would not have been convincing, and so what was there left but to kill his wife as well, maybe take a few items of value from each residence, all in the hope he would not be suspected of the original killing by carbon monoxide poisoning. It was odious and crazy, and it didn't make any sense to Eugene, but it had made sense to his daughter. She had reached for the gun tucked inside her husband's pants, and that's when Riddell had exploded and struck her with the steel barrel. Once, twice, and then a third time. Maybe in the end he would not have shot Paulette. Maybe not even Connie. Perhaps his assault on Paulette was nothing but an extraordinary reaction to a tragedy that he had conceived but was never intending to fulfill. Yet Brownie and the story of the grandmother suggested to Eugene there was only room for the smallest argument.

His thoughts stretched no further because Lila was guiding the car into the dedicated lane that led to the emergency entrance. She brought the vehicle to a stop behind the ambulance that had delivered Connie Reardon several minutes before.

THIRTY-FOUR

The bloody, weakened appearance of Eugene's daughter caught the attention of two E.R. nurses. They abandoned their assignments and swept across the floor to remove her from the embrace of Eugene and Lila.

As they ushered her to a section on the west side, in a corner partition on the opposite side Eugene spotted Connie who she sat on the edge of an exam table. Not long after, her brother entered the E.R. and Eugene imagined that she must have come awake in the ambulance and asked that Allan be summoned.

He waited with Lila next to the exam room holding Paulette. It was several minutes until the doctor emerged. Half Eugene's age, he scanned the room with a disturbing eye. "Did her husband do this?" he asked.

Eugene nodded without reluctance. "But I don't think she's going to press any charges."

"I already gathered that," the doctor said, not hiding his disbelief. "She's a little delirious, but that came through loud and clear."

"I'm her father. What happens now?"

"We'll dress her wounds and keep her overnight as a precaution since she isn't talking sense. The lacerations above the eye are potential trouble spots. In fact, she's lucky to be alive. The luck ran out for a woman delivered here last week who'd been struck in the head."

Eugene recalled the lead-off story on KDKA of a boyfriend who had clubbed his girlfriend to a pulp with a ball bat.

Lila glanced at a clock nearby and stepped silently away to a corner. She opened her cell phone and tapped in a number. As the doctor slipped back inside the partition, she rejoined Eugene.

"I have to get back," she said. "But I'll stay if that's what you want."

"I'll be fine," he said.

"Are you sure?"

He nodded

She reached for his hand and wrapped the fingers around the keys to her car. "One of my boys will be along to pick me up in a few minutes. I'm going to wait outside."

"What do you want done with the car?" he asked.

"I'll come by your place this evening."

"All right. And thanks, Lila. For everything."

She kissed him on his cheek before making for the exit.

He watched her go and then, while Paulette was getting stitched up, moved across the room to the east end of the E.R. where Connie was.

"Hey," he called in a somber tone from the doorway.

"Oh, Eugene, I'm so relieved to see you."

"I'm relieved to see you, too. I'm especially happy to see that you're awake and talking. A little while ago, you weren't either."

A nurse attendant at the back of the room signaled that it was okay for him to come inside.

"Where's Allan?" he asked.

"Right behind you."

Allan entered the room, holding a styrofoam cup of coffee, which he handed to his sister.

"You must be wondering what happened," said

Eugene.

"Allan said your son-in-law forgot to shut off his engine to the car after pulling into the garage. But I must have already dozed off while waiting for you. Otherwise, I think I would have heard a car running beneath me."

"Apparently, he's extremely stressed out," Allan remarked.

"How's that?"

"Your son-in-law. He's been working a lot of hours?"

The question surprised Eugene.

"Yes, being a dispatcher keeps him busy," he offered, just to say something.

"All the same, it's not a defense. He could have killed Connie."

Eugene had been agonizing right along what he would tell Connie Reardon. Neither she nor Allan knew that his daughter was at that very moment on the opposite side of the E.R., receiving treatment for wounds from an attack by Riddell. Neither did they know that Riddell, in an effort to silence his dog Ringo, had left the motor of his car running intentionally. But now he was wondering where Allan had found his explanation, and if he hadn't glanced to the outside of the room at that exact moment in time and seen the oldest of the paramedics leaving the hospital, he likely would not have remembered the young female paramedic who had presumed Connie was his wife. He realized suddenly and intuitively that the woman knew his son-in-law better than what he had assumed. She certainly knew him well enough to make up an excuse for Riddell's potentially murderous act.

"No, it isn't," he said to Allan. "It's not a defense."

"Eugene, the doctor has said he'll release me, so I won't being staying overnight. However, Allan and I have already discussed things and we're going to drive back to St.

Andrews this evening."

"So I guess that means you've lost your appetite?"

She half-smiled at him. "I'm afraid it does."

"What was on that menu of yours?" Allan Hardinge asked with a genuine smile. "Anything good?"

Grateful for the change of tone that he wasn't expecting and which meant no further questions were likely to be asked about his son-in-law, Eugene grinned and said, "I make a first-rate beef stroganoff. And I would have made certain that I delivered Connie back with a plate for you."

THIRTY-FIVE

Besides the gruesome halftone, the story published in the *Star-Enterprise* more than three decades earlier had provided scant reporting and hardly more than a rehash of the headline: "FOUL PLAY SUSPECTED IN COMPANY OFFICIAL'S DEATH."

Nevertheless, the news would generate an endless buzz of presumably insider information within the plant every day for a week, Eugene reminded that he was the only employee who was keeping quiet and not asking questions or furthering along the words of his fellow workers, and paranoid at the same time that he might appear suspicious because of his silence

"The cops don't believe it's a suicide and that's because the gun wasn't found next to the body. His fingerprints are all over it, but so are prints belonging to someone else."

"Did you hear that luxury sedan of his was parked a hundred yards off the road?"

"Who takes a car like that into the woods in the first place?"

"And what of *this* strange little item? Its key was found lying in the dirt, tucked under a tire. Like someone put it there on purpose. And that's straight from my neighbor whose brother's on the force."

At the entrance to the kitchen the dog lay couchant, its

eyes set on Eugene.

"Ringo boy," he said waving a chef's knife at the dog, "I'm putting together this dish despite the cancellation by our guest. Except I won't be making use of all the meat. Now a number of us have had an absolutely horrible day, and that includes you. So treats are in order."

He used the knife to scrape two handfuls of the diced-up beef cubes from the cutting board into a bowl and set it on the floor. The animal went to work at once in making the meat disappear. As he rose back to a standing position, he noticed something that had gone unnoticed. At the far wall in the adjoining room the CD player remained faintly aglow with the number "17" on its display. He hadn't paused it. Most likely one of the EMTs, he figured, had pushed the pause button in place of turning off the power. He rinsed his hands, patted them dry, and strode from the one room to the other. He touched a finger to the arrow icon and his favorite opus resumed. So, too, did the subject that his mind had been working on for the past hour.

Would his daughter inform the police of her husband's attack on her and demand that Riddell be locked up? Given what she had said on the way to the E.R., it seemed unlikely. *But what about yourself, Eugene? Might you want a little justice? Lila, too? Your son-in-law, after all, had threatened you with a loaded gun, and who was to say he would not have used it if the two of you had not complied with his demands. Who was to say he wouldn't have shot you both and then gone back inside the house and finished off Paulette?*

And yet, wanting Riddell to serve a little time and actually getting it done, he wasn't fooling himself. In fact, it was this uncertainty that was forcing him to scrape through his memory, not so much of the incident itself as he had done when Barbara Lennox had shown up at the apartment, but of how it had been treated in the media and discussed around town and inside the mill. Was there any substance to Riddell's threat? That's what he was attempting to determine.

From what he was able to recall, most of his neighbors and co-workers were convinced the man was murdered, although not a one of them would venture a reason with the exception of those who knew the abductor in some small personal way and had harbored suspicions about his sexual proclivities. And what of the gun? Was it, as Riddell had said, still in the hands of police? Was it possible, too, that fingerprints would linger on a surface for all that time? Were his prints on file? That seemed more than probable, although no name would be attached identifying their owner. Was there a box or a storage bin in the basement of the police station which, to this day, held the abductor's gun and knife and maybe other evidence? Like casts of his and the girl's footprints? Casts of tire tracks from his own car? And who knew what else? He certainly didn't.

But what he did know was this: if the coroner had never ruled the death an accident or a suicide, then the police considered it a homicide. And that meant it remained unsolved. It further meant the case, however cold after all these years, was still open to investigation.

A knock, as if made mistakenly from habit because it was cut short like a half note, sounded on the apartment door.

"Come in! It's open!" he shouted from the kitchen and the cutting board to which he'd returned. He rinsed his hands under the faucet again and dried them in a cloth.

He then popped back into the front room, expecting to find Lila. He stopped short.

"How is she?"

Eugene scrutinized his son-in-law to learn if the gun remained on his person.

"She's breathing," he finally said. "They both are. Not that I think you give a damn about either woman."

"What did Paulette say? Did you get her to make up a story?"

"She's fortunate to be alive! There's no time for stories."

"She didn't say anything?"

"Son, you'd already be under arrest if my daughter was intending to accuse you of trying to kill her."

The dog rose up off the floor like a surfing wave. It advanced a step toward Riddell and a violent rumble, like a storm on the horizon, emanated from deep inside its throat.

"You haven't said why you're here. What is it you want, Riddell? And if you came back to apologize, you can go straight to hell."

The dog took a second step. Its movement was slow, deliberate, even calculating.

"You have control of that hound?"

"He's an old dog."

"Meaning what?"

"He acts on his own."

"Like you I suppose."

"I'll ask again. Why did you come here? And if you haven't an answer, then get the hell out!"

"Careful, Eugene. I own this property. Don't forget it."

"I won't be forgetting anything. You can be sure of that."

Each man then stood in place for several seconds and stared at the other. At last, Riddell attempted some kind of grin and his hand waved in a manner to signify a recognition of the futility in their confrontation. With an eye to the dog, he slowly backed out of the room and across the threshold without saying anything further. Once on the landing, he spun about and ran down the staircase. Eugene moved unhurriedly across the room to the open doorway.

From there he watched Riddell scramble to the top of the driveway where his car idled in the dark with its ambers lit. The dog padded over next to him and nudged his leg.

"You knew his intentions earlier in the day, didn't you?" he said to the dog. Together they watched Riddell drive off, then went back inside.

The whiskey he had sipped with Nemerov weeks before was his first in years and because he had enjoyed it, the following day he'd stopped by the local State Store in Arlion and purchased a liter. He went to the cabinet now where he'd stored the bottle, removed it and poured himself a drink. Before long there came another knock on the door and this time it was Lila, who was there to claim her car.

"How's Paulette?"

"They stitched her up and are keeping her overnight. She wasn't making a whole lot of sense, as you know."

"And your friend? Is she going to be okay?"

"The hospital released her," said Eugene. "Lila, I am so glad I returned to the apartment when I did. And I'm thankful that you showed up. Another ten minutes and the paramedics might not have revived her." He held up his glass. "Can I get you some of this?"

"What is it?"

"Whiskey. Maybe you don't drink whiskey."

"When you're a general contractor, you better drink whiskey. Throw a little ice in mine."

He found another glass like his own and dropped in two ice cubes from the freezer.

"You know Riddell came by," he said as he offered her the drink.

"To the hospital?"

"Here. About an hour ago. Ringo had him in his sights, so his stay didn't last very long. Maybe a minute or two."

"Eugene, I feel I have to apologize for my cousin."

"Why? You're not at fault!"

"Even so—"

"—Forget it."

"Well, I appreciate that," she said.

"Really. Just forget it" He waved off any further expression of regret from her. "However, I am interested in hearing your thoughts on why he returned here this evening. Earlier in the day he was talking tough when he had the gun out, but he was frightened as well. We heard him even muttering to himself. I don't know if I was expecting to see him ever again. But certainly never this soon."

Lila shook her head out of her own confusion. "I can't predict what Riddell's thinking is. Still, I do know this. Everything he owns is in that house next door. Plus, he's been with Hollowell for so long, it's impossible to believe he would abandon everything he's gained. I mean, where would he go? And if the doctor who treated Paulette at the E.R. recognized that she wouldn't be bringing charges, he must have come around to that conclusion himself."

"So are you suggesting that perhaps he showed up here expecting that I might somehow confirm it?"

"That would make as much sense as anything."

"Lila, let me ask you another question. Do you agree with Riddell? Do you agree that no one would believe my story of what happened years ago?"

She sipped at the whiskey and afterwards rattled the ice at the bottom of the glass. "On the way to the E.R. you mentioned that the kidnapper had children."

"Two sons and a daughter as I recall."

"Well, today they're adults. And if this were to surface, do you honestly think they will allow a stranger, which is what you would be to them, to denigrate the memory of their father and their children's grandfather? Without witnesses to support your story, you must know they'll create a version of their own. A version that's a fiction, for sure. But that fiction will turn magically into fact, and there won't be anyone but yourself to dispute it."

Eugene swished around the whiskey in his own glass as he considered her words.

"You're a smart woman, Lila," he said after a time.

She turned a palm upward as though to say *maybe, maybe not*.

"Have you eaten?"

"Another day. Hubby's waiting."

"More whiskey then?"

"Thanks, but no."

"All right, if I can't string you along here talking with me, best not keep him waiting. You'll find the keys in the console."

"You remember to keep me posted now on everything that's happening," she said as she finished her drink and handed him the empty glass. "This isn't over, you know. Your daughter was attacked. My cousin did it. Where's the resolution?"

THIRTY-SIX

The capacity to recognize the truth behind the utterances and facial expressions of others who were attempting to deceive him—it was a remarkable phenomenon; and although Eugene had never once expected that it would endure until his death, all the same it came as a surprise when it began to collapse. The first sign had surfaced at the funeral home.

"About what, Allan?"

The ambiance was all of solemnity and muted conversation, and a humorous grin or anything resembling it would have seemed out of place. Yet that was the clear expression in the facial features of Allan Hardinge when he informed Eugene that his sister wanted to speak with him, and it had moved Eugene to respond with his question wrapped in a tone of more than normal curiosity.

Allan had shrugged his answer, which was no answer at all, and the humorous grin had remained in place.

But, led aside into the empty viewing room by Connie Hardinge and anticipating that he would encounter a similar expression on her countenance, Eugene discovered nothing of the sort. No longer was the magical screen in place that would wipe away the subdued, deceptive rays of light that were meant to fool him. What he saw in her face was pensive and earnest, and it told him that Allan had meant to show his humor—nothing had been wiped away because there wasn't anything spurious to erase. With Connie it was otherwise. She did not want Eugene to know that she was having a laugh on him.

He could only speculate about its source, what there was about him that was providing amusement for her, and one thing alone came to mind, though it was hardly amusing to himself. Ever since his visit to St. Andrews, he had wondered why a woman who was his wife and with whom he had lived for more than thirty-five years was not the most significant person in his life. He felt shamefully certain Connie had been wondering the same. Who wouldn't? And why wouldn't any person laugh? If not to your face, at least to themselves.

● ● ●

The E. R. physician ordered an extra night's stay.

"I want to be on the safe side," he said to Eugene who had called before leaving the apartment to confirm the pre-scheduled trip to pick up his daughter. So it wasn't until the next morning that Paulette was delivered in the Plymouth from the hospital and back to her home. Although she remained bandaged about the head, the delirium of her speech from two days ago was gone.

"I'll try not to be a burden, but if I need something, Daddy, I'll let you know," she said to Eugene once they were inside the house.

"I'll hold you to that," he replied. "And don't think of yourself as a burden. You're my daughter, remember? Now what about my grandchildren?"

"What good would it do them to know their father is responsible for this? I won't be calling them, and I don't want you to get in touch with them either."

Eugene nodded, although not in a manner that

suggested his complete agreement, but rather to show that he would honor her point of view.

Seating herself on a chair at the kitchen table, Paulette looked utterly drained of emotion to Eugene who regarded her for the longest time as a worried father might. She held her hand to her forehead and because he could see how terribly exhausted she was, he weighed if he should tell her that Riddell had paid a visit. In spite of what she had gone through, perhaps it would lift her spirits, he thought. But in the end he kept the message to himself because he did not want to be a conduit for Riddell's apology, if that was what the visit was even about, and he did not believe it was. Instead, he left her to be alone, reminding her again that if she needed anything, anything at all, she had only to let him know. And on that he retired to his apartment above the garage.

That day was Saturday and the rest of it would come and go in an ordinary fashion, and so it seemed would Sunday, until late in the lazy afternoon. Standing at a window and observing a pair of gray squirrels leap from tree to tree, he was surprised when his son-in-law's car turned into the driveway. Without appearing to show even meager compunction, Riddell rolled the vehicle into the first bay and pulled the door down behind it. If Eugene wondered if he had observed his father-in-law at the window, Riddell gave no sign. Without a moment's hesitation he walked a brisk step to the house and never looked around at anything to his left or right. He remained inside until the following morning when Eugene watched him drive out in the direction of the terminal. Drive out as though last week and this one were the same. And if the attack were only forgettable, Eugene would have been obliged to say it was because the everyday actions and interactions of his daughter and her husband were once more underway and they would continue into the week.

On Thursday as the noon hour approached and he was gathering his books for their return to the library, Paulette opened the apartment door and stepped inside. Her face was drawn and serious.

"Something wrong?"

"I'm low on groceries, Dad. Last week the van was giving me trouble and I never got to the store. Riddell was going to have someone look at it—"

"—Except he never did. It's quite all right," he said with a series of nods. "These books can wait. I can take you wherever you wish. Just tell me what you want off the shelves and from the freezers and I'll run inside on your behalf. Do you have any coupons? If you do, let me have them." He flashed an upbeat smile.

"What I want," she said, "is for you to take the van and get it repaired."

"Oh," he said. His assumption that she didn't wish to be seen in public with a bandaged head was off-the-mark. "Why don't you just remind Riddell of his promise?"

"He's agitated. I don't want to put anything more on him."

More on him! On Riddell! Eugene forcibly denied himself a scowl and allowed her statement to pass without comment.

"Does the van run at all?" he asked after a while out of a businesslike tone.

"There's no guarantee you'll make it to a garage."

"In that case I'll just have to hope for the best," he said. "I'll leave for the dealership in a few minutes. If it's nothing major, perhaps I can persuade them to fix it today."

Then Friday came, and with it was another difference.

Riddell, after returning home from the terminal and parking his car in the first bay, did not march to the house and his wife. On this occasion, he mounted the stairs to the apartment two at a time and barged in on Eugene.

"I want you out! Out of the apartment and off the property!"

Never having anticipated the decree, Eugene did his best to cover his surprise.

"Why? So you can do the same thing again to my daughter, only this time without anyone around to question you?"

"Nothing would have happened, Eugene, if you hadn't been living here."

"You're blaming me?"

"A real tenant wouldn't have had a dog. I wouldn't have allowed it."

"What's my daughter say?"

"You've two weeks."

"You haven't talked this over with Paulette, have you?"

"Two weeks! You find yourself somewhere else to live."

"I won't find anything in that short amount of time. What are you thinking?"

"There's homes for sale."

"No one closes in two weeks."

"You find a house and force the seller to close. That's what you do."

Later that week, when his son-in-law was away from the property, Eugene walked over to the house.

"Your husband wants me out," he informed his daughter.

"I know," said Paulette. "He's told me."

"But it's all right. I've thought it over and I'll concede the man has a point. If I hadn't been living here, what happened, would not have. That isn't saying I'm to blame and it's not excusing what he did to you."

"Dad, you don't have to go."

"You're the one who has to live with him. Although I am surprised that you're not seeking a restraining order and a divorce. But since that doesn't seem to be in the cards, I'll leave and that should make it easier. However, I will require your assistance in getting your husband to understand that any purchase of a house will take longer than two weeks."

He started his search the following day by stopping at the office of a local real estate agent who had been in the business for years. He gave the woman some idea of what he was after and the next afternoon she escorted him to several small homes in both the Brells and in Arlion. Unfortunately, the structures demanded serious repair or were too adjacent to a high-crime area in which a recent home invasion of an elderly couple had made the news. Others that appealed to him carried price tags far above the value at which he figured them. Then one evening while he was walking the dog, a wild idea crossed his mind. He would get hold of Connie and inquire if she might like to travel the country with him for a time. He would purchase the travel trailer with his savings, and they could take turns driving and getting it to wherever they wished. They could see the U.S.A. and Canada in their waning years. He mentally played with this flight of fancy countless times, even told Ringo to pack his favorite cushion, and was about to test its reality with a phone call to St. Andrews when his son-in-law disappeared.

As usual, Riddell had left the house one morning, and it was expected that he would return later that same day, except he didn't. There was no sign of him the following day either, or the one after that. At first, Eugene simply figured he hadn't been paying much attention and had failed to notice his son-in-law's daily return from his job at the trucking terminal. Lately, he had been getting out more often with frequent stops both at the library and Gino's Luncheonette. Plus, while at the mall he had run into the Shank brother who had given him his first job and soon found himself visiting a popular bar in Arlion and enjoying a few beers and some laughs with the man as they talked of earlier times. So it would have been easy not to have taken any notice of Riddell's coming and going. Finally, one evening, when he still hadn't seen Riddell, he looked into the window of the garage's first bay and saw that it was empty. Before this moment he hadn't considered asking Paulette about her husband and his whereabouts, and even now as he was about to go across to the house and do exactly that, it struck him suddenly that his son-in-law had disappeared at other times in years past and that it was really nothing new. On each of those occasions the dispatcher had been called on to temporarily abandon his desk job in order to slip behind the wheel of a big rig again. The first time because of a Teamsters strike. The second because of a flu outbreak among the company drivers. And even without the work stoppages and debilitating influenza, Riddell had said often the company was forever in need of additional drivers, so much so that those on the roster routinely extended their over-the-road-time beyond what was legally permissible.

However, on day four of Riddell's absence, while returning from the local mall, Eugene surrendered to his curiosity. He made an abrupt turn opposite his normal one and wound his way out by the trucking terminal. He slowed the car while he passed the array of brick and metal-sided buildings of Hollowell Cartage and searched carefully for Riddell's car in the large gravel parking lot. It wasn't there. Soon after, he returned to the apartment and minutes later overheard a diesel truck bobtail to a stop at the entrance to the driveway and apply its air brakes. Recognizing the one-of-a-kind sound, he stepped over to a window and watched his daughter emerge from the house at the same time the driver of the truck descended from the cab.

He moved to the door, opened it, and leaned against the jamb, watching and listening. The driver gave a once-over to Paulette's face and skull. The bandages had been removed, but not yet the stitches, and these looked bizarre as they stood out like tiny insulators in the middle of the long patch where her hair had been shaved off above the left ear.

"What happened to you?" Eugene heard the driver ask.

Paulette waved off the real answer. "Nothing worth repeating," she replied.

"Riddell hasn't been showing up at work, and no one picks up the phone when we call. My boss wanted me to come by to see what's going on. Is Riddell here?"

"He's left me," Eugene heard his daughter tell the trucker.

"Left you? You mean split, sayonara, I'm outta here?"

"That's what I mean," said Paulette.

"Well I'll be. You're not kidding?... No, I can see you're serious."

The trucker's eyes rose ever so minutely so that he could steal a second glance at Paulette's injured head.

"You think he'll be back in a day or two, or are you telling me he's gone for good? They're not too happy with him, but if he isn't away too long, I imagine he'll keep his job."

"He won't be coming back," Paulette said firmly.

The driver shook his head. "Well, I'm sorry, I really

am."

She didn't offer a nod or any farewell to the man, but turned and headed back down the driveway for the house.

The trucker turned away himself. He shook his head a second time to the unexpected information. After that, he seemed to assess the road and the driveway, and Eugene realized he was trying to decide if there was sufficient room to back the big cab around and return the direction he'd come.

Eugene left the apartment and quickly descended the staircase. He reached the top of the driveway just as the man was grabbing hold of the chrome bar at the right side of the door to assist entry back into the cab.

"Hold up there!" Eugene called out to him.

The man released his grip on the vertical bar and swung back around. He pointed at his own head and circled a finger. "Riddell do that?"

"He did," Eugene said.

The man glanced at the ground about his feet. "No excuse for that kind of thing, even if she pushed him to it."

"Are you saying my daughter got what she deserved?"

The trucker vigorously shook his head and raised a hand. "No. I just mean we never know what's really going on inside the minds of others. Look, I know who you are because Riddell used to talk about you. So what can I do for you, Eugene?"

"When's the last time you saw my son-in-law?"

"Just what you would expect, the last time he was at work. He'd been grumbling to everyone that he was uptight and needed to go fishing, which he's done a time or two before. We all figured that would be a little down the road, but when he didn't show the next morning, we actually laughed among ourselves and said Man, I guess he is uptight. And then when he didn't show up the day after, we laughed harder and said he must be even more uptight than we all imagined. But we quit laughing on Day Three. Where the hell is he, we started to ask. And then like I said to your daughter, no one at the house here was answering the phone. I guess she's been resting and all and just ignoring it. In any case, we didn't know what to think, which is why I'm here.... Hey! Look, if Riddell shows up, tell him to get his ass to work. Freight is piling up across the river and his assistant can't handle it by hisself."

Eugene gave a positive sign to the trucker who then climbed up into the black cab and drove off.

THIRTY-SEVEN

Paulette was sitting slumped at the kitchen table with nothing in front of her but her bare arms when Eugene walked in. Dirty pans and tableware lay stacked in the sink and on the counter, and a few crumpled paper towels were scattered across the floor. Nothing loomed in the drying rack but a fork and a wooden spatula. A sponge mop had slid from the wall and rested on the tile.

"I'm waiting on Pippa," she said to Eugene's questioning eye. "I'm to watch Marshall. Her mother can't do it today, and she can't reschedule her gynecologist."

"Why is that funny?" he asked, detecting a tug of self-amusement.

"She and Lila must have talked."

He shook his head.

"They think my mind needs to be on something other than myself. Their idea of therapy."

"Marshall will guarantee that," he said drolly.

"What is it you want, Dad?"

"I overheard you talking to that Hollowell truck driver. Why didn't you tell me that Riddell had left you?"

"Haven't you had your fill of us?"

"You're still my daughter," he said. "What happened? Did he threaten you?"

"You and Lila were right," she said. "I was in denial. But Riddell is gone now, and he won't be coming back. So let's leave it at that."

He did not move and he did not look away because there set before him in his daughter's face were the purposefully carved fissures and indentations that defined maybe a lie or some attempt at subterfuge, that were telling only a part of the story, certainly not the whole truth. There, too, marbleized in with her words had been the subtle inflections to put off the listener, to instill in him a false belief that honesty alone confronted him. Because these additives to her countenance and voice were not wiped away, as had been the case when he had been the audience to prevaricators in recent years, he knew, first, that this was further confirmation that his beneficent afflictions were now a thing of the past; and, second, that what, in fact, he was seeing and hearing were the familiar vestiges of a little girl and later teenager who had lied about the smallest things, and even a young unmarried woman who was afraid to tell her parents that she was pregnant.

What had really happened, he asked himself. Was it that her admission of denial, while honest, was also shameful, and she had felt the need to minimize it to others, especially to the man who had raised her? Had she, however, come to her senses and in so doing ordered Riddell out of the house, threatening that if he ever came back, she would be certain to call the police? Or was it much the other way? Had Riddell tired of her? Was he sick of the extra weight? Sick, too, of her compulsive picking with the fingers? He remembered that even as a toddler, his daughter had demonstrated the annoying habit of removing things from the garments of visiting friends and relatives. And yet, maybe it was none of this at all. Maybe sex was the problem that kicked the marriage to the side. Not enough of it for one or the other. Maybe not the right kind of sex. Perhaps a fetish of one the couple couldn't agree on, and the half wanting it would not give it up, so goodbye forever.

He didn't know what to think had taken place between his daughter and her husband, and so he broke off his attention to her and lent it to the room.

"Go on," she said, taking note of his action. "Get started with your inspection."

"Sorry, it's an old habit. Marshall isn't quite the little boy anymore. Perhaps an inspection isn't required."

"I haven't been fulfilling my womanly duties of care and upkeep to the house and I know you know this, Dad, because I watched you spy the dishes in the sink the moment you walked in. So do your thing. That way, we'll all feel safer." She wagged an impatient hand to the air. "Go ahead. Do your thing."

Eugene squeezed out a smile because of his daughter's read of him.

It was a good decision, in any case. In the bathroom, sprinkled bath powder coated a section of the floor and when he stepped onto the tile, the sole of his shoe slipped from under him and he was lucky to regain his footing. He could easily picture Marshall running unawares across the spot, losing his balance, and cracking the back of his skull on the hard surface. In the hallway leading to the bedrooms a closet door was open and several wire clothes hangers were linked together on the floor with their ends pointed at the ceiling. In what was his bedroom before he'd moved out to the garage he found an assortment of boxes. The tops were not taped shut and he took this as an invitation to open up each box to inspect its contents. Much of what the largest contained was old clothing, sheets, and drapery, but another box held numerous items for a kitchen, including a long serrated knife and one for boning, each missing a side of its handle. He removed the knives and refitted the flaps, closing the box.

Where his daughter and her husband had slept, in the master bedroom, the blind was raised, but he could see that the cord had not been wound around the metal cleat at the window's edge and it hung almost to the floor. More likely a potential for the strangulation of a dog or a cat, but not an impossibility for a child Marshall's age. He looped the cord around the cleat with his free hand until there wasn't room enough for the insertion of a youngster's head. That completed, he moved to what had been Riddell's closet and set the knives on the shelf at the top where the .22 revolver was eventually hidden following Marshall's very first visit. He felt about for the gun, not believing it would be there now, as it was a thing he was sure Riddell would have taken with him, and he was not disappointed. He inspected the top drawer in the nightstand as well, where Riddell had originally hid the .22, expecting again that it would not be there. And for the briefest moment, this expectation appeared to have been met as the gun was spun around so that his hand, reaching in, contacted the barrel and front sight first and not the handgrips. The cylinder, too, had been released and lay open to the side.

With some hesitation formed of disbelief at what he'd found, he reached further into the wooden drawer and took the small-caliber revolver into his hand and removed it. Out in the openness of the room, it surrendered the smell of a gun that had been fired recently. In the scattering of the ammunition at the bottom of the drawer he discovered two cartridges that were empty.

He elevated the pistol to eye level and aimed it at a window. Bright backlighting illuminated powder specks inside the barrel. Deposits were present also in a pair of cylinder chambers. He brought the gun to his nose and sniffed at it several times. Besides that of burnt powder, a second smell was trying to mix in. It came off the grips, but he was unable to say what it was. He snapped shut the cylinder, stepped back to the closet and placed the revolver on the high shelf.

Whatever was behind Riddell's absconding, the gun must have had a role in the story, he surmised. Had he threatened to shoot Paulette, and did she stand up to him? In light of the trouble that had already taken place, that seemed a plausible scenario. And if he were to judge by the pair of empty shells in the nightstand, Riddell might have twice discharged the gun in an attempt to frighten and intimidate his wife. He searched the surrounding walls for a bullet hole. When he left the bedroom and re-entered other parts of the house, his eyes continued to scan the walls for a mark that was out of the ordinary.

In the meantime, Pippa Goodwin had arrived with her son Marshall, and Paulette met them at the door. As they stepped inside, Eugene appeared from the opposite side of the house and came up behind his daughter. Both their faces lit up when they saw him and he responded in kind, even asking a few questions that inquired of the well-being of mother and son. He stayed very briefly before excusing himself. While stepping off the tie landing at the front of the house, Paulette called from the threshold.

"Dad?"

He stopped but did not turn completely around. "What is it?"

"I never thanked you."

"Thanked me for what?"

"For getting my van repaired. It's such a relief."

Throwing a perfunctory gaze over his shoulder, he uttered, "No thanks needed," added an abbreviated wave, then continued off the landing and on past the line of maples.

Upon reaching the apartment staircase seconds later he paused and grabbed hold of the railing. He took a step upward, a second step, and yet a third step, only to hesitate and pause again before the next step. The feeling that had made him leave Connie unconscious and under Lila's resuscitative efforts in order to check the hood temperature on Riddell's car, that shaky feeling of apprehension was curiously back for a second visit, and it was urging him to once again enter the garage whose bay doors this time were down.

He swung about and, while remaining motionless, questioned in a frivolous way why he was affording any thought to an inclination that could be defined as paranormal. And yet he knew that he would obey the impulse. He stepped off the risers onto the ground and opened the door to the walk-in entrance. Shutting it behind him, he stood in place a long time. Up and down and across the walls and through the space between them he ran his eyes. But what they were searching for or what he was expecting to uncover, he hadn't a clue. In the middle slot this day was parked the runabout, strapped in its trailer, and he eventually moved across the concrete floor to examine the boat. One of the tires, he immediately saw, was flat and in need of air. For no definable reason he inspected its rubber and ran a casual hand over the exposed tread. He then straightened himself and inspected the boat's interior. He pressed his fingertips into several spots of the stiff fiber rug and curled them over the edges. The seats were cushioned and he picked at their wales. He slid a palm across their flat surfaces, then slid it back. Everywhere the fabric was dry. Other than the faint scent of motor oil there was no odor coming off the boat.

He next backed away several paces so that he could examine the hull of the white fiberglass watercraft. He searched for a mud line or a blade of a previously submerged weed, now dry and turning brown, which would suggest the boat had been recently in the water. But there was nothing like that and so he moved around to the stern to examine the outboard engine, an old but well cared-for Evinrude. But, again, there wasn't even the smallest string of vegetation wrapped around its prop.

The boat is much too clean, he concluded. It was unlikely it had been on the water in recent weeks. *But does that mean anything?* It was another question he was unable to answer. All he knew was that something had encouraged him to enter the garage and that's what he'd done. But he remained in the dark regarding what had stirred the impulse.

He stepped further away from the boat and let his eyes for a second time revert to the walls, the shelving in particular and the countless items set upon them by Riddell across the years. This consisted of Mason jars filled with nuts and washers, plastic coffee containers relabeled with the penny size of the nails they hid, a collection of files for use on wood and steel and a chainsaw, two staple guns, various tools for mechanical repair, others for work in the yard. He loosely shook his head after a time and laughed at himself and was even about to give up on his effort and exit the building when the second odor that he could not identify at the house encroached on his sense of smell, except this time it was not altered by the lingering wisp of burnt gunpowder. He raised his nose like an alert animal to fine-tune the draw. It was water that he detected, he realized, and not water from a faucet. Water not from rain, water not even from a stream. This smell that was wafting to his nose reeked of water, algae and mud, fused with a splash of bait and fish.

He turned away from the walls and their shelves and

looked to the van as the source. The blue vehicle sat in the last bay this day, its flat front end pointed to the rear of the building, and the window on the driver's side was halfway down. He walked up to the vehicle and pushed his nose into the half-opened window, inhaled sonorously, and pulled on the outside latch.

The smell was emanating undisturbed from inside the van. He surveyed the dashboard, the gauges, the radio and CD player, the inset on top where the time and outside temperature were told when the key was turned. Just dust and dried insect wings were stuck to their surfaces. He ran his gaze over the front seats and at the floor. He stretched himself over the driver's headrest and peered at the bench seat in the rear. Nothing. He pulled back, shut the door behind him, and moved then to the rear of the vehicle. He unlatched both doors and opened them to their widest.

And there lying in two sections with the spinning reel attached to the thicker lower piece was Riddell's graphite fishing rod. He reached in and picked up both ends. A tiny chunk of nightcrawler, soft and pink, lingered on the hook. He lifted the rod's handle to his nose and sniffed the cork.

The smell was all over it.

"What are you doing, Dad?"

At the other end of the building the walk-in door, without Eugene's knowing it, had opened and closed.

"Dad, what are you doing out here?"

"Where's Marshall?"

"I asked you a question."

"That truck driver said Riddell had told the others at work that he was going fishing."

"His boat's here, you can see that."

"But he might have decided to fish from the bank. He's done it before."

"And yet you're holding his fishing rod in your hand."

"I pulled this rod out of your van," he said, pointing the end of it at her. She started to counter again, but he threw up the other hand to cut her off. "It has a worm at the end." He shoved it out front to afford her a closer look from which she shrank. "Paulette, why did you come out here? You know, when I was checking on things inside the house a few minutes ago, I found Riddell's pistol in the drawer next to the bed."

"I'm sorry," she said, shaking her head. "I forgot to put it out of reach."

"Stop!" he said. "The gun was fouled. And walking my way back from the house I got to thinking that any man who was so consumed with a stain on a rug would not have left the gun in that condition. Your husband killed Brownie with a single bullet, and the following day he was already swabbing out the revolver's barrel with a solvent."

He waited for a response, but there was none.

"Paulette? What's going on?"

"Daddy, was Mom aware that you killed a man? Did you let her know? Or have you always kept it to yourself?"

"What?"

"When I told Riddell what I overheard you and that woman talk about upstairs in the apartment, he said you'd done a good deed. He said you'd rid the world of a child molester."

Eugene reached and very deliberately set the fishing rod aside, against a wall. He then just as slowly and deliberately latched the rear doors on the van before turning back to face his daughter.

"Let's leave your question for some other day," he said calmly. "Besides, there's yet another matter you probably know nothing about and we'll take it up at the same time. But for now, what I want to know is what happened to Riddell and why the gun is with you and not with him. I want to know who fired it recently and I want to hear the reason."

Paulette turned aside.

"Last week your husband almost killed you," he continued. "And he may hurt you again. As hard as it is for me to understand, I still can see that you might miss Riddell in spite of what he did to you. But as your father, I have to say I'm relieved that he's gone. I've worried things could escalate."

"Daddy, did you know that not once in our marriage has Riddell ever apologized. Did you know that? Not once. And I never asked him to. Not even when he knew he was in the wrong and he knew I wanted and needed an apology. He wouldn't do it, and I always let it go. I didn't ask, I didn't demand, I didn't sulk and deny him, even though I had every reason to. Only this time was different. This time I wanted my husband to say that he didn't mean to hurt me and that he was sorry."

"He owes you more than an apology," said Eugene.

"I shot him, Daddy. I shot my Riddell."

"What…? What are you talking about, girl? You're not making any sense."

"I shot my husband and he's dead."

Her gaze remained fixed in an opposite direction and Eugene had to step around to her front so that they were again facing each other.

"What are you saying, Paulette?"

"Just what I said. I shot him."

"You actually shot Riddell, and he's dead?"

She raised her eyes to meet his.

"When he walked out of the house that morning without giving the apology I'd wanted, I watched him through a window and I saw him in the garage place his fishing rod inside his car. I knew then that he wasn't going to show up at work that day. He'd done it before without reporting in and got away with it simply because he was a really good dispatcher and the company was willing to put up with his occasional absence.

"At first I didn't think about following him, about approaching him at Crooked Creek and its muddy lake. There wasn't any doubt that was where he would go. I didn't think about confronting him and pushing my need for an apology. I thought it was something that could wait until he returned later in the day when he wanted his dinner. But after a while, the more I thought about it, I realized I could not wait. I'd waited long enough. I'd waited years."

She looked off into the air and through a window, and sidled away several steps.

"It was noon when I got to the lake, and the only car parked there was Riddell's. He was sitting in it on the passenger side, eating a sandwich that he must have picked up along the way, and the door on each side was open as the day was warm and he was letting in the little breeze there was. I could hear the car radio and the hourly news broadcast from a local station, the only one he liked to listen to. I saw him glance over his shoulder at my arrival, only he kept his attention to his fishing pole, which he'd planted on the shore with several rocks. The bobber was floating on the lake's surface a hundred feet out.

"I circled the van and parked to the left of the car and Riddell reached across the seat to close the door on the driver's side so as to keep me from entering, only it was out of his reach and I was out of the van quickly. I slid in behind the wheel and said, 'Riddell, why are you doing this? Why won't you apologize? I need to hear you say you're sorry for hurting me. It's important to me.' But he wouldn't even look at me.

"And he didn't say anything. He wouldn't say a word. Instead, he opened the glove compartment, reached in and took out the gun. I thought he was going to shoot me, Daddy, I honestly did. And I just reacted and slapped at his arm. The gun went off and the bullet went through the roof of his car and I think this surprised him so much that he lost his grip on the gun, and just like that I was fumbling for it, and it went off a second time in my hand and this time the bullet hit Riddell. But it didn't kill him, I'm sure it didn't. Still, he slumped and fell forward and that's when the car began to drift. He had bumped the shifter out of gear. The shore there is steeper than it looks and before either of us realized it, the car was in the water and the door on his side had closed on him. I yelled for Riddell to get out and tried to pull him out my side where the door was open, but even injured he resisted and was pushing at the door on his side. But the water was coming in fast and the car was disappearing and turning onto the side I was at. I had to leave, I didn't know what else to do, but I kept yelling at Riddell.

"He went under with the car, Dad. I watched and waited, I don't know how long. And I prayed that I would see him swim to the surface. Only he never did. Riddell never came up. And within a minute, that lake looked like it always does. Absolutely still and just plain muddy.

"I didn't know what to do. The only things that didn't belong there were Riddell's fishing rod and a can of worms, and I tossed the worms to the fish and put the rod in the van. Then I drove home."

She turned back to face Eugene and her voice dropped. "Dad, I didn't know what to do. Calling the police wasn't going to help Riddell. What would you have done?"

Even though she was leaving it unsaid, he understood on its face what she was asking of him. And was it any different from what he had asked of himself once upon a time? If the car were pulled from the lake, Riddell's body would undergo an autopsy, and the gunshot wound would receive special attention, as a gunshot wound was wont to do. And he knew exactly how the authorities would work it into an analysis of the victim's death.

He understood it, also, because there were no tears wetting his daughter's eyes and that detail alone would place the focus of the police on her. That observation by itself would make them think that this was yet another of the many spouses who had murdered their significant other.

And wasn't he really wondering the same thing? With an incident of this magnitude, an unexpected death in an unexpected manner, he was unable to determine if his daughter was in any way lying to him. Along with the absence of expected tears, there were also the small details in her story that was prompting his musing. It was true that he hadn't much to do with guns. Nonetheless, he had some knowledge about them. He knew, for instance, that a .22 was not a gun often used to murder someone, mostly because of its small caliber. Yet a bullet from it could definitely kill a person if that bullet penetrated the most vulnerable places like the brain or the heart or a major artery. Similarly, he was aware that pistols—revolvers, in particular—in order to be fired either had to have their hammers pulled back and cocked each time, or the trigger must be pulled for each round released. Single-action and double-action, these were not altogether unfamiliar terms to him. Still, in either case, the action was not an easy one; both were actions with resistance. Which is why it was hard for him to believe the gun had fired accidentally not once, but twice. The first, certainly he could make a case for that. Riddell might well have intended to shoot his daughter. He might well have cocked the hammer and had his finger on the trigger when Paulette slapped at him. But how then was it fired a second time in their moment of turmoil. Yes, it was possible, a second accidental firing, and he wanted to think it was even probable, but the stretch in credibility was thin.

And all the more so because of those dry eyes that were continuing to peer at him. What was it that Riddell had done in prior years to deprive him of her crying after he was instantly and tragically gone from her life? What terrible acts had he committed for which his daughter needed an apology? Eugene could think of one only and that was infidelity? And it was only the shortest space of time that passed before the young EMT came to his mind, the young woman who had provided his son-in-law with an excuse for his heinous behavior that might have killed Connie and his dog. And was she that same woman who lived elsewhere in the neighborhood and whose husband abused her? Who, whether headed up or down the street inside her vehicle with the demonstrative light bar on the roof, who returned but the most cursory greeting to his daughter and even to himself? A small mystery it remained, which brought up from a few years earlier another equally as small—Dara and her erroneous belief that he was father to Riddell. Had his son-in-law gone to bed with her and told her a few things, one of which she hadn't taken in correctly? Maybe it never was love they had, his daughter and Riddell. Perhaps from the very beginning, from the first time the boy had arrived at the house on his motorcycle, each believed that one possessed the other. And when it came time, as it too often did with couples, wasn't it always easier to rid oneself of a possession than it was a love? And if any of what he was thinking was true, might he have had a part in it? Had Paulette known in an intuitive way while growing up that he too often was thinking not of her mother, but of another woman? And if there was any truth in that, what, then, were her thoughts of Ginger? Of him? Of Ginger and himself as a married couple?

"Excuse me?"

Pippa stood at the walk-in entrance with her hands resting at the sides of her son's head.

"I really have to be leaving, Paulette, or I'll miss my appointment, and you know it isn't easy to get another."

"We're finished," Eugene said.

Paulette nodded the same and moved toward the open door. "Come along with me, Marshall," she said. "Let's see what's in the house that might be fun to eat."

She pushed the boy at the shoulders and they headed off and away from the garage.

Pippa stayed yet a moment. "What do you think, Mr. Banish? Do you think we'll we ever hear from Riddell again?"

Eugene hesitated before he answered her question. Instead, he returned to the rear of the van where he glanced at the fishing rod and reel against the wall and at the small piece of worm still secured to the barbed hook.

He reached out and took the worm between his thumb and forefinger and rolled it from the hook. "No, Pippa," he finally said. "No, I believe this is something Riddell has been planning for quite some time. I believe he's gone for good and we won't ever see him again."

Outside the garage, as he was returning to the house with Paulette, Marshall shot a look back over his shoulders. It extended past the maple trees and seconds later he started pointing at something, somewhere.

www.ingramcontent.com/pod-product-compliance
Lightning Source LLC
Chambersburg PA
CBHW020411260626
47156CB00007B/2336